Praise for

The Dying of the Light

"This sweeping and layered tale follows the life of Diana Cooke Copperton Cooke—a Southern beauty who is sacrificed by her family to repair their fortune—as she experiences and inspires love, desire, jealousy, and rage. The characters are memorable, eccentric, and all too human as their needs and passions draw them together and tear them apart. Goolrick shows real insight into the workings of the human mind, particularly when he demonstrates the chasm between what his characters should do and their inability to do it, even when they know it would make them happy. Passion, loneliness, decadence, and sexuality are all powerfully portrayed in this beautifully written novel."

—Sara Gruen, *New York Times* bestselling author of *Water for Elephants*

"The unique intense richness of *The Dying of the Light* makes this novel a fevered dream of sacrifice, sex, luxury, manners, honor, violence, submission, tragedy, destiny, secrets, beauty, and melancholy that holds you in an embrace that tightens through the novel, leaving you spent and transformed. Few writers approach this level of detail, but Goolrick's story is also very human, and the culminating romance both fills and breaks your heart."

—Joan Juliet Buck, former editor of *Vogue Paris* and author of *The Price of Illusion*

"Robert Goolrick has created a mesmerizing, evocative novel brimming with passion and tragedy. His portrait of a depleted Southern family, hoping to reinvigorate itself and its magnificently neglected estate, is at once thrilling and devastating. We can smell the decay of the house, feel the worn velvet, visualize the peeling wallpaper. But, most of all, we can empathize with the doomed characters as they walk the hallways and the grounds, desperate to find what they are looking for—love? hope? redemption?—or maybe that thing we all seek: a place to call home."

—Garth Stein, *New York Times* bestselling author of *The Art of Racing in the Rain*

"Goolrick's best book yet. A brilliant mashup of all the old greats, Faulkner and Fitzgerald and D. H. Lawrence, *The Dying of the Light* reads like *Absolom, Absolom!* meets *The Great Gatsby* meets *Lady Chatterley's Lover.*"

—Philipp Meyer, *New York Times* bestselling author of *The Son*

THE DYING OF THE LIGHT

ALSO BY ROBERT GOOLRICK

The Fall of Princes

Heading Out to Wonderful

A Reliable Wife

The End of the World as We Know It

THE DYING OF THE LIGHT

A Novel

ROBERT GOOLRICK

HARPER

NEW YORK • LONDON • TORONTO • SYDNEY

HARPER

A hardcover edition of this book was published in 2018 by HarperCollins Publishers.

FIRST HARPER PAPERBACKS EDITION PUBLISHED 2019.

Designed by Fritz Metsch

Library of Congress Cataloging-in-Publication Data has been applied for.

ISBN 978-0-06-267823-2 (pbk.)

19 20 21 22 23 LSC 10 9 8 7 6 5 4 3 2 1

For Ameena Meer

With my love forever

بحثتُ عن ملاكا في الجن ..

فوجدت واحدا بجانبي هنا على الارض

And for Peter Kahn

Without whom, this would not have happened

וכל המקיים נפש אחת ,מעלים עליו כאילו קיים עולם מלא.

There is a river, the streams whereof shall make glad the city of God, the holy place of the tabernacles of the most High.

God is in the midst of her; she shall not be moved: God shall help her, and that right early.

The heathen raged, the kingdoms were moved: he uttered his voice, the earth melted.

Psalm 46:4–6

Prologue

IT BEGINS WITH a house and it ends in ashes. There's your opening, you think. You can wrap it up and go home now. Phone it in. And you haven't even set foot on the property. But it's true. That is the complete family history. Except. Except. Between the building, in 1748, and the burning, somebody, or a number of people, people who weren't supposed to die, died in this house in a disastrous fire on December 5, 1941. This is all you know, all anybody knows, all there is to be known. The rest is detail, just local color. Of course, that's why they sent you, to sift through the ashes, to somehow find a bone in the ash, a bone that would unravel a mystery that has stood silent and unbreakable for almost sixty years. You are standing at dawn on the prow of an oyster boat you've hired for the day, moving, trailing a wide wake in a calm black river, under a sky the color of unpolished silver, to get there, the only boat on the lazy river, the fish running somewhere else, finally to reach the house, the remains of history, the remnants of her life. You are trespassing, even now. The house, barely glimpsed from the prow of the oyster boat where you stand, making its slow way down from Port Royal, the house, even in silhouette, is huge, unimaginably large, foursquare. Saratoga, the name coming from the old Indian language, means the hillsides of the quiet river, the hunting grounds by the water. It's not as though you haven't done your homework.

The house had been modeled after the gigantic house of the Earl of Shaftesbury, St. Giles House, and though slightly smaller, it was still the biggest house in America, with uncountable rooms and a grandiosity that quickened the heart of all who saw it. The cost was enormous, the first and greatest of many folies de grandeur that left the owners in a state of bondage and near poverty only redeemed by the labors of, at the most, nine hundred slaves who picked the cotton and cured the tobacco and boiled the peanuts and, for generations, cleaned up their messes in a silent, sly rage. Robbed of their humanity, these nine hundred looked at the house from the start and envisioned it in flames, hearing in their wistful hearts the terrible screams of their oh-so-white masters. Not able to flee, sold like dogs in the street, robbed of their children, babies ripped from their mother's arms in Natchez or Memphis.

It was a house built on tears.

Did four die? Three? Or just one—Diana Cooke Copperton Cooke?

Was it accidental, or arson, as the inept sheriff's office proclaimed?

Whoever was there, the fire burned flesh to bone and bone to ash and the ash blew into oblivion.

If she had somehow lived, she would be ninety-nine years old now. Unlikely, but not impossible. And, in the unlikely event that she was alive, where would she be? She was declared dead after seven years, in 1948, and the son took control of what was left of her money, not much, which he used occasionally. But where did the rest go? There was supposed to be a fortune. Fortunes like that don't just disappear, and she couldn't have spent it all.

So perhaps there was no arsonist except herself.

But inside the doll of her life, there was another, and another and another and another, smaller and smaller, all fitting together, and somewhere in the tiniest box was her soul and her affections. There was her son, Ashton, far away, never forgotten for one minute, the only thing that made her heart continue beating.

Mostly she dreamed of Ashton, her only boy, his handsome face and infinite charm. Because he had spent so much of his life apart from her, his face appeared as a slide show, not a movie. Ash at eight, getting on the train, weeping at the window of his compartment, and then after that, jumping from vacation to vacation, his growth a shock every time, pretending at affection during these short visits when in reality she knew less and less about him. Even the bills for his clothes went to his trustees, so that when he arrived in a new coat, it was always a shock.

You are speculating from what you know. You are seeing it for the first time, and yet it is not new to you. Hours spent poring over books and articles and stacks of photographs have led you to expect exactly what you are now seeing, and you are both satisfied and disappointed that there is nothing more than this, making you wonder why you have come all this way, and yet it *is* new, it is somehow unexpected, perhaps simply by virtue of the fact that you are here and it is larger, wider, than you had thought, the wind more brisk, saltier, everything surprising, the way it feels when you first see Niagara Falls, expecting only tourists and disappointment and finding wonder, wonder at the power and the size of it, a child's delight. And here, as there, everything else washes away, the crew of the boat, the flights of gulls, the expectation of thunder, lost in the mystery of the attainment of this one small goal, and the mystery, the thing that made you get out the magnifying glass and study the pictures under a light, all that wakes up in your heart, and your heart beats in your jaded throat, just for a minute, until you remember that it is only this, only a job, a job that will get done, as they always do, done and left behind, measured by the number of Internet hits, the number of shares. You have nothing new to add. That much seems certain.

You had felt you knew her, as much as could be known. Now you see you know nothing.

There it is, a silhouette in the distance at the end of what was once a long yard edged by gardens. Some say she still lives there, ancient, in the gatehouse, but there is no movement, no sign except the white tail of a deer flashing as it breaks into the bracken, nothing but the ruin of the house that was built three centuries ago and was called and still is, even in its ruination, Saratoga.

You have come a long way for this, and you have come by water because that's how they came, the first ones, and because the mile-long drive to the road that leads to Port Royal, the nearest town, is so overgrown as to be impassable.

The blackened house, almost unrecognizable as brick, sits in what was once a grant of fifty thousand acres from George I to one John Cooke—King Cooke, they called him, call him still around here, the first of three. The first men who came with him had come here, come to nothing, and cleared the land with mules and blacks and sweat and lived in lean-tos in the winter months, barely surviving, Americans before there was an America, strong backs and legs, and they fought the red men who owned the land since time began and they cleared the trees with mules and sweat and opened one acre after another until they could build the first house and farm the first fields and send for the women from whom all the rest of them descended. Blood was everything to them, cousin and kin, a line of Cookes who went on to found the great capitals and name the nation they had ripped from the land and its native owners.

They signed documents, and their signatures are under glass in museums; they made speeches, and some of their words ring in the mouths of patriots even today, often misunderstood, misused, vicious, and vindictive, when it had all begun in such hope, such stitching, and then waving of flags and banners.

There are no banners now, not here. There is no sound except the wind, and the water lapping at the boat, no sound, no human cry, no laughter or weeping or speech, just this, this monument to a family's life of work and folly, to their joys and struggles inside the four walls when the house was still standing, endlessly gossiped about in the town, before the awful fire, the fire that melted the silver on the sideboard, that turned the mahogany and damask to ash. The pickers came after; nobody stopped them, once the embers were cool enough to walk across with stiff boots and still it was hot, almost too hot to bear, burned the soles of your feet all to hell, and the rest they took, the ivory from the piano keys, the shreds of Oriental rugs and, here and there, a sterling candlestick, a punch ladle, a baby cup with initials, a Canton platter.

Landscape diminishes as we approach. First the vast line of green, indistinguishable, seen from out at sea, then the particularities of coast and tide, and the trees themselves, pines and magnolia and dogwood, the elms and maples fallen into the dull sand, giants toppled by time and neglect, and then what would have been the lawn, the long flat up to the house where she may or may not still live, for there is no way to know; if she lived, no one would see her, if she died, no one to mourn, unless they, the two servants left to her at the end, now long dead, had not moved on, but had found a way to cling to the land, to wrest copper pots and vessels from the ash, for carrying water and for cooking. Had she lived, she would be ninety-nine, and the servants, all of her contemporaries, would be long dead.

And you, here, now, 1999, before the century's turning, with your lined notebook and your Nikon, in your Top-Siders, new, what were you thinking, knowing more about this house, and about her, than almost anybody, but still not knowing the thing, the core of the mystery. You've seen the house, ghostlike, in the museum in town.

There is a plan, a group of men and women who are raising millions, although they are millions away from what they need to do what they want to do, which is to build around the ruins of the house a glass model of Saratoga as it was, every staircase, every fireplace, and a cruel magnificent thing it would be, this jewel box, if they were to get their millions, but they never will. Not enough people care enough to get them what they need to build their glass dollhouse of one of the most important Georgian houses ever built in this country. Nobody cares about history now. Nobody gives a shit.

On the table, in the museum, there are even tiny people, in their frock coats and sweeping silk dresses, strolling the lawn, dancing a minuet in the first ballroom in any house in America, thirty by fifty feet given over to graceful pleasures and nothing else, giving a synecdochic idea of the vastness of the rest of it all, if that much space could be devoted simply to the pleasures of the dance. There was a huge columned downstairs hallway, watched over by a butler, with a double staircase that led up to a gallery and the sleeping quarters. Upstairs there were twelve bedrooms, downstairs an orangery, facing west, with oranges and lemons and limes in profusion even in the winter. There was a dining room that could seat forty, a sitting room for the women, a study for the men and their cigars, a study with a pool table, every stick of furniture brought in crates from England and hauled up from the river on the backs of slaves and polished by them every day, watched over them by the women who became more wan, more etiolated, as every generation passed, and, on every side of the huge house, the rich fields that produced the tobacco and the peanuts and cotton and pigs that made it all possible, cash crops that thrived, that thrived for generations, that finally began to rob the soil of its nutrients, the earth growing as wan as the women, producing just that much less every year.

The broad round of the treacherous trees, giving no purchase, provides the only access to the land, the long, broad yard where she may or may not still live. Once, you are told, there were two docks, and a long sloop with brass fittings, polished every day, the brightwork, gliding, lit, up the river on summer nights to catch the breezes, people drinking and dancing on the mahogany deck, and a more rustic boat for the fishing and oystering. As you walk the tree, balancing with your arms, batting away the eternal infernal mosquitoes and vicious black flies, crabs scuttle, gliding sideways, and jellyfish float, ghostlike in the shallow water, and then you take a great leap and you are on the land and already fighting brambles, feeling them tear at your clothes, grabbing for your shoes, but you have come all this way for this, this end, and, blood soaking your pants where the thorns have torn the skin, you push on because you have to see it, this wreck, this history of one family in one nation that is called America, in this one state that is called Virginia.

This was just an assignment from the paper, the style section, reviving, as they did about every ten years, the fragile, tissue-like memory of her, best in show, one of the century's extraordinary beauties, fabled Diana Cooke Copperton Cooke, and the unsolved mystery of what became of her, her son Ashton living out a full life and dying alone at seventy, his liver the size of a football, without once mentioning her name, except perhaps in his nightly prayers, as though there were any more to know, as though you could glean one final scrap of information from the rubble that would make it all make sense. That rubble has been pored over time and time again, just as the photographs, the famous photographs, by Hurrell against draped brocade, by Horst, she alone in a forest of white cubes and a single calla lily, casting its shadow, she in a simple white crepe evening dress, diamond bangles up her arm from the wrist to above her elbow, white light so bright her face is almost in flames. Cecil Beaton, who saw in her something of his own sister, Baba, photographed her in her suite at Claridge's, the Prince Alexander Suite, the one she took for six weeks every winter after her marriage. She is wearing a flimsy ankle-length real silver dress, almost transparent, an agony to wear, cut low to the waist down her beautiful athletic back, down which hang two strands of gigantic fourteen-millimeter natural smoky gray pearls, held at the throat with an enormous diamond rose spray. The pearls had been called the Linley pearls for generations; they had sat in a vitrine in the Victoria and Albert for eighty years, except on three occasions, when they were taken out by the family to be worn to court or, once, to a wedding, until Diana's husband bought them for her at auction, only the second time they had ever been sold, still in their original leather and satin box, and promptly renamed them the Copperton pearls, an act that stunned and embarrassed both all of London and Diana herself with its vulgarity and disrespect. She had, in her way, shown the spirit of the new age by wearing them languidly down her back. Hoyningen-Huene, so courtly and correct, pictured her in the best of the new collections every year for *Vogue*, and Man Ray made the trip all the way to Virginia, even though he feared the country, the wilderness that startled him and filled him with dread and an unbearable, almost sexual excitement at the same time.

She was a darling of the camera. So many pictures of her had filled your nights, yet oddly, now, so close to where she grew up and lived and probably died, you can hardly remember her face. An arch of her neck, yes. A gesture of the hand. A shoulder, draped in chinchilla. But the face, only through a fog.

There she stood as debutante of the year in 1917, at the Bachelor's Cotillion in Baltimore, the International Debutante Ball in New York, the deep bow, forehead touching the floor, and still later, pictured in fur at the Ritz in Paris, at Claridge's in London, crossing on the *Queen Mary*, the famous diamonds, the parure from Cartier, the swanlike neck, the inquisitive eye, the utter calm that comes from knowing that you can have anything, from knowing that you can invite anybody to dinner in the certain knowledge that they will eagerly come. The enviable Diana, whose name, you must point out in parentheses, was pronounced Deeana, was named and raised for one single purpose: to marry brilliantly and revive a family's fortunes, gone through overplanting and various forms of careless and licentious behavior. The article would be accompanied by the inevitable interactive slide show, portraits of Diana, Diana riding sidesaddle to hounds, Diana at Lakewood with her Langhorne cousins at their marvelous house Mirador, Diana with the movie stars who visited to sail the Rappahannock in the twilight, Douglas Fairbanks and Mary Pickford and Charlie Chaplin, champagne glasses in hand, music from a crank phonograph playing, the sound spreading across the water in waves all the way to Urbanna, to play croquet in white wool slacks, the house itself, and, finally, the blackened, skeletal remains of the house after the great fire that burned for three days, during which there was no sign of Diana herself, as there was never to be any trace of her ever again, no trail, no obituary, no movement of money, nothing to indicate either her life or her death.

You are not the first to have looked for her and come up empty-handed. The paper you work for expects more, some shred not found yet, some scrap of history that would shed a laser beam of light on the mystery, that would bring Diana Cooke Copperton Cooke out of the darkness and the grave and into the light. This is your forte, your métier, to turn over every rock, each turned over time and time again, until you feel the scorpion's sting, the searing truth that makes the fable undeniably real, that makes the dead move again with the jeweler's loupe of your own insight. Perhaps you have already seen it, in the photographs over which you have pored for hours, watching her expression as it changed over the years, watching as the jewels slowly came to outshine her eyes, as a kind of desperation crept into the calm, so that her serenity became merely a sort of freeze in her features. Maybe it was her marriage, by all accounts not a happy one, Captain Copperton, sportsman and drunk. Whatever it was, somewhere along the way, the green lawn of her life had turned into acre after acre of bracken and thorn.

You stare at the blackened bones of Saratoga, once the biggest house in the state of Virginia. The rafters lie in ash in the middle of cruel weed and wreckage, the land returning to what the first Cooke first saw centuries ago, the odd stand of tobacco or cotton or soy poking up through the weeds, even now, the house built to last a thousand years gone in three incendiary days, the heat enough to melt the glass in the windows into glittering crystal puddles in the black of the brick. Like icicles in the flame.

The closer you get, the more the bones are lost. The outer walls are just too far apart. You hack your way into the darkness of the house. You stand in what was once the entrance hall, the rosewood parquet, the famous curving staircase, and you are there, with them, through the centuries.

And you stand in the black rubble, like the ashes in the urn from the crematorium, and you think, Where is the hidden door that leads to the secret room, the trapdoor, the safe that holds the long-lost letter that tells the story? Where is the crystal icicle now to point the way? But there is only this, this mess of history and the wind from the river and the gulls crying.

Then it happens. The silence opens, and you hear their voices. A jazz band plays. A boy dives, knifelike, into the suddenly crystalline aquamarine pool, leaving only the slightest ripple. Cary Grant makes his wicket, and the girls swoon at how beautiful he is. Suddenly, gamine, as light as meringue, as cool and crisp as mint, she appears at the top of the stairs and begins to descend without the slightest hint of haste. Diana Cooke Copperton Cooke welcomes you to Saratoga. She invites you into her house. She is wearing a long silk dress with pants, recklessly tied at the waist, the streamers trailing behind her on the stairs, the dress swirled diagonally with wide black-and-white stripes, to the left on the legs, to the right over her full bosom, a double strand of magnificent pearls trailing down her back, and it is as if she were made, put on this earth, just for this moment, just so that the shaft of late sunlight might catch her in just this way, already laughing, her Manhattan already icy in her hands, her jewelry already jangling like Eastern music as she reaches for the banister, as she comes to greet you as she has greeted hundreds of others to this, her house, her realm, this Saratoga. Her breathless laugh drifts down the stairs, there must be forty, and she takes her time, for no one is ever late at Saratoga, time is infinite in the glass house, the scent of Jicky, falling like rain from heaven, all of it like water to a man dying of thirst in the desert. Like every man who stood at the bottom of the stairs fifty years before and waited for her descent, you fall in love with her instantaneously and you know that you will never recover your heart. Not in this life. Diana Cooke Copperton Cooke. She is everything every man wants. She always has been. In a black-and-white dress any woman might wear but none ever has, not like that. And now she will descend and you will wait, just like this, for as long as there is breath left in your body. She the enchantress. You the bedeviled. And now you both will be that way forever. History has been written and has moved on. There are other histories, but this history will only happen once, and, once happened, it will happen forever, both fluid and static.

"Welcome," she says, laughing, "there are scads of people here you simply must meet. I don't even know who half of them are myself." And she pulls you inside, and there is no going back.

I

COPPERTON

1

SHE WAS BORN with the century. She was born as well into the memory of two wars—her grandfather had been Jeb Stuart's aide-de-camp, her father had lost a leg in the Phillipines—and then, when she was fourteen, she knew the agony of the Great War. Her whole childhood was touched by the present evil of war, as it was war that killed all six of her cousins, Penny, Carter, Stuart, William, Augustine, and Uncle Charlie, who was called that because by the time he was born, his oldest sibling already had children of his own.

The memory of the Civil War still hung over them all like a shroud, as present as yesterday, and the Great War stabbed at the heart of the great families as sure as a bayonet. The cousins had been such handsome, kind, fun boys, the youngest only eighteen, her favorite playmates and her idols, so brave in the uniforms. Heroes. Two died on the same day, at Verdun.

It seemed the walls of her house, Saratoga, were lined with portraits of heroes of the life's blood of America itself, and now only she was left, a girl, the last Cooke, her sex a disappointment to everybody. She now held the place of honor, which was a source of pride but also a shackle, tied as she was to upholding and carrying on the family history. Sometimes she looked at all the portraits and felt she was choking. There was not one place in the house where their bright eyes did not follow her, and she wanted, more than anything, to escape.

Now nineteen, she stood at the top of the stairs, suitcases and servants surrounding her. She wept into a small embroidered, lilac-scented handkerchief her grandmother, Miss Nell, had made for her. Her father had said the night before that the world waited for her, was hers if she wanted it, and she had screamed at him for the first time in her life to let it wait, she was happy right where she was, thank you. Saratoga was everything. It was her world. What would she do without it? Her glory. Her burden. And he had reminded her with enormous sadness in his red-rimmed eyes that unless she did this thing, got on the train with him, observed the rituals, and won the victor's spoils, there would be no more Saratoga, that they would lose it all. A husband. A very rich husband. That was all that stood between them and total ruin. She had been given everything, every advantage. They had put everything they had into the making of this moment, and now it was time for her to do the one task she had been raised to do. They both knew what task he was speaking of.

She was headed off on the train to Baltimore to the first of twelve debutante balls. They were the first since the beginning of the war. During the war, darkness fell, and long-necked aristocratic beauties found their husbands however they could, at drab little dances held almost in secret, with only the most clandestine show of lavishness. All the handsome young men were gone to France, few to return. An entire generation of beautiful boys lost. Boys who might have been husbands. Now, with Germany collapsed and a peace treaty signed, people of means and breeding felt it was all right to dance again, to have the debutante balls that were such a necessary part of the social construct of the world they lived in. There was almost nobody younger than thirty who would be suitable, so behind the smiles she was going to meet the survivors and the memory of the dead.

Accompanying her on the social march would be her father and a hired chaperone from Richmond, Miss Lucy Ackerly, whose sole skill in life was shepherding young girls through the vagaries and complications of balls like these, for which there was a single purpose: to find a rich husband, a man who had escaped death in the war, either by luck or by cowardice—claiming flat feet or a mother whose sole support he was. Her father's only purpose was to lend an arm to lead her onto the floor so she could make her deep curtsy to society.

The curtain had lifted on a new world of gallantry and luxe. Miss Ackerly, nervous as a bride's mother, was there to see that, throughout the exhausting season, Diana Cooke did not put a foot wrong, ever, that she knew the name and lineage of every man she met before she met him, that she didn't put her heart in the wrong hands before she knew her mistake.

It all was costing Arthur Powell Page Cooke, her father, a fortune, the last of the money that could be scraped together. Twelve dresses, made by Diana and her mother out of bits of wedding dresses and family lace and peau de soie from Washington that nearly broke the bank and caused Diana's father to stay up especially late with Sir Walter Scott and one of the last bottles of the really good cognac. A small morocco leather case with a lock, containing the jewels she was to wear, the last the family owned or could borrow from relatives, nothing flashy—the pretty but insignificant pearl necklace, of course; diamond earrings; a thin circlet of a tiara from Mappin & Webb that her mother and her mother's mother, Miss Nell, had worn at their debuts and on their wedding days, cascading family lace draping behind, a tiara like a Greek warrior's laurel wreath, which had to be woven, not pinned, into her dark hair, in an arduous process that took hours—every piece planned and labeled for the dress it was to be worn with. Twelve pairs of satin shoes, from Montaldo's in Richmond. Her grandmother Miss Nell's demure mink coat for chilly nights. Twelve pairs of opera-length gloves, kid and satin. The full equipage of the debutante. Her father was gambling everything on her, and losing was unthinkable.

Everything in her life had led to this moment. Surrounded as she was, it was she who would step on the dance floor alone, leaving her father's trembling arm, she who would take the hands held out to hers, it was she who would have to separate the dross from the gold and come home with the husband who would save them. The point of finding Prince Charming, for Diana, was not to live happily ever after; it was to save the house, to secure the five thousand acres, and in so doing find a man with whom to live out her days who was not too disgusting or vulgar. Love, she understood, was not part of the equation.

Her father had been willing to sell another thousand acres, to send her to New York to the finest stores, the best designers, to acquire everything she would need, but she had sat down gently on his lap where he sat in his wicker wheelchair and said to him, handing him a brandy, "We're country folk, Papa, we'll do it our way. We'll make it ourselves, out of what we have. And it will all be fine. Divine. You'll see." And she kissed him tenderly on the forehead, sitting on his lap in his wheelchair, weeping for what he was willing to lose for what he hoped to gain.

As she was leaving him to his book and his brandy, he called out to her softly, and she turned to find tears in his red-rimmed eyes.

"Diana? Darling?" And then he stopped, as though that were the end of what he was going to say.

"Yes, Papa?"

He looked up at her. "You don't have to do this if you don't want. You know that, don't you? I hate the idea of offering you up like a calf to the slaughter. You are too precious to me."

"Papa . . ."

"Yes, we need saving. But there are ways, other ways. I could sell all the paintings, the silver."

"And what happens when that money is gone, Papa? What happens when the money is gone, and there's nothing left to sell, and I'm too old to be a calf, as you put it?"

"I'll think of something else."

"No, Papa. It's up to me now. The weight of Saratoga is on my shoulders. You rest, darling. It must have been so hard for you, all these years, watching it go in dribs and drabs. You kept it from me, my darling Papa. I thought we were rich, because you made sure I had everything I wanted, down to the most trivial little things, a fox muff, all that claptrap I needed, or thought I did, to fit in with the rich girls at Farmington. The worry you spared me from. Let me take it now. I love you and Mama with all my heart. I know now why Mama so rarely comes out of her room. Every foot out of this house costs money. I sorrow for the fear that keeps her spellbound, a prisoner in her own house, overlooking the tattered rug, the frayed curtain. It was all for me."

"We did it because we wanted to. In my heart, you will always be Cinderella."

"Well, the carriage awaits. At least until midnight, let's try to have some fun, and I will bring down the richest turkey in the flock with a single shot."

Her father laughed.

"You are a remarkable shot."

"Every man left around here, every suitable man, is a cousin. I have to get out in the world. I tremble with excitement. And I *will* win the day. If I can carry a book on my head for two hours at Farmington while reading Madame Bovary in French, surely I can bring down some unsuspecting billionaire."

Her father laughed again. "I know you can do it. I've seen you. But men are wily creatures. A harder shot than a whole rafter of turkeys."

"We'll see about that, my darling papa. Rest now. Do you want another brandy?"

"I always want another brandy."

"I'll get you one, then go help Mother make these damned dresses." As she handed him the brandy, she kissed him and smoothed back his thinning hair.

They say he was once the best rider in Caroline County. He was master of hounds for the Saratoga Hunt. To watch him ride, both assured and reckless, was something that was still talked about today at hunt meets. Now, a legend confined to a wheelchair, he sat alone most of the time, drinking himself to death in the largest and most beautiful house in Virginia, a house that had hung around his neck like an albatross since he came of age. And soon it would hang around hers. Forever and ever.

The invitations came, from people she'd never heard of. She was invited solely based on her lineage. She was a jewel of American society, whether she knew it or not. The Bachelor's Cotillion in Baltimore. The St. Cecilia Ball in Charleston, the Veiled Prophet Ball in St. Louis. Twelve in all. So she and her mother had sat for hours, planning each dress as each invitation arrived, looking through books of designs from Paris and New York, searching through the trunks upstairs for pieces of dresses that might be usable to make other dresses, going into Richmond to bargain with hawk-eyed shopkeepers for silks and satins of pure white, laces of a delicacy that frightened her. And they had constructed the dresses, each to be worn once and only once.

She knew that she was being put on the auction block, like one of her grandfather's father's slaves, brought to market and weighed and inspected. She was appalled at the thought—her family tree looked up and discussed and found to be a kind of American perfection, nobility and grace, unspoiled by too much sophistication and therefore malleable. She realized that her whole past had led to this moment, this shamefully mercenary endeavor, but she knew her worth, at least in the eyes of the American blue bloods. She'd been invited to the ancient rituals only because of her name and her great hulk of a house. The fact that she was southern was, in their eyes, a plus, as long as she wasn't a clumsy cow. She was slender, with lovely breasts and wide hips, good for bearing children.

And she knew, even as she imagined her teeth inspected by dowager after dowager, that this had to be done. It was what she'd been raised and educated for, to capture the brass ring of the nouveau riche, vulgar, pretentious aristocracy who had everything except what they vulgarly called "class." She had class to spare and no money. It would be like shooting fish in a rain barrel, and her hostesses felt their mouths water for their first sight of her.

Girls in her situation were marrying dukes and earls and even princes because the royals lived in these big piles they couldn't afford to heat. But these were rich girls, the awkward daughters of the new robber barons. She was poor. They had lived by their wiles and an aristocratic condescension even the rich girls couldn't muster.

She thought of her grandmother's fur coat, and she smiled.

Her grandmother's fur came from Montaldo's; she had gone all the way to Richmond to buy it. She charged it. Three years later, a woman from Montaldo's had called, gently reminded her of the purchase, and politely asked when they might expect payment. Her grandmother erupted in full dowager's rage. "How dare you harass me in this way, as though I were some common streetwalker?" she said, and slammed down the phone. She could not fathom why a store would dare to call her and ask for their money, even after three years.

So the rest of the family had to get together and scrape up the money to pay Montaldo's in cash, like sharecroppers.

Still, the invitations that came in, envelopes inside envelopes, like wedding invitations, on thick stock the color of fresh cream, came not because Diana was rich or well known but because her family tree had been studied by people who do those things. She could trace her ancestry all the way back to Pocahontas, the Indian princess who saved John Smith but married John Rolfe and was taken back to England and paraded at court in full regalia with a ruffled cuff around her neck, choking her. There Pocahontas, now christened Rebecca, bore one son, Thomas, from whom they all sprang. She didn't even speak English, and the ladies of the court got together and embroidered her prayers on all her nightgowns. She endured the cold, damp English winters, died of pneumonia on her way home, before she even got out to sea. So Diana was a kind of royalty, her family tree an American perfection, and she was asked by committees of people she didn't know to dances in places she'd never been to not for who she was but for what she was, an example of the finest bloodline America had to offer, breeding without blemish.

In fact, she saw herself as a slave to her own lineage.

Now she looked down the stairs at her family waiting below. She was wearing a trim periwinkle-blue traveling suit, with a cloche hat, kid gloves, and the one strand of real pearls the family had left.

They all looked up the stairs at her, as so many would look

up so many stairs at her in the months to come, dressed in one of the twelve dresses in the twelve boxes spread out around her.

"I've always said you had a pretty foot," said her mother, hardly looking up from her needlepoint, and after that moment Diana Cooke lost all hope, all reason to believe in romance. Her hair was carefully arranged around her face in a sweep of dark waves, her face without makeup. Her eyes sought the light, drew the light to her. She was, at nineteen, a stunningly gamine creature who was just setting off to burn the topless towers of Ilium, and all she had to go on was the knowledge that she had a pretty foot, the Tidewater's prettiest foot, now in pale-blue suede shoes that buttoned across her arch.

She realized that, for all her expensive refinements, her French lessons, her schooling in the ways of the horse, her readings of the classics, read while walking around a large cold room with a book on her head, she was what she always was, always would be, just a wild child from the Middle Peninsula of Virginia. She had practiced and learned every sophistication—how to serve a tea, how to rule benignly over servants, how to waltz with a precision known only to Swiss watchmakers—but she was still and always the little girl who ran barefoot through the fields and barns of her beloved Saratoga.

She had grown up alone, the only child on five thousand acres of field and forest and bright river. Her father had adored her, and that made up for his hurt in not having a boy, a boy child to carry on the name, the lineage unbroken for three hundred years.

There were to be more children, a brood, boys, but after he lost his leg in the Spanish-American War, a change came over him, and brandy and cigars replaced desire, and she was left, the only heir.

When she was seven, she was in the very first car accident ever to happen in Port Royal, Virginia. Her father, having not much to do, loved to drive into town, strapping on his painful and ill-fitting prosthetic leg, and get the paper and spend the morning talking with the boys on the porch of the general store. It was practically the last place he was treated with deference, and he liked that. Diana liked to go with him and take the nickel he gave her and dip her hand into the iced water of the metal box and slip out a soft drink and sit on the steps of the store, drinking a dope, as they called it then, and listening while the men talked about the war, their hopes for their crops. One day, for no reason she could remember, she set down her Coke and ran into the street, where the car ran over her. Cars in those days were so light and flimsy that it bounced over her without doing any damage at all, but it mortified her father that he had taken eyes off her, and so he told her she could have anything she wanted.

"I want to have my hair cut like a boy's" was her instant answer, and she and her father went to the barbershop, and they wrapped paper around her neck and draped her in a clean striped cloth, and they both watched with a combination of excitement and horror as her long, dark curls fell, one by one, to the floor. The barber swept up the curls and gave them to her in a paper bag, although what she might do with them wasn't clear to anybody.

They drove home, and Diana felt a freedom she'd never felt before, as though the tomboy in her had been let out of its cage. There was a gladness in her heart. At the door, her mother took one look, shrieked, and ran for her bedroom, but not before Diana could give her the paper bag filled with the hair she had only recently had on her head, as though her mother might find some way to get it all back on or, failing that, find some use for it.

Diana was sorry to trouble her mother, but it was the first

confirmation for her that if the fruit was forbidden, it was only because that fruit was the sweetest. She and her father sat at dinner with her red-eyed mother like the only gladiators who had escaped the Colosseum.

From a very early age, she was fearless, almost feral. She was a wild child surrounded by wild children who lived in the adjacent great houses of some of the finest families in the state. She pretty much did as she pleased without attracting the attention of the preoccupied adults in the house.

She had a governess, a thin, plain woman from France who taught her to drink red wine and know her domaines, to read Latin and to speak French passably well. When Mademoiselle Simone wasn't looking, or was taking her little nap after lunch, she would dash into the little alcove in which the telephone table sat, and make a clandestine call to another child in the neighborhood. "Indian Rock," she would whisper, or "Eagle Beak."

The word would spread, and each child—the Carter children, five of them, the Tayloes, ten, if you counted the cousins—would call one other, until they had twenty or more. She would hitch up her beloved pony, Pickle, to her wicker pony cart and race off, following trails through the woods that only she and the neighboring children knew, stirring up a fall of woodcocks, a herd of deer, the whispering glide of eagles resting on the draft high overhead, the majestic pines—she yelled it—"The majestic pines!" She listened as the ravens fluttered from the perches, black high up in the black, then settled again, the woods alive with animals only momentarily disturbed, and the boys and girls, ages eight to eighteen, would meet, each carrying a Mason jar full of clear liquor, moonshine bought with their allowance from the stable boys, trotting along through the dense woods in overalls, barefooted, imagining attacks by red Indians, enraptured by the flights of bald eagles high up in the tallest trees, no matter how many times they saw it, the way they floated on the breeze without a care, their astonishing seven-foot wingspan, the unimaginably beautiful symbol of their beautiful country since 1782.

When the pack of children reached their destination, cove or cave, always by the river, just at the water's edge, they would have their tea parties, eating ham biscuits, exchanging the news of their neighboring estates, always astonished at the business of running the great plantations, the peccadilloes of the workers, the tyrannies and lassitude of their parents, an unending gazette of the comings and goings of the farms, lying on the warm rocks, sipping from their Mason jars and passing them back and forth, letting their bare feet hang in the water, smoking the occasional purloined Cuban cigar. The willows trailed their tendrils in the water, the sun making explosions of fire on the tiniest ripple, their toes nibbled on by minnows, boys and girls in the wilderness, the best families in the tidal estuaries of Virginia, drunk at ten and eleven in the endless sun-blasted days.

Once, the boys huddled and came up with a powerful dare. For every girl who took off her clothes and showed them her naked body, one of the boys would do the same. It was unthinkable. Nudity in front of boys was practically a mortal sin, even if you were drunk and even if the sun was warm and lovely on your back, and even if you swam every day of your lives, boys and girls together, in your underclothes, the bigger boys repeatedly dunking the smaller girls.

Diana leaped at the chance. She longed, at eleven, to see what the stable boys called a man's member, and so she stood alone, alone in a circle of aghast girls and boys who had already gone shy and regretful, and dropped her clothes piece by piece carelessly in a circle around her. And she liked it, all those staring eyes, although many suddenly found a reason to look away, to look anywhere but at Diana Page Powell Cooke. Diana laughed, and twirled for them. Her whole body so smooth, slightly pudgy still, but lovely, her short hair making her nudity even more shocking, nothing hidden. She loved the freedom, she loved the fact that she knew it was a dirty, filthy thing to do, pulling back her skin so they could see the pink smile of her hairless vagina, and so she did it until she was tired and everybody had lost interest. She hadn't even reached puberty yet, and her summer body, all almond and cream, was so white, most alive in its secret bits.

She finally sat, and put her clothes on, and pointed to Billy Carter. "I pick you," she said, in a triumphant voice, but he merely laughed victoriously and said, "Are you crazy? I wouldn't do that for anybody."

And they all shyly backed away, leaving Diana to dust off her bottom as they left her alone, so that it was darkening and she was alone as she climbed into her pony cart and, smashing her Mason jar in betrayal and disgust against some rocks, gave Pickle a flick of the whip and started home through the gloom, barely making it to the table in time for dinner.

"And what did you do all day, young lady?" her father asked, pouring his claret.

"Oh, I behaved excessively badly, Father," she said, sitting straight-backed, all starched pique and lace, a ridiculously large grosgrain bow pinned to her short hair. "Quite horribly."

"I would expect no less, my dear," her father said, "Not one iota less."

"Disgraced the whole family."

"Diana!" Her mother sat up regally straight." I'm sure you didn't, darling, but this is not a subject for mirth." Diana thought of all those children going home to their own dinner tables and telling of their day's adventures, with Miss Cooke as the centerpiece, and wondered how long it would be before her mother heard the Awful Truth.

"You must never, ever forget who you are, who your people are. Your great-grandmother was a duchess. Your grandfather was the governor."

"And the duchess, who bought her title for cash, was a terribly mean old woman who cheated at cards and practically ate and drank us out of house and home," said her father. "And as for the governor, my father, I'll just say this. He robbed the state blind and spent it all on fancy women in Philadelphia, where he spent most of his one term. Useless excuse for a human being. He wasn't even rich by the end. Worst seat on a horse I've ever seen, and all we got out of it was that string of pearls you've got in the safe, which his long-suffering wife, my mother, got as an expiation for his infinite peccadilloes."

"You mustn't talk that way, dear. Diana, you come from people of quality. You must behave accordingly at all times, whatever the circumstances. I know you're joking, darling. Just keep your jokes confined to the family. And Father, don't lead her on so."

"She's a wretched child, and she'll probably end up in prison."

"You really think so? Oooh, I can't wait. Do you think I'll get to wear one of those black-and-white-striped things and work on the roadside picking up trash, chained to the man in front of me and in back of me, while another man with a shotgun watches over us in case we escape?" Diana roared with laughter, and her mother, resigned, returned to chewing her bite of roast beef one hundred times before swallowing. "At least I won't have to worry about what to wear. And I'd meet all sorts of interesting people. And I bet I could escape."

And still they laughed as they always did, that loving laugh that only fathers and daughters know. "If anybody could, you could, Diana Page Powell Cooke."

Her mother, at her end of the table, just assumed her usual air of amused tragedy, expecting correctly that there was more truth in Diana's confession than was ever acknowledged by father or daughter. She had grown up on the river herself, and knew its chicaneries, its innocence and its too-early experience. Children play. Here, what did they have to play with except each other, what toys except their own bodies?

But Diana never forgot it, her first betrayal, and she never forgave the cowardice. She loathed cowards, and she honored courage. She still went to the river in her pony cart every day, as though nothing had happened, and it pleased her to notice that she and she alone held her head high when her eyes met the eyes of her friends. Her humiliation was, after all, her victory.

Her father carried on with a distant good humor, reading Sir Walter Scott after dinner with his brandy until Clarence, his manservant, had to carry him to bed. Her mother was still praised for her seat at the hunt and for her clear soup at the dinners they gave for thirty or forty, but they all knew the terrible truth: the money was gone. The superb wines came from a cellar that was only depleted, never resupplied. Every penny that was left went into Diana's clothing and education. Unless she caught a good, a very good husband, Saratoga was lost.

And that was her mother's ultimate victory. When Diana was fourteen, she came home to dinner one night and threw up in her vichyssoise and then laughed. For the first time, her father was truly horrified by her behavior. Her mother sat up as straight as a plinth in her seat at what became the head of the table in an instant. She said only a few words, but she said them clearly, indelibly: "Farmington. As soon as possible." Diana promptly fell off her chair and had to be carried up to bed herself. Even her father knew it had gone too far. Even he, so jocular, was not amused.

She would go to Miss Porter's in Farmington, the girls' preparatory school and prison, whose sole purpose was to turn unrepentant little hoydens like Diana into graceful women who more closely resembled American versions of Princess Elizabeth of England. Diana wept, she yelled, she kicked and screamed and said vile things to and about her mother, the gentlest and most long-suffering of souls, who had, herself, been through the rigors of the school, and thought with a certain glee of the strict rules that would turn her wild savage into a woman of grace and, most of all, marriageability. "The most beautiful voice in the world is that of an educated southern woman," said Winston Churchill, and at Farmington, as any graduate called it, Diana would become that woman, ramrod straight, both on the dance floor and on the back of a horse, graceful at tea, charming at table, never lacking for a topic of interest, her vowels beautifully rounded, her *r*'s soft and sweet as rain, her every utterance a sign of where she had come from, a beauty mark of a certain nobility—in short, an educated, gifted, beautiful lure with which the Cookes would bait the hook.

She became all these things and more in her miserable days at Farmington. She learned that just because you're miserable, that doesn't mean you can't have a wonderful life. She pushed her southern accent as far as she felt it could reasonably go, and they, in turn, from New York and New Canaan, looked on her as a kind of exotic pet, brought from the wilds of Borneo or someplace, simply for their amusement. No matter how much she might cry herself to sleep at night every night, she left a trail of laughter wherever she went. She had an impeccable seat on a horse. She could dance a waltz with a book on her head.

Yes ma'am and no ma'am, a struggle for many of the girls, were second nature to her from the cradle. Her classmates vied to lure her to their palatial houses for the weekend, houses where Daddy went to Wall Street and Mummy went to Saks and the new wonder of fashion, Bergdorf Goodman. Her school chums, on the other hand, particularly the Jewish girls, had an irrational fear of visiting her, possibly out of fear they would be cornered and devoured by Negroes. She wrote perfect, charming thank-you notes in her graceful hand within minutes of returning.

In other words, she started to become the woman she was to be, the woman who would dazzle a century, instead of the girl who seemed so jejune (her new best word) to her now.

She had walked, kicking and mewling, down those long steps of home in the fall of 1914, a rough, untidy, charming but unfinished girl, her face a squall of fear and rage. She walked back up them in the spring of 1918, just as the Great War was coming to its end, everybody expecting victory any day—an ancient, as they say in Farmington, pulling off long kid gloves, chic in a red suit without being showy, a tall, willowy girl whose dark hair swept her shoulders, her eyes bright, her life an ascending stairway of illumination. She embraced her mother, she kissed her father, noticing in him the age and exhaustion the years had brought to his once jocular face. She had gone to Farmington on the eve of the Great War, nine million dead in Europe, and many at home exhausted, financially and emotionally, by the conflict. Some of her childhood friends—two Tayloe boys, one Carter, and several others—were lost in the mud of France. The days by the river seemed very far away. They'd still been so young, each one dead within days of his arrival, so quick to the slaughter in the greatest slaughterhouse ever known, as a somberness descended on the great houses of Virginia. Each one a local hero. There was talk of a monument to them, to be erected by the river they had loved so much, to stand where they could see the wide water, its tides and currents, its blues and greens and grays, its flurries and flights of plunging birds when the fish were running. But there was no money for monuments. Monuments cost money; grief was free. Everybody was broke. Everybody carried on, or tried to, as though nothing had happened—but the whole world had changed, and Diana had changed along with it.

Into this mourning she walked, red on black, a big feathered hat on her perfectly held head, a hat so large she couldn't really get close enough to kiss the faces she loved, so she laughed and threw it off, down the stairs, and gave them all proper kisses. She had not been home at all in her Farmington years. There was no money to ferry her back and forth during those holidays, and so she had spent them as a guest in one of the great suburban sprawls of the north, where her charm and manners only expanded, her seductiveness grew, her power to flirt and attract bloomed like the roses on her cheeks. The northerners were captivated by her accent and the perfection of her handwriting when she wrote her thank-you notes, all of which made them want her back immediately. Everybody who saw her fell in love with her. She ate delicately and sparely. She played poker with the men. She rode cross-country, taking the fences with wild breakneck abandon and delight, and yet everything she did was pervaded by a delicacy, a gentility, that was never stale. Every day seemed fresh to her, a new chance for fun. She would appear for breakfast and, as she sat down to her place, look around with wide-eyed wonder and declare, "I'm having fun already!" She was the darling of every heart. The downy-cheeked boys at school dances knelt at her feet and wrote her notes of unbridled passion, which she politely but distantly answered.

Her heart was far away, at the river, a jar of moonshine at her side, her friends around, the days endless under an azure sky that would never grow dark. Her heart was at Saratoga. She never spoke of it, for fear that even a mention of it might cause it to fall apart, wither, disappear into the fog that sometimes rose out of the mysterious blue depths of the Rappahannock.

And now she was home, the war nearly over, walking up the stairs, pulling off her kid gloves, taking off her hat, and calling out, "Whom does one see to get a martini around here?"

Her mother said, shocked, "It's four o'clock in the afternoon."

"Time means nothing, dear mother. A martini means everything. Is there gin, Father?"

Sitting with her father in his study, sipping her chilled martini under her mother's withering gaze, all she would say of her years at Farmington was "Well, the school motto says it all. 'Puellae venerunt. Abierunt mulieres,' which makes us sound rather like mules, don't you think, Father?"

He chuckled. "Are you weak in Latin or just weak in the head?"

She laughed. "They came as girls. They left as women. Or mules, depending on how you translate it. I rather prefer being livestock. Women are treacherous creatures. Livestock you can pretty much depend on, and if things get tough, and they do, they always do, livestock is at least edible. This martini is divine. It is the most divine martini I have ever had, although, to be truthful, I've only ever had one other. Is there time for one more before dinner?"

"Do not, and I mean not, get drunk before dinner, darling."

"That is my whole intention, my dear mother, after four completely, and I mean completely, sobering years at Farmington."

"Wouldn't you like to see your present?" her father asked.

"There are presents? How thrilling. First the present, then a quick divine martini, then a supper where I promise I will not fall off my chair. I have at least learned *something* at Farmington."

Her mother and father led her out to the barn, and there he was, well over fifteen hands high—Phaeton, her father told her, was his name—an enormous black Arabian stallion, a true exotic beauty, really, purchased with what funds she dared not surmise, although she had noticed a large pale space on the staircase where the Landseer had always hung. Best not to think of these things; better just to look at her stallion in wonder, to run her hands across his muscular flanks, to peer into his bottomless black eyes.

"Oh, Mother, Father, he is the most beautiful thing I've ever seen. We can't possibly afford him—but, oh, I do, I do want him."

"He's called Phaeton. I went all the way to the Middleburg sales three times before I found him. Just don't go and break your neck."

"My neck is now the most expensive single thing in Caroline County. I will take extra good care of it. When can I ride him?"

"Not tonight, I think. You *will* break that pretty neck. Particularly after a martini."

"Martini! I completely forgot. Father, rush to the bar and start pouring that gin. Mother is so rigid about the dinner hour. Eight o'clock and in your seat or death," father and daughter said in unison. Diana turned to her stallion, idling in his stall. "Good night, sweet prince, and flights of angels sing thee to thy rest. Until tomorrow." And she kissed him on his muzzle and backed away, her eyes glued to his.

She could have predicted dinner. Ham. Sally Lunn, a bread that had defeated many of the best cooks in the South, green beans boiled to an indescribable color of gray, floating in ham fat, and for dessert, bread and butter pudding. She ate ravenously.

"You mustn't put on weight, darling," her mother said.

"I have an eighteen-inch waist," said Diana, "and it will stay eighteen until the moon turns blue."

After dinner, a brandy with her father, who held the *Richmond Times-Dispatch* in front of him, slapping the page with irritation as he read of each new outrage in the Commonwealth. Women wanting the vote. People wanting to ban hard drink. It was a cold, hard world, and he wanted no part of it.

Then they retired, but not before Diana sneaked out, as she had so often, this time to lie on the floor of her stallion's stall and gaze up at him in wonder. "Oh, my darling, what places we'll go."

Hearing her name called distantly from the house, she reluctantly rose, the smell of hay and horse and dung clinging to her traveling suit, and made her way into the house in the dark. And so to bed.

THE SUMMER WAS all riding and answering invitations to debutante balls, invitations that they could not afford but which would not stop coming.

It was time to go to work. She now realized what the years at Farmington had been for. Her one job in life was to save Saratoga from the creditors, to save for her father and mother a comfortable old age. It was to sniff out, like a hound after a fox, a man with huge amounts of money, and make him, force him, to love her. Her life was meant not for love but to save Saratoga.

They left on a bright late-fall afternoon, her father, Miss Ackerly, and herself. They boarded the train for Baltimore on the first overnight sleeper, and into the world.

They stayed in a hotel that was not the finest. It was proper, but it was not elegant, one step removed from a boardinghouse. Her room was large and spacious, and looked out on train tracks that seemed to go on forever, that could take her anywhere she wanted to go. She had two dollars in her purse, her father not much more.

In the evening Miss Ackerly came to help her dress, and to weave the tiara, the insignificant laurel wreath of small but not great diamonds, into her hair. While dressing her, Miss Ackerly told her, as she had so many times before, exactly what to expect of the evening, the formalities, the intricacies of the etiquette, set in place decades ago.

By the time nine o'clock came, she knew all there was to know, and she was as ready as she could be. She felt that every nerve was on fire. She had twelve chances. She held twelve cards in her hand, and one of them must trump everything else on the table.

There was a dinner. She was seated next to some young banker, filled with ardor and charm, who unfortunately would not be coming to the ball itself. No man under thirty was considered old enough to have established a firm footing in the world, certainly not firm enough to have acquired the requisite pile of money to take on a bride. These young men were like delicious hors d'oeuvres, taken away exactly at ten, at dinner's end, to be replaced by more substantial fare, older men who had the resources and the place in business to take on a wife. The older bankers and lawyers and landowners stood at the edges of the grand ballroom, filled with dozens and dozens of red roses, like horsemen at the sales at Keeneland.

For a long interval, one divine girl after another, carrying the bouquet of red roses they had all been given, was led onto the floor by her father, who then left her alone to make her exquisite curtsy. One girl fell down, and then it was Diana's turn.

She made her entrance out of the shadows, through the velvet curtains, onto the floor under the scrutiny of all the regal eyes, of all those handsome men. For a moment she stood, freed from her father's arm as he wheeled himself back from her, until she was alone in the light, eyes lowered demurely, under the hundreds of candles in the seemingly hundreds of crystal chandeliers, the luminous room catching the glitter from her warrior's tiara, her luminous, flawless skin, and then she bowed her head, her swan's neck bending so that her chin touched her neck, and made the curtsy that was so elegant, so graceful, it was forever to be named after her. She bowed to the floor and rose like an angel, shining eyes wide open, rose into triumph, rose into legend, rose into a beauty that was never to be touched or equaled. And then she stepped back, her head high, like a rider approaching a jump, looking past the hurdle. And then she just stood, seeming to look into every eye, her gaze piercing every heart. The most beautiful girl in the world in white satin, holding a bouquet of red roses, perfectly still, knowing that she had done it, done the thing she was supposed to do, and if not now, then on some night like this, Saratoga would be saved once and for all.

Her father wheeled forward, gently took her arm, and escorted her from the light. Once they were out of the eyesight of the crowd, he looked up at her from his chair, tears in his eyes, and patted her arm. "Bless you, child," he said, and she kissed his forehead. There was such a deep and loving understanding between them, there was no more to be said.

2

SHE HAD WON the season, she had won her place in every season to come, and she had won her place in the eyes of Captain Copperton, who approached her that first night in Baltimore like a snake in a barnyard, handed her his card, and said, "I'm Captain Copperton, and I'm going to marry you."

She laughed. "Don't mock me. You think I'm just a simple country clod. But I have fangs. And I can shoot the head off a turkey at a hundred yards."

His card was oversize, as the Europeans make them. The first thing she noticed was that there was nothing on the card except his name, which was fancifully engraved in copper ink. The second was his hair, which was the same color as the large carnelian set in the signet ring into which his seal was deeply engraved, bright rust-colored, the seal that she would only later learn was, like everything else about him, completely fabricated out of his own sprawling imagination.

There were so many of these evenings to come, every one alike, the fanciful dinners at which charming young men sat on either side, filled with talk of college and rugby and rowing. And then the dance itself—rich older men, that being the whole point of coming out; to go right back in, into a comfortable, fulsome marriage, into the babies and the nannies and the servants and the summers at the family cottage in Maine, vast, sprawling, mildewed places where families of thirty or forty would get together for the month of August. All this awaited her, and the goal was clear—to marry the richest man she could find so that Saratoga could be saved—she never took her eye off the gold ring that awaited. Still, the young men were more fun than the fossils she met later in the evening, at the actual ball, and she blushed with pleasure when one or another of them shyly slipped her his card. But then there was the rest of the evening to get through, on her father's arm, regal in his wheelchair, and then alone in the middle of the floor at Savannah or Richmond or St. Louis, the curtsy, the rise, her neck arched as though her face were a flower, turning toward the light.

And Copperton. Always Copperton.

She had been a wild success. Debutante of the year, they said, a jewel out of nowhere, all the rarer for that, for the fact that although her bloodlines were impeccable, her presence, herself, her infinite charms, were fresh, never seen before. Her homemade dresses endeared her all the more, her undeniable beauty making the other girls look awkward and overdressed. She had been photographed so many times she had forgotten how many, and she drew to herself the handsomest and the richest and the most refined. In their etiolated manners, so perfect, so ancient, she found no joy. She was—Farmington be damned—still the girl who took a dare down at the river. These boring men wanted to trot; she wanted to gallop.

Now here was Copperton. A big fish on her first cast. The notorious Captain Copperton. He stood before her in all his full-blooded vigor, the vastness of his wealth trailing out behind him into infinity, every penny of it brand-new, a strange figure out of nobody knew where, out of the ordinary and into the splendid sheerly through the vastness of his greed, his way of grasping at anything and anybody who would make him money, his fortune, like his hair, as red as a newly minted penny. Miss Ackerly, watching him follow her, had warned that he was not the sort, not *our* sort, a carpetbagger, entirely nouveau in money and manners. Diana looked at his splendid blue eyes and said demurely, "Do you have any hooch in that flask in your jacket?"

"You have a sharp eye," he answered.

"It comes from shooting Indians in the wilderness from which I have no doubt you know I come."

"There is brandy on my right, and whiskey on my left. When my evening clothes were made in London, I had flasks in both pockets when they fitted me, so they could fit the coat to make them invisible, just as they fit the coat with your arms up, as though you're dancing, so it hangs right."

"Not entirely. Invisible, I mean."

"They hadn't encountered you, Miss Cooke. So I am well provided for a lady in distress."

"Because I am dying for a drink as a man in the desert is dying for lack of water."

"That can be arranged easily enough."

"Can it? My chaperone . . . the Gorgon, my father."

"I will be outside on the terrace in ten minutes. You will, no doubt, find a way. Clever girl like you."

"What makes you think I'm clever? I could be just another unschooled idiot from the sticks."

"In that case, I will have to make you sophisticated. You don't have to be clever for that. You just have to read magazines."

"At Farmington, we only read movie-star magazines. And that only under cover of darkness. By daylight, we read Latin and Greek. Neither clever nor sophisticated, I'm afraid."

"We are alike, Miss Cooke."

"And how is that, Captain Everybody-Knows-Who-You-Are Copperton?"

"We are entirely made up. Out of whole cloth. Out of nothing. Out of darkness we have become dazzling beings. From the moment you made your first curtsy on this ridiculous circuit of virginity, yours was the only face in the room, the rest just moon-faced hopefuls who will sink back into the tide of ordinary lives from which they came. You are a brightness on your way to a greater brightness. All you need is money. I am made entirely of money, you of beauty. And I mean to have you. To make you one of the great women of the world."

"I believe that is entirely in my hands, Captain Copperton. Entirely. At the moment you have only one thing I want. And I will somehow meet you on the terrace in ten minutes and have it. Good evening."

In ten minutes, she was there with a thirst that seemed insatiable. They drank from the silver flasks and talked about it all.

"You're a princess from the country, and I'm an utter black-hearted cad, and I mean to sweep you off your feet and marry you as soon as possible. I've done my homework. I will show you the world, dress you in the couture of the moment. You will be the beauty of the age. For every acre you have, I have a million dollars to back it up."

"I have five thousand acres and a famous house that eats money."

"I know all this, and I know you're sinking like the *Titanic*. The band may still be playing, but there is nothing but ruin ahead. Besides offering you love, or what I call love, I offer you a fortune that is endless. Coal mines. Oil wells. Forests to cut. There is no end to it. I want somebody to love me, to have my children. I'm forty-two years old. I have flitted like a butterfly from this heiress to that, and now I want to settle in with a woman of quality.

"I saw you rise from your curtsy, and I offer you my fortune, my heart, and you have to offer nothing except the sweetness of your love and the fruits of your loins. Let us be a happy, comfortable couple. I offer you everything I have, and all you have to give me is your heart. A fortune waits for you, anything you want, and my heart.

"I'm not good at this. I have many flaws. But, flaws, flaws and all, it's all yours for the taking. Your father is free to get in touch with my solicitors. They will verify everything I have said. Marry me, Miss Cooke."

"Oh, stop. You're being extremely foolish. I don't even know you. What are those medals for, anyway?"

"It did sound sort of like malarkey, didn't it? Except for the you-*are*-going-to-marry-me part. But first, we'll have dinner tonight."

"Impossible. Miss Ackerly, my chaperone, shares my room."

"I should think that after four years of sneaking out after curfew at Miss Porter's, evading that old mummy will be a cakewalk for you. After this travesty of a ballroom has turned into a wilted bloodred mess, I will pick you up at your hotel. Leave this dress in a puddle on the floor and meet me in something black and sexy."

"It's . . . I don't have . . ."

"I know where you're staying. And I bet in that luggage you have something suitable for melting a red-haired cad's heart. Lose the tiara. Your hotel has the stench of sad desire about it. It was once grand, you know, like so many things. Let's be grand again, for one night. Midnight. Good evening, Miss Cooke."

Her heart suddenly beat faster. She was Red Riding Hood, and she had met the Wolf.

An hour later, having tucked her father in with his brandy

and gotten out of the dress and the crinolines and the bustle that held it up, and gotten into her nightgown and feigned sleep until Miss Ackerly was, indeed, sleeping like a mummy, her long, stringy hair splayed across the pillow, soft wheezing sounds coming from her nose, her nostrils flaring with each intake of breath, Diana got up and, in the light from the street, interrupted only by the sounds of the passing trains, got herself into a midnight-blue silk dinner dress, the simplest of shapes, and her pearl necklace, and descended the stairs to the shabby lobby where the night porter slept and found Copperton waiting, top hat in hand, still in white tie and tails.

There was something so clandestine about it all, so sinful, it made her blood rush.

"Beauty descends," said Copperton. "We have a taxi waiting to take us to Marconi's, ironically on Saratoga Street."

She had never been in a taxi. It seemed indefinably luxurious, watching the lights of the city going by, taking her far from the grime of her hotel and leaving them in front of the brightly lit grandeur of Marconi's. They walked up marble steps, scrubbed to a blinding whiteness, and into the small foyer where the maître d' greeted Copperton by name with great deference.

"Captain Copperton, my friend, it's so good to see you. Your usual table?"

"I think something more intimate. Somewhere where we can talk. We have much to discuss. This is Miss Cooke."

"Pleased to have you, Captain," said the maître d' with ultimate slavishness. "And Miss Cooke, I looked to heaven for an angel, and then she walked through the door of my restaurant. I hope we can please you." Diana blushed, flushing from the neck up. Mr. Marconi—she assumed that was who he was—led them to a quiet table in a small but grand room, chandeliers casting a perfect light on every face, the pale green of the walls making everything a kind of perfection she had never seen before, the tuxedoed waiters moving so silently it was like a magic act, eight waiters delivering eight dinners to eight diners at the exact same moment. She had never seen anything so grand in all her life. Men and women sat at tables for two, the men in evening dress, the women in dinner dresses that far surpassed her own, wearing jewels that made her own small pearls look like something a child would wear for her First Communion.

But word had already spread. Many of the diners had been at the ball. They strained their necks to catch a view of her, the already infamous Diana Cooke. They knew who she was and where she came from. They knew she was the jewel of the season, and of course Copperton had wanted her, and what Copperton wanted, Copperton got.

When they were seated, and she had taken in the dazzling array of forks and knives, some almost a foot long, she raised her head and looked him straight in the eye. "First of all, where does the Captain come from?"

"The Crimea. The Spanish-American War. The endless struggle to stamp out the devil. Who gives a rat's ass? Next?"

"The medals?"

"Marksmanship, Whittling balsa-wood airplanes at summer camp. Saving my men in the Charge of the Light Brigade. General heroism, like the heroism it takes to ask the prettiest girl in the world out to dinner when her legend already precedes her like a lightning bolt. What right do I have? Ask my solicitors."

"Your people?"

"They are the best-kept nobodies in the world."

"And home, where is home?"

"I grew up in Cadstown, USA, and attended Cadsville University, from which I graduated with high honors. I fought a duel and killed a man."

"For what reason."

"He bothered me."

And where is home now?"

"Any place that doesn't bore me."

The waiters brought the menus, and Copperton waved away hers. "I'll order. I know what's good. By the way, as an hors d'oeuvre, I have a little something for you, to commemorate your triumph." And he pulled from the pocket of his uniform a blue velvet box and handed it to her.

Hesitantly, she reached across the table and took it. Inside was a broad band of diamonds, a cuff for her wrist. She immediately closed the box and handed it back.

"Captain Copperton, would you call me a cab?" She rose from her chair as a tuxedoed waiter instantly appeared. "I've lost my appetite for supper."

"Oh, Lord, don't be such a bumpkin. It was meant—"

"It was meant as payment to get me into bed with you. Even you should know that ladies don't accept jewelry from men they're not married to, and, in this case, hardly know. Even the most cloddish of bumpkins, thank you, knows that. I wish to leave. Do you just carry these trinkets with you like Hallowe'en candy to amuse children? Are you so unloved?"

He looked in her eyes. The lights from the candles on the table flickered in his own. His face collapsed, took on a new, less arrogant expression. "Miss Cooke, if you wish, I will escort you home. But if you stay, I will give you wonderful food, and I will drop the facade of my life and tell you the whole story, whatever you want to know. I am the most honest man you will ever meet, and I will invite you into my hardscrabble world, and I guarantee you every word will be true and honest and from the heart. I give you my word as a gentleman, which, whether you believe it or not, is true as scripture."

She started to sit down and then stood up again, the waiter moving the chair in and out,

"What is your name?"

"You must promise never to say it again. Never. That person is long gone."

She sat, and the waiter heaved a sigh of relief as he put her back in her place, asked if she wanted a pillow for her back, and then walked away to his clamoring chores.

"I promise."

"Billy Lux. William. That is the first and only time that name will be heard."

"It's a beautiful name."

"Or Charlie Mann. Or H. L. Mencken, or Harry Houdini. What does it matter?"

"Where I come from, it matters a great deal. You promised the truth."

"And that is the truth. What does it matter? I am Captain Copperton from now to the grave. No fixed profession, no fixed abode, useless in every way but one."

"And that would be?"

"I have an endless supply of money, and an endless ability to make more."

The food began to arrive, along with copious amounts of champagne the Captain had somehow ordered.

"And if that's not good enough, go off and marry George Washington the eighteenth or somebody."

"He's very charming, but he's my cousin."

And for the first time they both laughed, conspirators in courtship.

"And he doesn't have a pot to piss in. I, on the other hand, am also charming, and I happen to be the eighth richest man in America. You have nothing. Marry me, and you will have everything, things you can't even imagine. Your father will live out his days in splendor. Your mother can do her needlework just as easily on the first-class deck of an ocean liner."

Oysters on the half shell were replaced by quail, followed by Dover sole. She was beginning to feel both drunk and faint. Then there were filet mignons, bloodred, and, finally, the lobster imperial for which the restaurant was famous. And through it all, an ocean of talk. Witty. Lewd. Seductive. It was almost three in the morning, and the dining room showed no signs of closing.

Diana was tired, but Copperton's energy didn't seem to be flagging, and through it all his intense blue eyes never left hers, sparkling with merriment, the eyes of a seducer.

It came time, finally, to leave.

"Remember," he said. "My heart, and my fortune, are yours for the taking. You may resist, but I mean to have you, and I didn't get so rich by not getting the thing I want."

Drunk, she answered, "Talk of money is vulgar."

"Dear girl, when you have it, you never have to mention it again. It's only poor people who talk about money."

In the cab, he kissed her; his hands touched her body, and she let him. In the lobby he clicked his heels and bowed, offering her a perfectly gauged and perfectly polite good night. She held out her hand, and he kissed it.

The elevator doors slid shut, and she watched as his flame-red hair fell away from her, floor by floor.

She slipped as quietly as she could into her room, where the Gorgon slept her holy sleep. She undressed, making sure to put everything away neatly, so that no one would know she had been out.

She laid the things in her purse on the mirrored vanity table. There, in her purse, was a blue velvet box she had seen before.

There was no need to open it. She knew what it was.

3

THERE WERE ELEVEN more balls, just like the first one, the red roses, the satin dresses, the gasp as she rose from her curtsy and her face caught the light. But in a sense, for Diana, the season was over. She had broken one of the cardinal rules of southern womanhood—she had accepted a lavish present from a man she hardly knew. She was famous now. Debutante of the year. She was on the cover of magazines, which outraged her mother, who believed women should be in the press only when they married and when they died.

And he, this Copperton, if that's what he wanted to be called, stalked her like a wild animal from city to city; in every city, he the wolf and she the rabbit. It was always the same: a swig from a silver flask, the clandestine dinner, the same flourishes from the waiter, food appearing from beneath silver domes, sometimes flaming at the table, the battle of wits, and somehow, at the end of it all, the velvet box she had to hide at the very bottom of her steamer trunk.

Was this love? Was it *like* love? She hardly knew. He brushed away any other suitors like flies on a peach, so he was all she knew.

After the last ball, she and her father made their way back to Saratoga, packing Miss Ackerly back to wherever she came from with a sigh of relief, arriving home to find dozens of invitations and letters of introduction from some of the finest American gentlemen, with bloodlines that stretched back to Plymouth Rock, filled with a kind of timid longing. But it was all set before it began.

Copperton made the obligatory trip to Saratoga in the company of two lawyers to meet with her father to describe, not his lineage, but his fortune. There was oil in Texas, wells that kept pumping and pumping, always more; there were copper mines and railroads, and vast forests of timber, and foreign investments, diamond mines and ships that carried cargo across the sea, a fleet of twelve tankers. It seemed endless, and it was.

"She is the dearest thing in the world to me," said Arthur sternly, tears in the corners of his eyes. "My wife is, well, she's my wife, and I love her, of course. We were engaged before we were born. The family has done great things, important things. I would expect the same of you, were you to join us. This house has stood for generations, and we are poor, as you know, but I would rather see it burn to the ground than have my daughter experience one moment's unhappiness."

"And there we are in agreement, sir," said Copperton. "I would throw my fortune in the sea for her happiness. Live in a shack by the river. But, as my lawyers will explain, it needn't come to that. I intend for her, and you, and your wife, to have the most elegant, the most luxurious, life possible. You will live in comfort for the rest of your life, and she will know a happiness that every woman in the world will envy."

Then the lawyers got out the ledgers and began to go over the long lists of numbers. It was more than impressive. It was unbelievable. When they were finished, and the ledgers were closed and put away in their black leather cases, Arthur wheeled himself to the drinks table and poured two brandies, and he and Copperton toasted and drank, and Copperton kissed him on both cheeks and called him Father, and so Diana Cooke was sold to the highest bidder.

After dinner, he knelt before her in the moonlight on the terrace, both of them slightly drunk, and slipped a ring on her finger, a six-carat yellow square-cut diamond surrounded by smaller crystal-clear white diamonds. And then Diana shocked them both. She led Copperton to her bedroom, the house sleeping, and she gave him her body before she gave him her hand in marriage. He made love expertly, passionately, and he made allowances for her virginity, and was sweet and gentle with her, and the new world of womanhood opened like a lotus blossom and she found the passion that had been coursing in her blood since that long-ago day by the river when she had stood naked in front of all her childhood friends, only to find that her naked body could be both a joy and a humiliation.

She was nineteen years old.

Copperton devoured her, celebrated her body, claimed her as his own, as he would claim an oil well, another coup for his portfolio. After the heat of passion had passed, they lay in the dark and cool of the night air, wrapped around each other, under covers against the night's chill, and talked about what fun they would have, a life of endless delights just waiting for them, trips and parties, and nights in hotels of such untouchable luxury that her breath would leave her body at the wonderment of it all. And sex, always sex, more and more adventurous, more intense. No two people on earth, he said, had ever enjoyed the pleasures they would find in each other's bodies.

And then they made love again, this time with greater intensity, greater freedom, and then again, until it was almost dawn, and Copperton slipped back into his clothes and back to his room, for an hour of sleep before it was time to appear at the breakfast table, where he showed up, freshly bathed and shaved, the picture of health and vigor.

At breakfast they made plans for the wedding, which he insisted would be held as soon as the dress could be made. It would be made this time not by Lula in the village but by the finest couturier in Paris, now that is was safe to cross the Atlantic again, the Armistice having just been declared in November.

In December they traveled first class on the *Aquitania*, with Diana's mother along to chaperone. On board there was caviar and champagne before dinner, and then course after course of culinary delights. Everything en croute, or covered in a delicate cloud of spun sugar. Her mother was dazzled into silence. Diana took few clothes. She took two empty steamer trunks, which Copperton told her they would fill in Paris. He had done his homework. He knew the names of all the dressmakers, and had made appointments with each of them.

Paris was alive and joyous with victory. People danced and kissed in the streets at night, practically having sex in public, shocking Mrs. Cooke. They stayed at the Ritz, glamorous beyond Diana's imagination, where Copperton seemed to have stayed many times before; everybody knew him. Diana's mother was stunned by the massive flower arrangements alone, and her room, with its majestic view of the Eiffel Tower, almost made her faint. They stayed in adjoining suites, so it was easy to slip discreetly between beds in the night; Diana's mother retired early after a long day of walking the city, guidebook in hand, and slept, oblivious, in heavenly peace until breakfast was wheeled into the suite at eight. She had never seen a croissant, took an instant liking to them, and could consume several while poring over her ubiquitous guidebook for the day's adventures, for which a sweet young English student served as her guide. In every room, by the bed, there was a button that merely read "Privé" that Diana was terrified to push, for fear of what it might summon. In her whole stay, she never pushed it, and she never knew.

As for Diana and Copperton, their days were spent visiting the couture houses one after another. Going into the first, the House of Chanel, Copperton said to her in a low voice, "Never ask the price. It's vulgar. Just nod at something you like. I'll take care of the rest." In each, they were brought by a trim, beautifully dressed middle-aged woman into a high-ceilinged, gilt-decorated room, seated on a sofa, and offered tea.

At Chanel, she sat primly in her red traveling suit. The clothes the models paraded before her were overwhelming. She thought of her tomboy days, and the thrill of wearing pants in the daytime, and she nodded and nodded, and then came chic little black beaded dresses for night, and even though she could not imagine much need for them in Port Royal, Copperton encouraged her to get three, and so she nodded at her favorites.

At the end, there were always the wedding dresses, amazing concoctions, like the spun-sugar clouds on the boat, but none was the right one, and she was careful not to nod her head.

After the first parade, she was led into the atelier, where the great Chanel herself, smoking like a madwoman, welcomed her with a warmth tinged with jealousy and took her measurements, writing everything on a yellow card, while a helper noted the numbers on a mannequin that had her name on it.

And then on to the next and the next, and more nodding and measuring, and kissing on both cheeks, and secret exchanges of money by Copperton and the stern-looking woman who appeared at the very end with a notebook marked with her name.

At the end of a long week, with no wedding dress in hand, they went to the boulevard Haussman, to the House of Babani, who, besides showing his own designs, marketed those of talented foreigners, principally Mariano Fortuny, an artist and designer who lived in Venice and who was rumored to make dresses unlike anybody else's. As soon as Diana saw the first one, she asked Copperton to wait outside. After only half an hour, she came out with a small bag, small enough to hold a bathing suit, and asked Copperton to go inside and settle up with Mr. Babani. There was a smile on her face, and she gave Copperton a wink as he passed her going into the shop.

There was nothing more to do in Paris. They embarked the next day for New York, and seven more days of lap robes, champagne, and meringues. Mrs. Cooke was weary of monuments and paintings almost to death. Diana herself felt perfectly well, something that was to be her specialty the rest of her life.

4

ON MAY 15, 1919, three hundred and fifty guests sat in rented chairs on the sweeping back lawn on Saratoga, having been seated by twelve groomsmen. On the bride's side sat one hundred and fifty representatives of the first and finest families in Virginia, families who had made the state, made the country. On the groom's, two hundred sophisticates who were as strange and out of place as peacocks in the desert. The two sides of the aisle looked at each other with curiosity, like animals in a zoo. Still, these strangers were staying in the great houses of the Northern Neck and the Middle Peninsula. There was not a guest room that was not full, and an uneasy truce had developed between the two sides.

The men and women were in their seats by four fifteen, and there they waited. And they waited, and they waited. Copperton appeared at exactly four thirty, with his best man at his side. He had wanted to accept the many offers they had had from magazines to have the wedding photographed, but Diana's parents firmly put their feet down and declared this an impossibility, and Copperton at last gave up. Still, the river was full of boats crowded with photographers hoping to catch a shot even at a distance, of the bride approaching, of the vows being taken.

Upstairs, at her dressing table, already in the dress that was to enhance her fame, Diana Cooke sat and looked at her face in the mirror. She knew they were all waiting for her, but she was frozen in place. At nineteen, she was about to enter into the rest of her life, and she was paralyzed.

By five o'clock the guests were getting nervous. It was cocktail time, and certain hands began to shake. Copperton, red-faced, stepped away from the flower-laden altar, under an arch of magnolia he had brought florists from New York to build, and walked the long walk back into the house. He stood at the bottom of the stairs and called her name, first softly and then with more force, so that he could be heard outside. "Diana? Diana, darling?"

She could hear him as though from very far away, but she couldn't find the strength to move or to answer. He loitered for a few minutes at the bottom of the stairs, where he was joined by Diana's mother. "I'll go up," she said. "Just go out and start serving champagne and give some humorous explanation, and we'll be down in a jiffy."

She went up, knocked softly on Diana's door, and, not getting a response, let herself in quietly and closed the door behind her. She found her daughter ramrod straight in front of her mirror in the famous dress, and she went and sat beside her on a low stool, and she just waited. After what seemed like an eternity, Diana said quietly, not turning her head, "I'm making the worst mistake of my life."

There were no tears, nothing to ruin her makeup, but there was a deep and terrifying sense of tragedy in her eyes. Her mother rose and held her softly in her arms for a long time, careful not to disturb so much as a hair on her head. "I know, my darling, I know. But the thing is done. Isn't it?"

"Yes. Done. Hold my hand."

And they held hands for a time, mother and daughter, and then the mother dropped her hand and slowly left the room, but not before saying, "My darling girl. You have given yourself to this man for all of us. It was a great sacrifice, and your father and I love you, as we have always loved you." She squeezed her hand. "This is your life. Your only life. Do whatever you want to do, my sweet lovely daughter. If you want to call it off, we'll find some way to do it. Even at this hour. Your father will make a little speech, and you will be free of it, of him. Our love will be with you just the same." Then she was gone.

Diana rose from her dressing table and moved to the window and looked over the waiting crowd. Waiting for her. She saw the boats in the river, the hungry-eyed cameras. Waiting for her. And Copperton. Waiting for her. She was wearing the diamond cuff he had given her a lifetime ago in Baltimore. She smoothed down her golden Fortuny dress, smoothed her hair, put her hand on her stomach, and breathed deeply. She threw open the window, and the sweet, warm spring air came in. She leaned out and yelled, so that everybody could hear, "Oh my darlings, forgive me. A case of girlish jitters. I am so sorry to keep you waiting. How rude of me, my darlings. If you'll sit for one more second, I'll be right down." Then she ran and opened the door and skipped down the stairs and out the door and into the golden light of the approaching evening.

On the stone terrace, with every eye on her, she took her father's arm and smiled a radiant smile, and together they moved down the stone steps and down the long aisle, preceded by twelve bridesmaids. The aisle was strewn with spring flowers, and Diana's radiance never faltered, never failed, as every woman, and some of the men, gasped at the daring and beauty of her, naked beneath the clinging, golden Fortuny dress. The shock that rippled through the crowd was exactly the reason she had chosen this dress, this one daring dress, over every spun-sugar confection in Paris.

Only her father knew how she trembled, how close she came to falling.

It was a simple silk column, golden, and pleated with what seemed like hundreds and thousands of pleats, the fabric so light it was almost transparent as it clung to her naked body. Glass beads weighted it down on each side and at the hem, which puddled around her on the ground, revealing golden, beaded silk shoes with every step. It was so light a confection it seemed the slightest wisp of air might have blown it away altogether, and she carried a single golden lily at her waist that hardly covered what every woman saw immediately: Diana Cooke was pregnant.

The cameras clicked so madly from the boats in the river that even across the water, everybody could hear them, like a swarm of bees, as she approached the altar, her veil of golden lace flowing out, sunlit wings from the beaded band around her forehead. She smiled lovingly at Copperton, who stepped forward in relief that barely concealed his irritation. He took her elbow from her father, and together they faced the minister.

Weddings are brief affairs, no more than fifteen minutes to seal two lives together for life. Diana and Copperton stood erect, facing the river, enduring the ceaseless clicking of the cameras, Copperton welcoming the notoriety, Diana horrified, and they spoke only when spoken to. They exchanged rings, hers tiny, his massive, and they said I do, and then they kissed, Diana's stomach churning, and then it was over. They turned to the crowd and waved to applause, and with ravishing smiles on their faces, walked the long, flower-strewn way back to the house. The crowd left their chairs and eagerly headed to any of the three bars that had been set up as the sun went down, and dozens of torches were lit to illuminate the reception, which was lavish beyond anything ever seen before in Virginia.

There were endless roast Rappahannock oysters, with their

slightly salty, almost buttery taste, ham biscuits, which the southerners devoured, and the Yankees eyed askance, because, as one of them said, "This tastes like something you'd put down on the driveway after a snowstorm." There were mounds of caviar, gotten from God-knows-where, since by the end of the nineteenth century the American rivers were almost fished out of sturgeon, and trade with Russia had only just begun. There were gallons of St. Cecilia's Society Punch, made famous in Charleston, and all the hard liquor the hardest drinker could want.

Diana rushed upstairs to change her clothes. The golden wedding dress was thrown on the bed, and she changed into a peach-colored evening dress from Lanvin, tier after tier of peach silk down to her ankles, with a giant rose at the waist, and two teal streamers that fell almost to the floor.

Then the guests sat down to filet and pommes Anna and Sally Lunn and magnum after magnum of Pommery, and the revelry went on and on, Diana the most boisterous of all, dancing with her new husband to a twenty-piece orchestra brought down from New York, playing swing music, the latest rage, and no one danced with more abandon than she did. There was a brief stop for the cake, a fantastic towering creation also brought down somehow from New York, covered in royal icing, shipped layer by layer and assembled in the great kitchen at Saratoga. At the top, Diana and Copperton in spun sugar, and they did the cutting with great hilarity, and then three hundred and fifty mostly drunk men and women each were given a piece, some in gold boxes to take home to say, "I was there, I saw it all, how it began."

The Virginia families left first. Copperton's friends stayed until the sun was coming up, the staggering men helping bedraggled women to their cars, so many beautiful dresses in ruins, and then it was over and it was silent. The boats had long since moved away and the river was smooth as glass as the sun came up and the gray turned to rose and gold on the water and one eagle swooped through the lovely moonshot sky as Diana and Copperton stood on the dock, arm in arm, silhouetted against the brightening water. And then they kissed at last.

Diana stood on the dock, the sun shimmering through her gossamer dress. Instead of tossing her bouquet over her shoulder, she dropped it with disdain in the river and watched as the tide quickly pulled it away. What had she done? Who was this vulgar stranger to whom she had sold herself?

Finally they went to bed, the wedding clothes swept to the floor, and made love with a mixture of ferocity and repulsion, and so it was to be for the entirety of their marriage.

The golden dress was wrapped in tissue in a box, where it lay until the night she wore it one last time, for Gibby, sweet Gibby, many years later, and then never again, given to a museum, the only people glad to have it.

Ah, Gibby. Even now, he sweeps over her like warm water. Gibby, her life, her love, her brief reward for her girlish sacrifice. Gibby the golden boy. Gibby the lost. Gibby in flames.

5

THEY SPENT THEIR honeymoon doing the two things they did best—having sex and shopping. Diana, until so recently ignorant of the ways of both, took to them with a vampire's eagerness for blood. She had been blind to sex before, but now that the veils were ripped from her eyes she saw everything as sexual—a ride in the back of a London taxi, where they kissed with a hunger that seemed criminal, an entrance into a Paris hotel where she was already known from her previous trip, and greeted with an obsequiousness that was mortifying, all these things did was make her want to rush to some private place where she could be relieved of the clothes that suddenly seemed to be strangling her. While the bellman stacked and emptied the trunks—there were four—she was almost at the point of screaming, whereas Copperton, to torture her, languidly dragged everything out, making conversation with the bellman, whom of course he knew by name, the bellman talking about his family and, with an apology lest the Captain think he didn't like his job, about the relief of his days off, his pleasure in his children and his wife, while Diana inwardly moaned, until Jean or Jacques finally left, a load of cash in his hand, and a nod to the Captain, and they were finally alone and she could lock the door and grab at Copperton, pulling him to the bed, where he came to life like a match struck in the dark and never disappointed, matching her desire with his skill. Sex between them was like war, she the conquered before the conflict even began, he the conqueror, with the freedom to enjoy the spoils of war at his leisure, picking through the ruins of battle, grabbing and biting, until finally he relented and gave her what she wanted, what she needed to have. And after, the joys of peace, her heart dancing in the streets, sipping champagne and embracing the sunset that would bring darkness and fiercer and more prolonged conflict.

She hated herself, hated her desires, in particular her desire for this vulgarian, but like a caged animal given its first taste of freedom, she spread her legs to the whole world and was only truly at home when violated. This was not love, as she had dreamed it. This was something hungry, atavistic, rapacious. She devoured small birds in restaurants, letting the juices run down her chin. Her skirts were the shortest, the very shortest in Paris, and she used her body to bring Copperton to the brink of ecstasy, the edge of despair.

Diana gave herself to her most fearsome and perverse desires, even though she was two months pregnant. There would be plenty of time for delicacy and rectitude. For now she was a warrior of love, blind to everything else. The rustle of the lavender silk of her evening dress only made her eager for the night to be over, for the sheets to be drawn back, the dress in a heap on the floor. The smell of the handsome waiters' hair pomade. The way the foie gras melted on her tongue. She would take off her shoes under the table and run her feet up Copperton's leg, without acknowledgment, without the slightest indication on his part that he knew she was doing it, increasing her furor to be alone with him. He seemed to take no note of any of this.

Copperton ate ravenously, asking the waiter many questions about each course, deciding carefully, drawing it out, the dinner, the dancing, the evening, knowing he was torturing her, and smiling his thin, graceless smile, winking at her from time to time. The diamonds around her throat were a noose, strangling her, and he knew it, and enjoyed the spectacle.

And when dinner was over, the last drop of *oeufs à la neige* wiped fastidiously from his chin, and an obligatory dance had been danced, he would suddenly and deliberately take her elbow and lead them from the orchestrated clamor of the dining room and up into their large suite of rooms, the one with the view, the one with the Whistler over the fireplace, the one with whatever distinction made it the best in the city, and in the shadowed light of the suite he would give her what she so obviously needed, as precisely as a brilliant general leading his troops into battle, and then and only then could she find peace, and lie with her head on his shoulder for a moment, limp, childishly pleased and smiling, but only for a moment, because soon he would rise from the bed and slip on his spotted silk dressing gown from Turnbull & Asser and walk away from her with a vague 'Good night, darling. Sleep well," and retire to his own room. What he did there, until late in the night—she could see the light under his door—was a mystery.

He thought it vulgar for a man and woman to spend the whole night together. He found waking up next to a woman, even his wife, repulsive. He, the parvenue, announced it to be crass and middle class. The morning smells. The dishevelment. The twisted sheets. She would not see him again until after breakfast, when he would appear, immaculately turned out, ready for the day, surprised to find her still in her nightclothes, her tisane and her single boiled egg untouched, and he, irritated, would urge her to bathe, dress, and meet him in the lobby. He was eager to get to the shops. And she would gulp down her still-hot tisane and comply, as she did in all things having to do with Copperton.

Europe was poor then. The war had left such poverty in its wake, and a man with cash could pick up treasures for pocket change. They came home with treasure after treasure—silver, furniture, a samovar four feet high that had belonged to the tsar—and with less love between them than they had felt when they left. The hollow between them had become a concrete thing, and they filled it with all the grandeur Saratoga had to offer, and all the baubles they could buy.

He had begun to hurt her. The withholding of his desire, his seeming obliviousness to her obvious invitation, was the first thing. But then he began to cause her real pain. He would bite. He began to slap her during sex, sometimes leaving marks, but never where they might show when she was clothed. Sometimes she had to beg him to stop, but once taken with his desires, he wouldn't stop. He tied her hands behind her back with the sash from his dressing gown; he tied her hands to her feet. He came at her from behind, a searing pain she, bound, was helpless to prevent.

"Come on," he said. "It'll be fun. Exciting."

Diana found it to be neither, particularly as his advances became more complicated and more painful.

He was raping her. Again and again, night after night.

One morning her chambermaid knocked gently on the door exactly at seven thirty, as they had agreed, to bring in her tea and croissant. As she opened the door, she shrieked "Mon Dieu!" as she saw Diana, tied hands and feet, last night's makeup smeared down her face in the rivulets of her tears. She quickly untied her and handed her her robe, and then she just sat on the edge of the bed and held Diana as she wept and wept into her shoulder. She finally got her to take a little tea and some bread, and Diana's embarrassment overcame her pain and humiliation, and she asked to be left alone.

She sat in the bath for a long time, nursing her sore wrists, her nipples, her violated body. Then, not knowing what else to do, she dressed and waited for her husband, telling herself that this was the last time, that she would not allow this to happen again, and knowing in her heart that it wasn't, and she would.

How do you walk out on the street after such belittlements? Surely the chambermaid had told the next chambermaid, who told the footmen, and so on, so that when she stepped into the lobby, everybody looked at her with complete knowledge of her imprisonment and her freedom.

After each of these episodes a box would arrive by noon, from Cartier or Chaumet or Rousselet with some more elaborate and dazzling jewel inside, a brooch, a necklace, another tiara for which she had no use or desire.

And yet she stayed with him. She didn't know any better. She assumed this was what marriage was, and in some small way, she felt that she deserved it. She had allowed herself to be bought, and now she felt owned, her body no longer her own. Somehow it felt right, as if it was all she deserved, having no more to offer than a pretty foot.

She was afraid of him. But she was bound to him. She had no other use. She couldn't leave. She had not a single dollar of her own. Her beautiful handbag was empty.

When they got back to Saratoga, and all the wonders they had bought were unpacked and placed, he ran the house like a military regiment. He was dismissive of her father once the ink dried on the contract. He was actively rude to her mother. They pretended not to notice, but they did, and it hurt Diana, who confronted him about it.

"Couldn't you just make an effort. For me?"

"Why on earth would I do that, my darling?"

"They did everything for me. You couldn't know the thousand sacrifices they made. It cost them everything."

"They didn't *have* anything, except some filthy old paintings. And now they have everything they could possibly want. Forever and ever amen."

He ran the house like a continuous party for a debauched set of people who arrived every Friday on the train from New York. Luckily, they had reached the part of her pregnancy where sex was inadvisable, so for the moment she was free from his desires and his terrors. She heaved a sigh of relief every night as she heard the lock turn in his bedroom door. He seemed to have lost all interest in her, and spent the days riding and shooting, in the brand-new clothes he had had fitted in London.

He still threw parties, inviting his louche friends every weekend, filling the guest rooms, and the dancing and champagne flowed from Friday to Sunday morning every weekend.

Pregnant, she watched the dancing, the whole bacchanal, from her balcony in her dressing gown, alone.

The family secretly prayed for a boy, an heir, and she, dutiful as ever, produced a boy, right before her twentieth birthday, a boy whom Copperton named Ashton Cooke Copperton III, another bunny out of the magic hat he had, the hat that was filled with infinite invention. Ashton III? Were there two others? It was never discussed.

And the minute he was born, she was so overwhelmed by his fragility that he was taken from her into the nursery, where she would visit him only late at night, where she would pick him up and wake him from a sound sleep. Eventually he started to develop mysterious rashes, until the doctor concluded that it was in fact Diana who was causing them. Ashton was, after all, being woken in the middle of the night by a total stranger, cooed at and coddled by a lady all in furs and diamonds and perfume, the fairy godmother, and then given a kiss and a "Good night, darling" and handed back to his mammy. Then he would spend the rest of his night and day in his crib, fed by his mammy, wondering who that woman was and whether she would come again, not sleeping until he involuntarily fell asleep, weeping at his abandonment, and then suddenly the room was bright and the queen, the queen of the night, swept down and held him in her arms for ten minutes, and then she abandoned him again to darkness. He didn't know who she was.

She was twenty-one, and she had given birth and then had been given no sense, no idea, what she was supposed to do with her son. The doctor simply advised that she not visit him anymore, and the rashes went away. Copperton, meanwhile, never missed an opportunity to belittle her parenting skills, her looks, whatever he could find. *I spent a fortune on that dress, and you look like a washerwoman in it. Change your shoes, darling, or we're not leaving this room. Most women look beautiful when they're pregnant—you looked like a bloated cow.* An endless string of small, unnecessary jabs.

As Ash grew older, he was let out of his crib, out of the nursery, was taken downstairs, and Diana was there, cuddling him again. But she was in tweeds and cashmere, not the lady who had come to him at night, and he had to begin slowly to realize that this lady was his mother.

But it wasn't until he was four that he looked at her across the breakfast table and said, his voice trembling, "Good morning, Mother," and she, as though this strange act had not played itself out over the years, looked up from her marmalade and toast and said, "Good morning, darling," and after that they were inseparable.

His name was Copperton, but Ash was Diana's son, and she vowed that he would know everything about the Cookes, and about Saratoga. Someday he would understand, as is common in many southern families, that there had been a stately marriage of blood to money, the Cookes to the Coppertons, but that of the latter family, she knew nothing. So for now, when he was all hers, she would just show him the property, the secret places. She went through the architect's drawings of the house, the original plans, drawn in 1789, and she shared with him her love of family and place. She went through the catalog of his ancestors, the duel that had been fought at dawn down by the river in 1792, a fight for the hand of his great-great-grandmother in marriage, who watched the whole thing from the very window where Ash had watched his mother twirl in her golden Paris dresses, massive jewels at her wrist and neck and ears, everywhere, really, diamonds and emeralds and rubies, and fountains of jewels sparkling in the torchlight that lit up the dance floor, watching, like his great-great-grandmother, who had had her portrait painted in that same window.

Remarkably, the great-great-grandmother had married the victor, and lived with him through a placid and altogether happy marriage for forty years. Diana taught him that from there to here was not a very long time, that the Civil War dead still sat with them at table, that they were his people. That they die, but they do not stay dead. He was part of something, a family, and that something meant something, something he had to live up to. It meant courtesy. It meant honor. It meant impeccable posture. It meant having a good seat on horseback. It meant treating a duchess and a kitchen maid with the same courtesy. It meant never seeming drunk, no matter how drunk you were. It meant going to the Episcopal Church, where his family had sat in the same pew for two hundred years. It meant a love of the land. There was a chain, she had told him, and he was the last of the links on that chain. And that meant everything.

All this to a bewildered four-year-old child, just out of the elaborate dresses boys wore then. By the time he was six, he would feel the weight of the past and the looming duties of the future. He would dream of the Civil War dead, the piles of bodies at Antietam, until the rotting mound of dead boys was replaced by the lady in diamonds and rubies who danced him through his sleepless nights.

6

HE HAD WANTED her so desperately. From the moment he saw her rise from her curtsy in Baltimore, he knew he had to have her. He researched who she was and what her lineage meant, and that only added to his desires. He immediately sent twenty dozen white roses to her hotel room, every white rose in Baltimore, in fact. And he stalked her as he would a deer or a bear. City to city, he would check in to the same hotel she had checked into, although they were never the finest. And, every time she reached a new city, a new room, there were massive bouquets, dozens of white roses with his card, which said simply, Copperton.

And in every city, he danced with her. Once. More would have been unseemly, and he meant to behave with perfect rectitude. Occasionally she would reach into his evening jacket and feel for the flasks she knew were there, and they would sneak out for a drink, and flirt. He had never been more charming, more alert to the tiny movements of another person's eyes. His goal, each time, was to make her laugh, just to hear the southern magic of it, and he always succeeded. And then she would leave him and return to the endless waltz with her dazzling smile.

And then there were the clandestine dinners and the little blue velvet boxes, presents decorum would not let her wear so that, in every city, with a new bauble hidden in the bottom of her steamer trunk, she made her curtsy, by now famous and widely imitated, still in the one good strand of pearls.

Her presence drove him mad. Equally so her absence. And once he knew who she was, who her people were, he realized that she was not only her beauty but also his elevation into a legitimacy of blood that he could not even pretend to have.

He knew that they didn't have a nickel to their name. Making her, in his mind, all the more easy to capture.

His ardor, then, was genuine. This was, he thought, the love he had waited for; this was why he had slaved through his twenties to amass his fortune—so that he might offer something besides his looks to the woman who captured his heart. And she had caught him whole and entire. They would marry. They would have children. The children would be called Copperton, but they would also be Cookes and therefore, by blood, members of one of the great families of America. If she were a washerwoman he would have desired her, as did every man in America with eyes and working organs, but now she was his lifeline into the long cavalcade of American aristocracy.

He would treat her with such sweetness, or so he thought. He would kneel at her feet and thank her every day from pulling him from the bog, the riffraff of the general public, the general milieu of men who came from nowhere to make fortunes that were everywhere for the taking.

So he traveled all that way, to Saratoga, and after his talk with her father, during which his lawyers patiently went through an endless list of numbers on pieces of paper, while Copperton quietly snoozed, at the end of which the father said yes as Copperton knew he would because he had to, he was set free to ask Diana to marry him. He found her alone in the yellow study, the sunroom. At first he knelt on the floor, and asked so tenderly, and with such a soft adoration in his voice, that he was shocked that she hesitated. He lay prone on the rug and begged her again. She laughed and said, "Copperton, my love, you look ridiculous. Get up off the floor and put the ring on my finger and I'll say yes, yes with all my heart. My papa has given you permission because he wants me to have what makes me happy, and you make me happy."

The fabulous ring was then put on her finger. His face was glowing with victory, as well as with love. The love that would ignite his life, and give everything else a meaning, and him a sense of place.

7

HE DID LOVE her, and he had meant to be so gentle and loving. But he was selfish through and through, and jealous of the one thing she had that he did not: respect. From the time he had nothing, through the years when he began to acquire more and more, vast holdings across the country, he had pushed and bullied and cheated and lied and grabbed, and taken the last dime out of old men's hands. Now he was splendidly and unassailably rich beyond measure, and he reveled in that, although he no longer had to pay much attention to it. That was done by other people like himself, which left him bored and restless.

So when he saw Diana Cooke rise into the brightness of the moon and sun, he knew she was the jewel in the crown and he pushed and charmed and wangled his way into her life, if not fully into her heart. He had adored her from the moment she flashed her dazzling eyes on the grand dames of Baltimore, her perfect skin rosy with candlelight on red velvet.

She had her own reasons for marrying him, and although he filled her with excitement, those did not necessarily include love.

She knew that beneath his veneer of politesse, his carefully learned manners, he was unspeakably vulgar, and that he was not, and never would be, as her mother would have said, "our kind." She had married him for his money, and the fact that he was tall and handsome and well-mannered and smooth as glass in public did not disguise the fact that he was the kind of man who would put his feet on the table and treat the servants badly. Her sexual need for him produced the same frisson she would feel having sex with one of the stable boys. He was forbidden fruit. Not our sort.

And this drove him wild.

Once he had her, once he was a part of one of the most distinguished families in the country, she and her parents slowly became like bile in his mouth. He knew they condescended to him, that they held him in a regard slightly lower than the servants, even though, without his money, there would be no servants, no house.

He worked hard to fit in. He hired an English riding instructor and began to ride, and ride well. He hired a valet to teach him dress and manners. He tried, laughably, to speak with a southern accent. He learned mostly from Priscilla, the housekeeper. He didn't know any better, so he came out sounding like the child of slavery.

But he did have one great virtue. He loved his son with a pure and innocent adoration. Even Diana was moved when she saw them, Ash and his father, walking hand in hand down to the paddock for the riding lessons. And it wasn't long before Ashton had a pony of his own, and beautiful riding clothes. Diana had grown up riding in jeans and ragtag shirts, and there was a sweetness in seeing her son at four in his boots and jodhpurs, holding Copperton's hand.

She began to join them. Phaeton was brought from his stall, wild from too much leisure, and she had to tame him all over again, but she knew more about riding than the instructor, so it wasn't long before he was easy in the hand again and they could all circle the ring of the paddock.

And when the horses were put away, Copperton would carry Ash back to the house on his shoulders, telling him all the way what a great rider he was on his little pony, and what a great man he was going to be.

"But Poppa," Ash would say, "when I'm a grown man, what will we do? Where will we go?"

And Copperton would describe India to him, or Venice with its gondolas, Greece with its white-and-blue boats in the white sun in the blue sky, pounding the octopus they would catch a hundred times on a flat rock before they grilled it, and Ash would laugh, saying he didn't believe any of it.

"Is it true, Mama? Is it true? Are there really such places?"

And Diana would laugh herself, such a relief, and say that yes, there were such places, and places even more strange and wonderful, she would show him in a book.

But underneath it all, Copperton seethed. There are so many ways that love can turn into carnage, marriage into casualty. He was unkind and abrupt with the servants. He was rude to his mother-in-law; he picked apart his father-in-law's war stories, proving to him that his heroism was a fable of his own invention, taking from him the one thing of which he was most proud.

There was a glass wall between himself and his wife, and he would never get through. But with a constant barrage of insult and obliviousness, he could crack the glass wall a bit every day. He was sickened by his own behavior, but it seemed to soothe his desperation. So the more cruel he became, the calmer his heart beat, the better he slept at night.

A man sees a beautiful flower on a tree. He reaches up and picks it, and then he crushes it into a soggy mess in his hands. There is no reason for his behavior. But he can't stop himself. Every day, Copperton rose from sleep and crushed the flower of the morning, the evening, and the night.

8

COPPERTON NO LONGER recognized the line between what was acceptable and what was sheer cruelty. He felt he had bought her, bought them all—the haughty mother, the crippled father, the house he was progressively filling with more and more servants, as he simultaneously filled it with loose and looser aggregations of houseguests. He bought the yacht, and a crew, along with a ludicrous captain's uniform for himself, and he would sail up and down the river, sometimes all night. One guest carelessly fell from the deck into the river's dark waters and wasn't even missed until dawn, when they had to send out boats to dredge her limp, blue, bejeweled body from the cold waters.

He would sometimes lock Diana in her room for days, until she learned, as he said, to behave, meaning, in his mind, to drink more, laugh more, have more fun, instead of showing to the world the perpetual shock and sadness on her face. So she became a fierce drinker; her laughter was vicious and neverending, her carelessness immense. She wept herself to sleep whenever he gave her a few hours.

At dinner one night, after he saw Copperton handling her roughly in the pantry, his hand beneath her dress, Diana's face covered with shame to be seen used this way in the shadows of her father's house, Diana's father shouted, "Get away from my daughter! You abuse her, sir. You mishandle her and humiliate her in front of her family. If I see that kind of thing again, I will shoot you to death right here in the dining room. I won't have this in my house."

"Your house?" Copperton laughed. "You pathetic old man, this has not been your house since the day I slipped the ring on your darling daughter's hand. Never forget that. You live here at my pleasure."

Arthur's shoulders slumped; his ashen face turned to stone. "I wish I could forget," he said. "As it is, I regret everything. This life has made me so weary."

"I can't imagine why," said Copperton, eating heartily. "You have a thousand niggers around here to do whatever you want for you."

"Sir! We don't talk like that in this house. Never. Do you understand me?" There was a pause. "*Do you understand me?*"

For once Copperton seemed cowed. He looked the old man straight in the eyes. "Yes, sir."

Then the real Copperton returned. "You do understand, I assume, that in actual fact I own everything here, do you not? I own this table, this fork, your daughter, of course, the hairs on your head. The drinks table at which you spend most of the day wearying yourself. Everything. *Everything.* Now do we understand?"

"Some of these families have been with us since before I was born. Since before the war."

"Ah, the sainted southerner who treated his slaves with compassion, except that decades later they're still here because they don't have a pot to piss in and nowhere to go. Nappy-headed slaves without the shackles."

"That is *enough.* You are trash, sir, and there is only one reason you're here."

"My unmatchable charm?"

"My daughter doesn't love you. She may have, once, but what she loves is this house. She had one reason to marry you. To save this house. So you live here at *her* pleasure. Do you understand that?"

Copperton stood to his full height, mockingly bowed, and clicked the heels of his boots. "Whatever you say, sir." He turned and quickly left the room.

Diana's father looked at his wife with a slight nod. "I believe we'll take our sorbet in the library." And his wife rose, and took the back of his chair and wheeled him from the dining room and into the shadows of the hall until they couldn't be heard any longer.

The next morning they moved their bedroom into a large, sunny suite on the third floor, stopped coming to dinner, and were rarely seen again, except in death, which came soon, but not soon enough to suit them. Her mother died sitting in a crewel-work slipper chair doing a needlepoint prayer for Ash, who came to see them every day. *O Lord, bless us and keep us.* She finished the last stitch, tied off her thread, said, "Arthur, I have always loved you," turned to look at the river, and died. After that, Diana sat by her father's chair all day long every day, sometimes with Ash at his feet, holding his hand, and read to him from Dickens as the girls ran up and down with fresh bottles of brandy until he poisoned his liver beyond repair and one day, looking up from her book, she saw that he was dead. It took only twenty-seven days.

Diana wept at their gravesides—so sweet they had been, so kind and loving to her—the river breezes blowing her black silk veil. Ash stood straight and confused. Where had they gone? People came from three counties. So many funerals of these great families. The old ones were almost gone now, and the rest hobbled up the hillside to the family graveyard, Diana's mother and father surrounded by graves from as far back as 1760.

Copperton did not attend.

As Diana walked back to the house from her parents' graves, holding Ash's hand, she could hear her mother's voice. *I've always said you had a pretty foot.* And she knew that, in her way, her mother had loved her.

9

COPPERTON HIRED TUTORS for the boy, dressed him perfectly, tucked him in every night, in effect cutting Diana out of his life. He bathed him, telling him stories of pirates at sea and lonely men lost on desert islands. After he was all tucked in, Diana was allowed her fifteen or twenty minutes with the boy, to say his prayers, to talk about his grandmother and father, whom Ash barely remembered but missed dearly—their scents, and the peppermint sticks his grandfather always seemed to have one more of in his pocket. He was so proud the day he could read his grandmother's needlepoint prayer over his bed by himself.

Every morning Ash came to breakfast before Copperton got up, blessed time she spent alone with her son. When his father appeared, Ash raced to get into his riding clothes and they ran down to the paddock and rode for an hour before Ash's lessons began. Then Copperton rode alone, faster and faster.

He had heard of endurance races, races that ran for fifty or a hundred miles, and he wanted to do one. The only problem was that his horse wasn't suited for them. They were races for Arabians, and Diana had the only Arabian in the stable.

He tried with his big gelding. Diana and Priscilla and her husband Clarence, whose duties were many but undefined, would stand at the kitchen door and watch him race the woodland trails, pell-mell, pushing the horse into a sweat, beating him mercilessly with his crop, wrecking his mouth with his cruel use of the bit. Priscilla and Clarence would just hold on to each other, as they had in times of trouble since Diana was a girl.

Copperton would beat the horse on his haunches, on his legs, and he would bring the horse back to the stables in disgust, whipping him one more time, the gelding's head bowed almost to his knees, the sweat of rage making Copperton's clothes stick to his body, and throw the reins to the stable boys, who applied salves and bandages and did what they could to get Copperton on any of the other ten horses for the week or two it took the gelding to heal. Except for Phaeton, Diana's Arabian. It enraged Copperton to see her cantering so freely across the fields, taking the fences, snaking the trails, always seeking the light, coming back to the stables, both rider and horse, rested and exhilarated. God, she loved that horse. Over the years, they had become almost a single being. The slightest shift of her hips was enough to turn him. Phaeton had a soft mouth, and had never once been whipped or used harshly.

The next night at dinner, Copperton said casually, "There's a fifty-mile race on Saturday. I was thinking of taking Phaeton for the day."

"You will absolutely not take that horse. I am begging you. Races like that take training. They take expert riding. He's mine. Nobody else has ever ridden him except me."

"Very well, my dear."

But the next night, "I think I really do need to take Phaeton. He can do it. Arabians were built for those races. Bred for them in the desert."

"Copperton. It would kill me."

"You've had your way your whole life. Sometimes you have to give in to the needs of others. Let's not be selfish, darling."

"I won't hear of it. This subject is closed."

Still, a few days later, she woke to a general clatter from the stables, and got to the window just in time to see the gates of the trailer close on Phaeton's magnificent rump. It was only just barely light.

She caught hold of the curtain to steady herself. Sometimes you just know it, and she knew this. This was the moment that changed everything. Irrevocably and forever.

As the truck rattled down the long dirt road to the highway, she noticed that one of the rear lights was out. Maybe they'll get stopped, she thought. But then, no, let them all go out. Let them travel in darkness. As she lost sight of the truck, she somehow knew that life as she had known it was over.

II

GIBBY

10

THERE WAS AT least this to be said. She managed. She kept Saratoga running against all odds. While the wallpaper peeled, and water dripped through the kitchen ceiling into a bucket when it rained, she kept it going. Through cracks in the plaster. Buckles in the floorboards. Through hurricanes, when the river came halfway up the long lawn to the house, the old house endured because she willed it so.

She had kept mourning as long as anybody in 1931 could have reasonably expected. Not out of love. Not that. Out of a perverse sense of duty. She was Victorian in her observance, and in her guilt. When Phaeton, the Arabian gelding who was the jewel of their stable, had shied at some imagined something at the thirty-fifth milepost of the fifty-mile endurance race and thrown the Captain, breaking his neck and killing him instantly, leaving him broken and dead on the side of the trail with no more visible wound than a small blue mark on his left temple, his little blue ribbon—the horse racing on, a harrowing sight, his leg broken, collapsing five miles past his rider, heart bursting—Diana Cooke Copperton put away her bright and diaphanous finery, the tea dresses and the furs and the hats from New York and Paris, and put on widow's weeds. She exchanged her diamonds and pearls for jet and black bombazine, gave up her dancing, her nights of gin and vicious laughter, her tortured passion. Instead she sat still in a blue velvet slipper chair draped with black lace for six months, knitting for the poor. She sat implacable, needles clicking as she drew the yarn from the skein. Nobody could have argued with her behavior, once so scandalous. She shut herself in like Aida in the crypt, and eventually the cards and letters stopped coming and the telephone sat mute on the table in the pantry. The fatal stone had closed over her, with no Radames to share her slow and agonizing suffocation.

She drew the curtains, rolled up the rugs, and locked the doors against the world, refusing all visitors. A quiet descended on the great house that seemed forever impenetrable, a lethargy from which it was impossible to rise. The servants put on slippers for silence and black armbands for respect; she even kept the boy at home and schooled him herself in the mausoleum the house had become, teaching him his numbers and the history of the Gallic Wars and the eloquent cavalcade of the English poets, the boy himself in black pants and jacket, hunched over his books in the darkness of the library, with its thousands of leather-bound books, looking out over the flats and marshes and scrub pines that surrounded the town of Port Royal, on the shores of the Rappahannock River, at the mouth of the Chesapeake Bay.

Oh, how she loved that boy. He clung to her, asking again and again where his father was, and if they would still go to all those wonderful places Copperton had described to him. And she answered, "Of course, my darling. Your father wanted you to see the wonders of the world we live in. Other people, remarkable places. As soon as you're old enough, we'll go there, go everywhere." He lay his head on her breast, and his quiet tears wet the black silk of her mourning clothes. She would try to give him the dream of a life Copperton had put in his head. God knows they were rich now, and no parents to watch over.

Then Mr. Ambrose came to discuss the will, and she discovered that the Captain had left her out of his vast fortune, of which he had lost not one penny in the Crash of '29, and allowed her just enough to live on comfortably, barely enough if, that is, she gave up the splendor of the life they had known together, the servants, the dressmakers, the wardrobe sent from Paris, the parties and the travel. She could live a modest, comfortable life, but her son, who was thirteen at the time, had become instantly the richest man in five counties.

She never said one unkind word to Ashton about his father. After all, it must be said, he had loved the boy with a fierce and mesmerizing power. And so, with a grief so heavy she thought she would die without a wound, she stood silent as his trustees sent him away to Exeter, which was also a provision of Copperton's will. Even this, the pleasure of raising her own son, Copperton had denied her from the grave. She could not afford to raise him as well as he could raise himself. The night before he left for school, Ashton sat on the floor in front of her in his bathrobe, fresh from the bath, his hair wet, and she brushed his hair dry, as she had done almost every night of his life. He purred like a cat when she did it, and she thought she would die of grief. She thought also she would explode with loathing for her dead husband.

The next morning Clarence drove mother and son to the train, both in tears, and she saw Ash off, his destination pinned to his jacket in a note, and then she went home, put away her widow's weeds, flung open the curtains, and began to fire the servants one by one, until only Priscilla and Clarence were left. She then walked down to the edge of the garden, waving goodbye to the gardeners, Paolo and Tomasso, who were packing up their tools, weeping in the peonies, burning the last of the leaves in a huge pile.

Autumn was coming on. Locked in her tower, she would hear them, the horns blowing, the beagles with their anxious yelping, the men and women of the hunt club, passing through her land. She didn't even lift her head.

Her fury was murderous. Her rage was without bound. Her grief was infinite and impenetrable. Her boy. Her beautiful boy, lost now also. Oh, there would be holidays, he would come at Christmas and Easter and in the summers, but he would come increasingly as a stranger as he grew into his own world without her. Would he still want his hair brushed dry? Would he still ask her to twirl in her party dress just for him? And what party dress, now, now that the party was over?

The house, Saratoga, was safe, at least; the Captain had made sure it was left in trust to Ashton, which meant she could live there, but as a tenant, a lodger in her own property, among the furniture and the silver with the Cooke crest, the large and fine family portraits, by Sully, by Stuart, the strings of pearls, none of it belonging to her in any real way anymore, although she bore the entire burden of maintaining it in some miraculous manner she couldn't yet envision. The Captain had thought these things just happened, the endless details, that copper pots got polished on their own and so forth, like a gigantic flower arrangement that never wilted.

She hated the thought of him. Had she ever loved him? Or was it mere gratitude for pulling her out of the march of the debutantes and saving her family from ruin, from loss of home and place? Perhaps she had loved him for that, but she was only nineteen and knew nothing of how quickly and violently love could turn to loathing. True, there was a fierce sexual passion, but he was her first and only, and perhaps she mistook that for love. And even that passion was a mixture of deep loathing and desperate longing.

Even now, in her grief and rage, the power of his seduction and his body would cause hers to warm, and she would writhe on her bed, wanting something she didn't know the name of. It wasn't him, but she felt whatever it was deep in her groin. Sometimes it became unbearable, and she had to be naked, her hands had to touch her body, she had to stand in front of a mirror and watch herself doing all of this, call it whatever you will.

Almost a year went by. On the first Saturday in October, she heard it: the familiar sounds of the Saratoga Hunt assembling, down by the boathouse. It was just after dawn. In the semidarkness of the library where she had sat up all night, half sleeping, Tennyson open on her lap unread, she heard the horns, pictured in her mind the bridles and the hot steam coming out of the horses' nostrils, the warm trust between horse and rider, and then, at the sound of the master of hounds' signal, off, off, off, into the bracken. She imagined herself among them, as she always was, always had been since she was a child. She felt it in her body, the dormant lushness of it all, the smells, the sounds, the power controlled through the slightest movement of the reins in her hands, the ultimate power of the horse beneath her, the saddle rubbing at exactly the right place, and she imagined herself joining the hunt to which she had belonged since she was eight, in her semiwaking dream riding naked, throwing her hat away, her hair streaming behind her, the bracken and branches of trees cutting into her arms so that blood trailed down to her hands. It was ecstasy.

Copperton had come back to her, with his velvet and satin ribbons, with his rape night after night of her young body on the crisp sheets of the Ritz Hotel or Claridge's, leaving her spent and alone as soon as he had taken his pleasure, gone back to his own bed, seeming never to sleep, left her with not so much as a kiss good night, the pleasure all his, left her tied for the maid to find in the morning, her lamentation, her prayer only that she be set free, but her body, throughout the night, electric, begging that he would return and take her again.

Copperton. Why wouldn't he leave her? She had come to hate him, and now she felt an urgent need for him almost all the time.

When he died, there was no one to get in touch with, no next of kin they could find. He had been, before their marriage, a man of no fixed abode, and it was hopeless to look for his family, so he was buried in the Cooke plot, where they had all been buried for two hundred and fifty years, an interloper even there. His coffin was very large, and he was buried in uniform, with medals, shiny elaborate things that turned out to be mostly geegaws for accomplishments like marksmanship in summer camp. Who had she been married to? She hardly knew, and this only added to her fury. She was so grateful for the things he gave her, she hadn't wanted to ask; she didn't want to know.

She heard the sound of a champagne flute breaking behind her, but she knew there was nothing there. She didn't even turn around. Memory was creeping in. She heard the laughter of the guests as the orchestra struck up a jazzy foxtrot. So often. So many nights. So many nights Paolo and Tommaso, twins who slept in the same bed in the gardener's cottage, had laid down the parquet dance floor at house parties where every one of the fourteen bedrooms was full, flasks on the men's hips, sometimes syringes wrapped in silk, suitcases taken as the guests arrived, taken downstairs and unpacked, everything pressed and hung on satin hangers in closets and armoires upstairs, ready to be put on, flawless, after soothing baths and emoluments and libations before dinner.

So, on that October morning, when she heard the huntsman's horn, it seemed no more real than her other fantasies.

She had lost track of time; one day was exactly like the next. She never bathed, unless Priscilla made her sit in the huge bath, soaped her, smoothed her skin with delicate oils, as Diana had always done, though now she never did anything unless at Priscilla's command. Her bed seemed too far away, and she mostly spent her nights in the chair. Some nights Priscilla would order her to lie down, and she would acquiesce. Priscilla had to help her up the stairs, brush her hair for her, lay out her nightclothes, even help her into them. She just didn't give a good goddamn.

How much time had passed? she would wonder through her sleepless nights. Days? Months? Seasons?

But the huntsman's horn and the baying of the pack of hounds pulled her up short. It was fall. Copperton had died in the spring of the year before. Enough time had passed. The season was coming for the Saratoga Hunt, founded by her great-grandfather when the house's acreage was ten, not five thousand.

There was a knock on the door. Priscilla answered. It was the master of the hunt, Roddy Powell. He had seen Diana naked, all those years ago.

"Good morning, Priscilla," he said. "Will Miss Diana be joining us?"

This, today, Diana knew, was just the first of the practice hunts. The real season didn't begin for a month.

Priscilla appeared in the library. Diana had heard the invitation.

"Give him my regrets. Tell Mr. Powell I'll be there on opening day," Diana said.

She heard Priscilla speaking, and some mumbling from Roddy, and then the big door closed. After a while Priscilla brought her the usual big breakfast on a tray, which she, as usual, took two bites of, and then left on a table. She went upstairs to get out her riding clothes, stored in neat boxes, wrapped in tissue. The jodhpurs; the scarlet jacket with its turquoise collar—mysteriously referred to as a hunting pink—that identified her as a member of the Saratoga Hunt; the bespoke boots. Then she unwrapped the jewel of her wardrobe, her sidesaddle riding habit, custom-made on a trip to London with her father, after Miss Porter's. With a pang of tenderness, she remembered where all the money had gone. It had gone to her—her education, her outfitting, with all its trappings—and she had never thanked him for it. Like all eighteen-year-olds, she was so heartless and self-involved, she had no room in her heart for anybody but herself; she had accepted all the things her father provided with a carelessness that now reddened her face with shame.

The clothes, jacket and skirt, were a flight of fancy, modeled after pictures she had seen of ladies of the peerage in the nineteenth century, all ruffles and pleats and passementerie, but all in black. A duchess in mourning for a state funeral. There was also a beaver top hat, veiled with brilliant beaded netting, that half hid her face; tulle wrapped around the brim, black fluff that flew out behind her as she rode. She hadn't worn the outfit in ten years, but she was going to wear it now.

THE FIRST SATURDAY in November, she was at the boathouse before dawn. She was sitting in her sidesaddle on Icarus, her most beautifully trained horse, black as sin and twice as lethal, but instantly obedient to her every move. She had made sure of that. A hunter needs to be strong, inexhaustible, and precise. She had spent months training him. Now horse and rider were one being, and she would trust him with her life. He stood, restless, his mane and tail braided immaculately, the hair intertwined with black satin ribbons, a job so fraught with danger the stable boys wouldn't even attempt it. Only she could get near him. All around her milled her pack of hounds. Lying on the ground at her feet, asleep, was her best dog, her striker hound Bluesie. In her black clothes, her black kid gloves, she looked like a dark queen, though in fact she was nervous, and the dogs and the horse sensed it. Icarus was a wild thing, but she trusted him completely to do exactly as she commanded him to do. He was the fastest, the best jumper. She wanted the danger, the speed, the flight when they hit the fences and brooks, never knowing what was on the other side, ditch or brook, jumping into the unknown.

She wanted a taste of danger. The smells, the skittish horse, the cold black morning—it felt like sex, and she wanted sex.

Her days of mourning had passed while she sat in the darkened house, reading Tennyson, dreaming of Copperton inside her, hating him, needing him. She ached for the feeling of the pommel of the saddle, its force and thrust, the scars and scrapes of Copperton's love.

Other horses appeared out of the fog, and the hounds. The men tipped their caps, impressed by her imperial look, more impressed by her magnificent jumper. The master of the hunt arrived, and the rattle and buzz in the air grew and grew, palpable—a camaraderie she had missed for all those months, as everybody sipped from the flasks that had been built into their scarlet jackets. Dogs were underfoot everywhere, and the children on their ponies, so sweet, so eager.

The veil over her face almost hid her from view, but they all knew who she was. They had been riding together for thirty years, welcoming her into the juniors as a wildcat ten-year-old on her crazy little pony. People greeted her, sometimes holding out a gloved hand as they tried to control their overwrought horses at the same time.

Then the huntsman led the dogs out, the horses, barely restrained, following. At last the dogs caught the scent. They were baying and barking, crazy to be running free and fast across the landscape toward their prey, but knowing not to move until the horn blew, and then it did, and they flew off, followed by the thundering wildness of forty horses, Icarus, unbound, leaping to the front, wild already, almost throwing her with every long stride, the reins loose in her hands, giving him his head, Icarus going faster and faster as though insane with speed.

How happy she was! She felt nothing except the speed and the tight muscles of the horse, the black flanks and withers, sweating already, the fence approaching, her head up, her body erect on the horse so that it looked as though she were leaning backward, every muscle of her body in tune with the horse, black on black flying over field and through bracken and jumping the sagging fences and the brooks.

It went on for miles, the hounds losing the scent, then picking it up again, the whole pack, horses and dogs changing direction time and again, her skirt flying, catching on a low limb, the hem coming undone, a branch sweeping across her face, tearing her veil and leaving a swath on her cheek, unnoticed in her focus on the one thing, the speed, the muscle it took just to stay on at such speed, the pack around her, and sometimes strung out behind her like savage warriors come to burn down the gates. As they caught the scent, it was Bluesie who was out in front, keen, close to the ground, not to be denied.

The fox, spotted and then invisible then spotted again, a flash of red seeking some way, any way, to go to ground and finding none, knowing somehow there was murder behind him, the savage teeth overpowering him and ripping him apart their only desire, blind with bloodlust, trained all their life for this one thing, this one show of blood.

Fence after fence, for miles they followed him, some riders even changing horses to keep up. Diana didn't need to change anything. Icarus was implacable. He was crazy, his eyes flashing wildly, following every shift in her weight, taking every jump at exactly the right second, no thought of stopping, his flanks lathered up, his nostrils flared with rage. Her whip in her hand, unused. No point.

Finally the dogs ran the fox to ground, and the terriers dragged him from his hole. As Diana watched the dogs tear the animal apart, her heart beat with a combination of exhilaration and disgust.

When there was nothing but a carcass, the master of hounds jumped from his horse. Dipping his finger in the fox's blood, he made a cross on Diana's forehead, to welcome her back, back to the hunt, back to the life, her circle of friends. Then he cut off the tail and attached it with a ribbon to her hat, because she was closest to the kill. The day's hunting was over, and the serious drinking began.

Diana spontaneously asked them all to Saratoga for the traditional hunt breakfast. She wasn't sure how Priscilla would pull it off, but as long as there was a ham—and there was always a ham—and eggs and biscuits, nobody would mind, because the bar was copiously stocked. She felt as though her nostrils breathed a new air, just as a fresh need ran between her legs and up her spine.

IN THE LONG months after Copperton's death, Diana would wake in the dark, as she always did, and wait for the sun to rise, huge and stunning. At first light Priscilla would bring her coffee on a tray, everything just so, her grandmother's Limoges coffeepot, and she would sip her coffee, burning her lip, and watch the smooth river turning from black satin to opalescent peach and turquoise, the blue deepening as the shoal dropped off. The tides would come in, as they did every day, endlessly fascinating, endlessly flowing, not just through its banks but through her heart, through her veins. She was a child of the river; the croakers and trout swam through her heart; the herons plunged there, their talons lethal. Ducks would float in a line, driven by some knowledge, some order that she was locked from ever knowing, and at some secret signal they would struggle into flight.

The window sash concealed the opposite shore, so she saw only water, and every day every single thing was new; the river smooth as glass or chopped and uneven, like unpolished slate. She felt so small, so insignificant, in her grandmother's big bed, with the monogrammed hangings, deep blue, like the river. She was all that was left of Saratoga's enormous history, except for Ash, and who could picture where he was or whom he would become?

Sometimes she would wake up even earlier, at midnight or two, lightning streaking the sky, the wind high and furious, Bluesie pacing, and she would let him get into the bed, where he calmed them both down, and they went back to sleep no matter how fierce the storm, breathing together softly, no longer afraid, waking to a pure dawn, the river running its placid course as though nothing had happened in the night. All the things we never know.

THE LAND WAS mostly flat—scrub pine and undergrowth, here and there the occasional dogwood, like a bridal veil in the spring. And her garden, so beautiful once, so fulsome, now gone to ruin; it was November, so nothing was expected, but she knew that only the very few strongest things underneath all those invasive plants—the vinca, the creepers, the loosestrife—would try to bloom in the summer: a rose, a lily, strange and mordant and muted.

It was time for her to get on her hands and knees, to plunge her hands into the dirt.

It was time for her to order plants and bulbs and put them in the ground in the hope that the moles and the deer would not get everything, that they would leave something to blossom in the spring.

And it was time for her to open her heart.

It was time for Diana Cooke Copperton to love again.

Let the river run.

11

WISTERIA BLOSSOMS BEFORE it leafs out, and so it was with Ashton. And now there was this: Ash was being sent down from Yale. The letter said that although his grades were more than adequate, he was too "dreamy." What did that mean? The world stood on the brink of chaos, and he was being asked to take a year off and return to Yale more focused. His work was perceptive and often brilliant, the letter said, in an off-kilter kind of way, but it was also often late, and filled with fanciful extrapolations that strayed from actual facts into pure imaginings.

In the nine years since the Captain died, everything had changed except Diana and Ash's love for one another. Ash grieved deeply for his father. Diana did not. They never spoke of it, each alone, in grieving or lack of it. But in every other thing they were allies. They wrote to each other almost every day, and saved the letters. They rarely spoke on the telephone. Only when she knew he was having a migraine did she call. "You're having a migraine," she would say, and at first he would say, "How did you know?" But then he just came to accept that it was part of the remarkable bond between them, that she could feel the searing pain on the right side of his head, an agony that began as an aura of sparkling light and turned almost immediately into nauseating, stabbing tremors. She just knew, and her voice was more soothing to him, as he lay in his dark room with cool cloths over his eyes, than any medicine. He was not wrapped in the solitude of his pain in those moments when she called.

They both lived for the days he could come home from school for his vacations. Even though, once he learned to drive, he spent his time largely staying out with his friends and sleeping until noon, they were happy being under the same roof, and Diana was pleased that, more and more, he preferred the nights when his friends came to Saratoga to drink cheap beers and listen to the phonograph and smoke cigarettes, although she wasn't supposed to know. She became, for his rowdy friends, their "other mother." And she was pleased that they could sit in the kitchen with her and discuss their traumas and distresses and the love affairs that were always knives in their hearts, even as their faces blossomed with agony and joy in discussing them.

Ash knew she was poor, and he vaguely knew that he was not. He noticed more than she knew, more than was ever spoken of. He was embarrassed for her, but had no idea how to help. The lawyers declined to send her money. He offered to pay for the phone calls, but she refused, and he didn't want to insult her pride by pressing the issue. He had only a vague memory of the way things had been when there were fourteen to help in the house, and he never saw his mother on her hands and knees, scrubbing the floors, or waxing the long table. He didn't see as his mother drove the lonely miles to Richmond to sell this diamond or that, wrapped carefully in a pristine handkerchief, not saying that she needed the money, just that she was selling a few pieces she didn't wear anymore. She almost believed it, since it was almost true; the days of the house parties and the ball gowns were over, long over, the orchestra packed up and gone home for good, the dance floor warping in the barn.

Now the big house was empty but for Diana and Priscilla

and Clarence. She began to take her meals with them in the kitchen; the big dining room was too lonely and too expensive to heat. It was awkward at first, very awkward. They didn't know what to call her. For weeks, they ate in silence. Then she became part of the kitchen landscape, and eventually Priscilla would have to ask her to pass the butter or the salt, and spoke to her as Miss Diana, and Diana answered her as Miss Priscilla, and that opened the gates, at least between the two women, who after all were now doing the same amount of housework. Unconvinced, Clarence ate in stony silence, glowering at them as they grew to talk like sisters. When the meals were over, it was still Clarence who cleared the table and Priscilla who did the washing up, although Diana put everything away.

The heavy silk damask curtains had begun to shred and sag in the harsh summer sun, but there was nothing to be done. She just closed room after room and turned a blind eye to all that was falling apart.

When Ash came home for Christmas or vacation, she'd open all the rooms again, but he never spoke of the destruction that was happening every minute all around him. He loved the house as he always had, despite its decline. She even gave parties, like in the old days, selling a brooch or a necklace to stock the wine cellar and lay good food on the table and fill the house with guests. Ash finally got his wish—to sit at the dinner table with the grown-ups—and he played his part well, with a natural charm and manners that went beyond anything you could learn. He had learned to tie a bow tie. He made people laugh. He often told hilarious stories about his adventures with his roommate. He enchanted women and men alike. He rode and hunted with the men, and the women who increasingly went in for sport, and he danced like an angel.

Ash slept in his old bedroom, and Diana still brushed his

hair dry before he went to bed, Ash sitting on the floor and leaning against her legs as she sat at her dressing table, purring like a dreaming cat as the soft bristles of his grandfather's silver hairbrush ran through his dark hair. Diana still made it a point to say good night to him before she went to sleep, even if the sun was already up. He never remarked on the plainness of her dress, her lack of jewelry.

But now this, this homecoming, this was a different thing. Things would change in the house that was, after all, his. She decided to move him into his father's old bedroom, with the heavy desk and bed, the gun racks and the mounted stag's head. She knew that he missed his father, had never stopped missing him. He often visited his father's grave up on the hill when he was home, spent long hours alone up there. He was his father's son, grown now, and it was only right he move into his father's room, with its view of the back lawn, down the long sweep of the lawn to the wide river where the sun rose every morning.

Nine years ago, now, they had carried Copperton home on the back of a flatbed truck, his body cradled in bales of hay. She had thought at first that he was drunk and sleeping. They had to explain it to her, and then, only then, did she notice the twist of his neck, the unnatural set of his head on his shoulders; only then came the sharp intake of breath that was all she did to mark his death. It was harder on the boy. He couldn't believe it, that his father was gone from this body so seemingly unharmed. Ashton had howled and fallen and been helped up and pulled himself together as he knew was expected of him. He behaved nobly throughout the funeral, greeting every mourner—and there were many—with grace and selfless kindness, getting this one a drink, that one a ham biscuit, holding every hand and giving, not asking for, comfort.

This river land, which Ashton now owned five thousand acres

of, spread out before her through the diamond panes of her dead husband's room. The land, so gentle to the eye, was less gentle to farm, punched with rock, mostly clay. Tobacco loved it, though. Cotton loved it. Peanuts loved it. She had lived her life by this river every single day, except for the trips to Paris and London and one disastrous trip to New York, where she had been so unhappy alone in their room at the Plaza, where the Captain had been abusive to a waiter at the Oyster Bar because they didn't have shad roe and had refused to tip him, causing the waiter to follow them onto the street, rip up the bill, and spit in the Captain's face. No, she had always been happiest here, even alone, by the long amazing shoreline, endlessly variable, its moods matching her own.

In valuing these old river houses, shoreline was everything. With every foot, the value grew. Saratoga had miles of pristine sand.

But she had not been happy in this room. She remembered the nights she had been called to this huge bed with the Captain, terrified, as he had forced his sex on her, his unforgiving body like green timber, his zeal frantic, her breasts scrubbed raw by the bristles on his chest, his thrustings, entirely forgetful of her, without patience or delicacy, ripping her nightgown to get at it, to get at her, to get it over with and be done with her.

She was so happy when she got pregnant; if it was a boy, there would be the end to it. And it was, it was Ashton, for some unknown reason called Ashton III. She would never answer the knock on her door again, or take the long walk down the dark hallway to Copperton's shrouded bed. Now she was spreading fresh sheets for her son, smoothing them so there was not a single wrinkle. She considered putting flowers by the bed, then changed her mind.

For all they had corresponded, she knew so little of him. She was, she had to admit, nervous. How would he find her? And what would he think of Saratoga, so diminished from what he knew? There was, in the end, the final question she couldn't even ask herself, as she smoothed out the heavy blue silk coverlet, embroidered by her with his initials: What if Ashton didn't like her, had forgotten his love, threw her out? What if he asked her to leave her own house? A vacation was one thing, an hors d'oeuvre, a folly. But this was to be their life, continuous and endless. Mother and son. When he married, what would become of her? He wouldn't make her leave this house, even if she had to move to obscurity on the third floor, like her mother and father. There was no reason to imagine he would cast her out. But still.

The letter from Yale had said that in the previous six months, he had rarely left his rooms, rarely bathed, ate with no one but his roommate, and had, on his desk, a stack of letters, all unopened, mostly presumably from her. Who else would be writing to him? Was there a sweetheart, some secret sorrow?

But not to open letters he obviously knew were from her? Which he obviously knew were expressions of her love for him? She never asked him questions about his life at Yale, and he never spoke of it, except to mention his roommate, Gibby, occasionally, and this or that outing they had taken together. They had roomed together since prep school. She wrote to him about the river, her endless fascination with it, its colors and tides, the way the light caught its risings and fallings, the ducks and swans riding the caplets and the troughs. She spent whole days watching the river, her lover, her friend. She ran to the window to catch every sunset, each one a miracle, different every day, entrancing long after darkness had sucked the last ounce of color out of the indigo sky. She never complained in her letters, never gave a hint of how hard it was to hold it all together—

the shredding curtains, the fractious tenant farmers, ready to rob a woman of every nickel they could, the hollow left by the ending of the dancing weekends. She always wrote brightly of her renewed love of gardening, which was only partly a lie. She always sent love from Priscilla and Clarence, and sometimes a ham on the bus. She told him never to forget the constancy of her love for him.

And now, the letters never opened, all her efforts to paint a bright picture gone into the oblivion of Ash's feverish dreaminess. Perhaps Saratoga and the river flowing once again through his heart could waken him from the dream.

NOTHING HAD CHANGED in this room since the Captain had died. Nothing had been moved on his desk. His cigars were still in their humidor, the sterling cigar cutter beside it still, polished and ready. His silk dressing gown still hung on the closet door, his slippers by the bed. The tweed hacking jackets and the gleaming riding boots, and all that paraphernalia, and the tuxedo and the tailcoat and the white dinner jacket, now yellowing slightly. Was Ashton supposed to simply walk in and be his father, in an instant? If that's what he wanted, every accoutrement was ready for his return. The entire equipage of the Virginia squire. Even his father's ebony razor from Geo F Trumper in Jermyn Street.

"Dinner be almost ready," Priscilla said.

There was no need to ask what dinner might be. Chicken. It's all they ever ate. Every afternoon Clarence would kill a chicken, and Priscilla would try to do something new with it, but whatever she tried, it was still and always chicken.

Tonight it was curried chicken with the standard boys—peanuts, avocado, coconut, chutney, rare treats for a rare night—and an aspic. They ate early, because there was a big storm moving in, and Clarence had to get out the Rolls and drive to Richmond to the train station to pick up Ash at eleven. They hardly ever drove the big old car anymore, driving the smaller and more practical Ford for daily chores, but this was a state occasion, the homecoming of the prodigal son, the return of the master of the house, and it seemed only fitting that he be met and ferried in style. Clarence had spent days cleaning and dusting the car, cleaning, as well, the engine, making sure there would be no mishaps along the way. They were all tense and ate little. They took up so little space at the ten-foot kitchen table. The house, usually dark, spread around them in its illuminated vastness, every light lit, room after room of things handed down and taken care of, the history of a family in which the Captain had been no more than a slight bump on the map of history, a life, a history, in which more was saved than was lost, each thing taken care of, nothing neglected.

They ate in silence, each thinking of something he might have overlooked, hearing the low peals of thunder coming from Richmond, closer and closer. The radio that kept them company was filled with news of the storm—bridges out, trees down, roads disrupted.

Diana went to call the train station as Clarence changed into his old driver's uniform, to see if the train was late, but the phone was out, and dinner was wordlessly over. Things were put away. She helped with the washing up, the putting away, but her hands shook so badly, she had to stop and let Priscilla take over. Priscilla had helped at Ashton's birth; she had wiped the blood and snot from his mewling body before handing the pristine baby to his exhausted mother. Priscilla did not for one second believe that this storm, or any show of the elements, would stop Ashton from returning to take up his rightful place now. White people were so delicate, so easily frightened. So foolish.

As Clarence appeared in his full chauffeur's regalia, the lights went out. They caught a glimpse of his gleaming black knee boots, his black jodhpurs, his smartly buttoned jacket, now too tight, cap under his arm, but just a glimpse, before they were sunk into blackness and the scramble for candles and matches began. There were hundreds of half-used candles from evenings a decade ago, but they were scattered in drawers all over the house, and it took some time, so by the time the kitchen was lit by the warm glow of candlelight, Clarence was already gone. The rain was coming down in sheets, drowning out any sound the car might have made, pulling down the drive.

Once the business of illumination was taken care of, the two women had nothing to do. They sat anxiously at the kitchen table, both still in their aprons.

"We need to find us something to do," said Priscilla. "It's no telling how long they'll be. Can't just sit here like lumps."

"We'll polish those candlesticks."

"All of them? They haven't been touched in years. Could take hours."

"You're the one who said we had time."

They heard the crack and crash of a tree outside, in the garden, struck by lightning that lit the room like daylight, like noon in July. They felt the chill air that suddenly filled the room, blowing in from the library, and thought the same thought at the same moment, "The books!" Diana jumped up.

They ran into the library, forcing open the broad double doors, to find the giant half tree that had been split by the lightning and crashed through the diamond panes of the windows, destroying everything, letting in the slashing rain, pulling books from the shelves, the soggy pages flapping in the wind, the rug soaked, the ruination of all that Diana held most dear. She gasped and almost fell, but Priscilla caught her, and another lightning flash showed them clearly, two women alone in a giant house, frozen in the face of what seemed to Diana to be the destruction of the library at Alexandria.

Frozen, but not helpless. "There's not a second, not a second to lose," said Diana evenly. "Get towels, get rags, get mops, get buckets. Now!"

They rushed around the house, grabbing blankets and trying to hang them in front of the broken windows, but the windows were fourteen feet tall, and it was a useless exercise, so they began to cart what books they could get to into a dry space, looking behind to see that there were still hundreds of books they couldn't get to. Water was now covering the floor, and books floated freely. The blankets, soaked, fell from the windows, and the high western wind was free to blow the blinding rain straight into the room. Diana screamed, and went back again and again, to little avail. They had pulled out perhaps a third of the books, and even those were sodden.

Priscilla caught her by the shoulders. "Child, there's nothing more we can do. Stop now. Clarence will get to work when he gets home. Any minute now. The boys will be here. Now we wait."

"We have to do something."

"Then we polish, like you said."

Diana busied herself, and got the polishing things together, turning always to look at the library doors, shut against the storm, listening for every clap of thunder, watching for every lightning strike, as Priscilla brought in the candelabra, two by two. There seemed to be so many of them. So much silver in this house. The long trickle of inheritance through the funnel of death.

They set to work. The minutes passed in silence, except for

the rubbing of the rags, the rasp of the toothbrushes in the hollows of the repoussé. They tried not to look at the clock, but they did, often. The train was supposed to arrive at eleven, so the car should be back at one fifteen. It was past that already. Then it was two o'clock, and they were done. They sat blankly, staring at their handiwork, six gleaming candelabra. Diana took off her apron, smoothing down her wet rose-colored crepe dress with a lace collar, no jewelry.

"Let's set the table."

"What for? Who for? It's the middle of the night."

"For his homecoming. For the rightness of the thing. Like in the old days. Because it seems like the right thing to do."

Priscilla, too tired to argue, just followed her to the dining room. The wind was wild in the house, glass all over the library floor, water everywhere. The books. Floating. Lost or salvageable? She felt an ache in her heart for her grandfather's library, for the comfortable hours of her childhood spent between the covers of those adventures and romances, curled up in a leather wing chair for the light. Wandering the alleyways of that history. But that was tomorrow, tomorrow's work; nothing to be done now. "Never cry tomorrow's tears today," Priscilla always said, and Diana clung to that. She had grown used to it. So much that could not be saved. Lost in a night, no matter how careful. The inevitable loss. Of everything, in time.

They opened the big closet that held all the linens. First they put down the pad on the enormous Duncan Phyfe table, and then spread a heavy linen tablecloth over it, embroidered with a tangle of vines and roses, ironing the cloth on the table so there wouldn't be the tiniest crease. Then they put their gleaming candlesticks down the center of the table, all six of them, with the best candles they could find, none of them whole, and then began to lay out the silver, the forks almost a foot long, all of it heavy, Victorian, coming gleaming from the blue felt bags in which it was kept to ward off tarnish. It hadn't been used in years.

"How many?" asked Priscilla.

"How many what?"

"How many place settings?"

"Eight. I think eight."

"You don't even know no eight people no more."

"This is not about that."

Eight places. Eight snowy napkins. And forty glasses—water, white wine, red wine, champagne, sauterne.

"Flowers," said Diana, and she rushed into the garden, into the maelstrom of rain and wind, grabbing at hellebores, and brought them into the dining room, still dripping, Diana dripping now, too, disheveled, her rose dress dark and damp, her hair wild, and filled the epergnes that completed the lineup in the middle of the table. Then the blanc de chine Chinese figurines. All of this in the ghostly semidark of the house, the electricity still out, now past two o'clock in the morning.

Suddenly the lights came back on, and the table was revealed in all its splendor. Like the old days; it hadn't been laid like this for years, and it gave her a thrill even though Pricilla was right—she didn't know eight people anymore. She had systematically cut them from her life. Still, if she did know eight people and if they came, she would be ready. The linens were immaculate, the silver polished. The wine cellar was filled with hundreds and hundreds of bottles of the Captain's excellent wines. Her dresses from fifteen years ago, dresses sent for from Lanvin and Patou and Chanel, hung in her closet still, like dreams you forget as soon as you wake up.

"Miss Diana," said Priscilla, "you're soaked to the bone. Run upstairs and change your dress. Run a brush through your hair. Mr. Ashton will be here any minute."

The wind wouldn't die, but somehow, mercifully, as she was upstairs pulling on a simple black dinner dress she hardly recognized as being anything that belonged to her, she heard Clarence drive up, and a door slam. Ashton was safely home.

Diana panicked: the table looked foolish. Priscilla was right. What had she done this for? What festive effect had she hoped to achieve? There was no festivity left in this house. It had slowly died, as Diana had slowly given up hope, had slowly relinquished her youth to a watchful age, becoming the caretaker of a house that she could be asked to leave at any moment. She closed the bedroom doors behind her and ran down the winding stairs in her bare feet, suede shoes in hand, to open the big double doors to the night and Ashton Cooke Copperton III.

He was too thin. Even under his perfectly tailored Chesterfield coat, his tweed suit and his perfectly polished brogues, she could see that he was too thin.

"You're as lovely as ever, Mama," said Ashton. "Give me a kiss."

He was at least six feet tall. He dwarfed her. His embrace was so forceful and warm, it was like being buried alive. She was lost in the darkness of the folds of his coat, and she barely heard him as he said, "Oh, how I have missed you. I have so much to tell you."

Turning back, she looked at Ash's beautiful face, "What happened to you, darling? Precious?"

"Nothing, really. And so much. I'll tell you all about it. Gibby has come to stay with us. Won't that be jolly?"

There was someone with him. A short, solid man with red hair. His roommate. Gesturing, as though they had never met, Ash said, "And of course you know my partner in crime, Mr. Gibson Fitzgerald Cavenaugh."

"Hello, Gibby," Diana said, holding out a trembling hand, which he grasped warmly.

"But, Mama," Ash said. "You look white as a sheet. And you're wet to the bone. What's happened?"

And she finally broke down and sobbed so hard she hardly made sense. "In. There was. Lightning, a tree crashed. Into the library. My books, floating . . ."

He didn't even let her finish. Taking her hand, he said, "Show me. Show me now." She took his hand and the three of them raced to the library.

"My God," said Ash to his mother, who hung back, as though she couldn't bear to face it one more time.

"What are we going to do?" she cried. "Ash, what are we going to do?"

When he spoke, Ash's voice was so calm, so comforting, almost a whisper, like a doctor at the bedside of a dying woman. "Mother, listen to me. Yes, it's terrible. Yes, it's a disaster. But there's a solution. But not now. It's the middle of the night. There's nothing to be done that you haven't already done.

"Here's what we're going to do. We're going to close the doors of the library, and sit down to supper—God, I hope there's something to eat, I'm starving—and in the morning, I will do what needs to be done. I will take care of everything.

"I'm home now, Mama. Your problems are my problems. I will fix this. You'll see. Can you trust me, just a little bit, just for one night?"

And looking into his bright eyes, she did, and she said so, and he took her arm, and the three of them walked into the dining room and sat down, the library doors and all the disaster inside, closed behind them until the next morning.

"Miss Priscilla? Would you open the windows to air out Mr. Ashton's room? The storm is passed."

"Yes, ma'am."

And Ash and Gibby bounded up the stairs, laughing and punching one another's arms.

WHEN ASH CAME down, twenty minutes later, in an immaculate white shirt, pleated gray flannel trousers, and black velvet slippers with his initials embroidered on them, Diana could see immediately what his greatcoat had concealed. He wasn't thin at all; instead she saw the contours of his beautiful, fit young body, tiny at the waist, broad at the shoulders, a boy who had the muscular chest and shoulders and neck of a man. A Greek god, with his curly brown hair and his laughing eyes, so like his mother's, his eagerness for life's pleasures, how unaware he was of what disappointments it might hold. He had what Diana had so bitterly learned; he had no regret. He lacked the sadness that turns a boy into a man, a girl into a woman. He was followed by Gibson, whose tweed jacket did little to conceal the power of his torso, just as his flannel trousers barely held the strength of his legs. Power and grace, he joined them as though he had always been there, showing a knack for making himself instantly at home.

Diana had brought up a bottle of Pouilly-Fuissé 1910 from the cellar, and Ash expertly uncorked it, poured a glass, and then one for his mother and for Gibby, offering it to Priscilla and Clarence, who both refused. He raised his glass in a toast to all of them, before taking a bite of food. "Here's to my beloved family. My beloved mother. My finest friend. My dear Priscilla and Clarence. I am finally where I am meant to be, in my heart's true home."

And then, with the wind still howling and careening against the trees outside, Ashton and Gibby drank deeply and began to devour their dinners as though they had never seen food before.

"But Ash!" Diana cried at one point.

"Shhhhhh. . . . Stay calm, Mama. I'm home now, remember? To protect and provide. Peace will reign again. A toast to peace."

And they drank, in the flickering candlelight of two dozen candles.

12

AFTERWARD, THEY SAT in the vast sitting room, warmed by roaring fires in the two enormous fireplaces. Diana hadn't sat in here in years, and only now, in the wavering light of the fire, did she notice how decrepit, how shabby, it had become. It was all cabbage rose and saddle leather, masculine and feminine in a perfect marriage of taste and style. It was at least dusted, kept up, the drinks table gleaming with crystal and silver. The Captain used to say that there were only two kinds of drinks, earth tones and clear, and she had plenty of both, the drinks table a monument to a time that was, most of it at least, ten years past. Liquor didn't go bad, and the bottles were dusted every week by Priscilla or herself, a temple to the sort of fun that was never had at Saratoga anymore.

Suddenly chilly, she shivered. Ash started to rise, but Gibby jumped up and wrapped an old cashmere lap robe around her legs. "Here," he said. She looked at Gibby and noticed how the muscles in his arms strained the seams of his jacket. Then, panicked, she looked at her son. She saw the glint of jealousy, just a flash, in Ash's eyes.

The red damask curtains sagged and shredded on their heavy wooden poles, the finials the size of grapefruits, and everywhere hung more family portraits, the men with their stern, handsome faces, the women pale, barely alert after all that childbirth, always against a velvet swag looking out on a bucolic scene, cows grazing, always, in the distance, the peaceful river flowing.

There was even a portrait by John Singer Sargent of herself as a young girl. So hopeful in white muslin and silken bows. She looked very much the same, even still. Brown hair cut in wings around her face, a brightness to her blue-gray eyes, the pale skin and the pink cheeks, the expectation, the firm jaw. There was a kindness in her aspect that she hoped she still showed, but she couldn't be sure. A string of pearls, the last one left to her. A pretty girl, a viewer might have said, not a raving beauty but memorably pretty, and with a charm about her, and a hint of the mischievous, a sparkle like the large yellow diamond that was later in her engagement ring. Out of the ordinary.

This visit was different from all of Ashton's other visits—the Christmas holidays, the spring breaks, the summer windfalls, the endless leisurely days when she sacrificed and opened the Olympic pool so he could swim laps every morning at dawn, determined to do ten more every day. This visit was not finite like all the others, was not momentary. Now he was actually here for good. Changes would have to be made. Secrets revealed about the true state of things. An accounting. Cards shown.

She sat on the immense brown mohair sofa, four cushions across, with her shoes off and her feet curled under her. She knew she looked good that way, gamine and carefree. Beaton had once photographed her in that pose, and she liked it, and struck it as often as she could. Ashton saw her just that way as he entered the room, carrying a stack of phonograph records.

"Ash, it's four o'clock in the morning," she said.

'New music and old brandy," he said. "The perfect ending to the night."

"I don't know if it even still works. It hasn't been turned on in years."

"Ah, but it has. It worked just fine at Christmas. Don't you remember? We kept you awake all night."

"You're a wicked child."

"You said you liked it."

"I did. I liked the fact that people were having fun in the house again. Even if only for one night."

"Is it that bad?"

And before she could stop it, the tears welled up in her eyes and coursed down her cheeks. Where were the mischievous eyes now, the cloudless sky? As cold and dead as the Sphinx, and as ancient. Ash was at her side in an instant.

"Mother, darling," he said, and she could feel the vibration of his voice in his chest as he stroked her hair. "I'm here now. I'm not going away. We'll make it all right. Just the way it was. However you want it to be. That's what all this money's for." And she felt something she hadn't felt in a long while: the kindness, the warmth another human body could impart. For the first time since she'd married the Captain, she didn't feel alone.

"I didn't want to bother you," she said. She looked up, and there were tears in his sad eyes.

"And I was too stupid to notice. But not anymore. From now on, I see it all through your eyes, and I see what it was, and I now see what it will be. I promise. I have a friend in New York, a guy I stay with sometimes, and he has the most amazing apartment, done by a decorator who he says is a genius. I will call her to come help us. Her name is Rose de Lisle. When she's done, everything will be splendid, more splendid than ever. Then we'll have people for dinner and dances, like in the old days when I would listen and watch from that window in the upstairs hall and it all seemed like a fairy tale. I would kiss you through the glass as you whirled by. You were the queen. Always the queen."

"Don't be silly. I'm hardly a queen."

Ash knelt on the floor in front of her. "Oh, Your Majesty, will you forgive me?"

"Then bring me a drink. Forgiveness never comes without brandy."

Ashton got up, went to the bar, poured two snifters of old, good brandy, and brought one to her. Gibby, who had been left out of all of this, who had found himself wishing he were somewhere else, got up and poured himself a brandy. Nobody noticed. He poured a big one.

"And now, surprises. Surprises and music."

In moments, Glenn Miller was playing softly on the phonograph, as the fire warmed the room, and the first sip of brandy warmed Diana. Before joining her on the sofa, Ash pulled from beneath the stack of records two official-looking documents, and brought them with him as he returned to sit beside her. One was thick, and tied with black grosgrain ribbon. The other was thinner, and tied in red. He gave her the thin one first.

She held it, not knowing what to do. "Go on. Open it," he said, and she untied the ribbon, unfolded the vellum, carefully read the document, and looked up in surprise.

"All you have to do is sign. It legally changes your name back to Diana Cooke. Mother, it's who you are. Father has been dead for nine years. I know there was not a lot of love between you. Children can tell more than grown-ups give them credit for. The marriage was a business deal between Daddy and your father, but this house has been a Cooke house for a hundred and fifty years. It's time it was a Cooke house again."

"But it is. You . . ."

"That's the other part." And he handed her the second, thicker document. It took her longer to read it thoroughly, but its meaning was clear fairly quickly. Saratoga would be in her name again.

"Darling, I know this is well meant, and I thank you with all my heart, but I can't do this. I have to say no."

"But why?"

"I can't afford it."

"You'll have all the money you could ever need."

"Where am I going to get it?"

"You're going to get it from me. As much as you want. I've got gobs. The house itself is yours now. Not a life tenancy, not anything tricky like that. Yours. As it should be. As it should always have been. I'm only putting things to rights."

"But your father wanted you to have it."

"And I loved my father. I loved him dearly, and I miss him every day. But the house was never his. It's yours. Now, let's not fight about it. Let's dance. I mean, if you're not too tired."

And he offered her his hand, and she rose from the sofa and they danced in the dwindling light of the fire to "In the Mood," and "When You Wish Upon a Star," gracefully and sweetly, until it was starting to be light out, and then they put the screen in front of the fire and left the lights on in the sitting room, something Diana would never have done only a day before, not wanting to waste a penny, and they went up the long staircase and into their bedrooms and then to sleep, warm and tired and happy, both of them completely at rest and content for the first time in a long time, for as long as either could remember.

Gibby lay awake in his room, remembering their dance. Each time her lovely face had passed, she'd looked at him, and each time the message seemed different. It changed from a cordial formality to the warmth of welcome, to that look a horse gives its owner, knowing there's an apple in the pocket, to hunger, to a hunger she had forgotten for a decade. Through Ash's arms, and into her bloodstream and her heart, Gibby had watched her come back to life. He knew he was not handsome, but with his forest-green eyes and his shock of red hair, he was sin writing itself on her heart.

And he was a green fire, waiting to burn her up.

13

SHE DID NOT sleep for long, but she didn't feel tired. She sat at her dressing table, crystal and silver bottles in front of the dressing-table mirror, brushing her shining hair a hundred times, as she had done every morning and night since she was twelve years old. As she reached eighty-seven, there was a soft knock on the door and Ash walked in, wearing a splendid paisley silk dressing gown with a fringed sash, his hair still wet from the bath. In his hand was the sterling boar-bristle brush that belonged to his great-grandfather, oval, shining. He held it out shyly.

"I've dreamed of this. You used to . . . Would you?"

"You were a child."

"It was one of the greatest pleasures of my life."

"The greatest pleasures of your life? Lord, silly boy. You must be very deprived of pleasures. Sit down." And he sat on the floor, his back to her. She could see, from above, his long strong torso, covered with a fine down. She took the brush from him, and began to brush his wet, curly hair. He sighed and closed his eyes.

"You've filled out, as they say."

"Captain of the rowing team, the riding team. Captain of the gymnastics team until I got too tall and Gibby took over. You should see him. A whiz. Still is. Father taught me a gentleman should be good at sports."

"He adored you. He wanted everything to be perfect for you, and he wanted you to be good at things—sports, dancing, horsemanship, even music and art, things in which he had no interest himself."

His hair was so thick on his head. He lay back, his solid neck in her lap, wetting Diana's velvet dressing gown. She didn't care.

"Except academics," she said. "He didn't much care for academics. He thought there was more use, in the life you were going to lead, in knowing how to inseminate a bull than in knowing how to translate the *Aeneiad,* and I suppose he was right. God, we were both so empty-headed and ignorant. That's what I've done in your absence. I've gone through Grandfather's library, book by book, year by year, and I've learned things, history and art and literature and poetry, and, well, I can talk about things. Not that there's anybody to talk to anymore."

"There will be, love. Wait and see. This will be the greatest house in all of Virginia, and dukes and duchesses will come to sit at your table and marvel at your wit and charm."

"God. What a flighty dreamer you are. There. All dry. Now go put some clothes on—work clothes, not fancy clothes—and we'll go down to breakfast. I'm sure Priscilla has been up since six, making enough for an army. I hope you're hungry."

"You know, I am. Ravenous." He laughed and jumped to his feet, leaving her alone, strangely enervated, to finish brushing her hair, and then to dress in her old house clothes.

She dressed and went down to the kitchen, where Priscilla and Clarence had been at it for hours, as she had known they would be. Ashton bounded in right after her, in his white shirt from last night and well-worn blue jeans and work boots.

"That's a new look for you, darling," she said with a touch of amusement.

"Well earned, I assure you," he said. "Two summers ago,

when I didn't come home, I worked in a factory, building airplanes. Someday I want to fly them. I don't want to be a gentleman of leisure, like my father. I want to do something with my life. You object to this, in some strange way?"

"I promise you I don't." But she smiled.

Gibby joined them, clean and dressed for the country, smelling like a baby after a bath, and when they were all seated in the kitchen, again set with fresh linens and the best silver, there was, in fact, an enormous breakfast. Ash looked at Priscilla. "Priscilla. This is too much. Until we get more help, and we will, I want you to take it easy. Let's live a little simply for a while."

Turning to his mother, he said, "What really happened to my grandmother? Grandfather I understand, demon rum, but Grandmother?"

Diana looked him in the eye. "Don't ever start drinking too much. It seems attractive at first, but drinking too much runs in the family—think of your grandfather, and his father before him. So be careful. Promise me."

"I promise. Now, Grandmother. First she was here, and then she wasn't."

"One day she said she was tired. She said she was more than tired. She said she was ill, dying. We called the doctor. He came. There was nothing wrong with her. She had already picked out the south bedroom on the third floor, and she moved her things, her favorite things, from all over the house up there, and she got in her favorite chair, mine now, and she never got out. There was nothing wrong with her. She just wasn't comfortable being in this house any longer, so she and your grandfather withdrew. She sat in that chair all day, healthy as a horse, only sixty-seven, and she did the needlepoint that hangs over the bed in your old room, your boyhood room, and she smoked and smoked. She only started when she was fifty-eight. She read all of Dickens from one end to the other, and then she started again at the beginning. If she wanted to see me, she sent a note by Miss Priscilla. Usually because she wanted to have a party. Her mind was going. She sent a note with the day and the time and the guest list, many of whom were dead, but we couldn't afford to give a party anyway, and I did nothing but ball it up and throw it away, after trying in vain to explain it to her, and on the day of the party she would put on a voile tea dress from twenty years ago and get your grandfather all dressed up and drunk as a lord and they would sit in that room and wait for the guests to arrive, which of course they didn't. She then carefully undressed, got dressed in a housedress and an old cardigan, undid your grandfather's tie, and hung up his suit. They would get back into their chairs, as though none of it had ever been mentioned. She had one old-fashioned every day at five o'clock. Clarence carried it up to her. Arthur, of course, drank continuously.

"Then she just gave up. She simply turned the faucet of her life off. And off it stayed. She asked for you twenty-four hours a day. And then she died. You lifted her into her wicker coffin. You lashed down the top with raffia. She died from sadness. And then your grandfather drank himself to death, quickly, in twenty-seven days. He didn't eat, he didn't sleep. He just held my hand as I read to him and looked at me with what was left of those beautiful eyes. And then he died. You came for that, too. So soon."

Gibby said nothing. Just sat and watched. He never took his eyes off Diana. Whenever she looked his way, there he was, calling out for her attention. And when she could, without quite knowing why, she returned his gaze. More and more fiercely.

Did Ash notice? Suddenly, he stood up. "I have two phone calls to make," he announced. "First, a call about the books."

"They're lost," said Diana, mournfully.

"We'll save them," he told her. "There are people who specialize in this. I'll make a call and find out what to do, get somebody to come, come today. Mother, don't worry, I come alive in a crisis."

"Call? Call who? Who do we know?"

"I don't know anybody. But there's a whole department at the University of Virginia that does nothing else. I'd bet on it. I'll get somebody here this afternoon. Just wait here."

And then she was weeping for her lost lands. Gibby came to her and held her, his strong hands on her shoulders as she lowered her cheek to bathe them with her tears. She covered his hand with her own. They stayed that way for a long time, Gibby's hand softly caressing her hair, turning her head so that she could look into his eyes.

She suddenly felt Gibby's touch and looked up, saw the tears in his eyes, and said softly, "Not you, too . . . ," and suddenly they both were smiling at one another, his funny face, his hands wiping away the tears.

"Excuse me. You make me feel . . ."

"What?" she said, drawing away.

"Something. Something." He turned away from her as though they had not spoken, as though he did not belong here, in this room, with her, the mother of his friend.

Ash came back into the room after fifteen minutes, flushed with excitement. "Lucius Walter. Grad student in library sciences at UVA. He arrives this afternoon. He says not to touch anything until he gets here. He'll stay as long as it takes." Gibby moved aside reluctantly as Ash stepped between them. "We may not be able to save them all. But I've told him everything. God, he's dull as toast points, but he thinks we have a good chance. Now we need some mops and two chain saws. Got to get these limbs and all this water out of here. Clarence!" And Clarence stuck his head through the door, and got his instructions, and reappeared with the chain saws.

Ash spoke brightly. "But first, the second phone call."

"To whom?" she asked.

"To my friend in New York. The one with a beautiful apartment, done by the best decorator in the world. I'm going to call and dangle gobs of money, and put her on the night train. She'll be here soon. Now to the chain saws."

"I somehow can't put 'chain saw' and 'the decorator' in the same sentence, coming from you."

"I've met her. You'll love her. She's extremely odd, instantly dislikable, but in time you'll find she has both exquisite taste and a kind heart. Give her a chance."

"What is this lovable person's name again?"

"Rose de Lisle."

What would she have done without Ash? She would have coped, as she always had. The books would have been lost. Whole beloved worlds would have been lost to her forever, but she would have managed. The slates would have continued to fall off the roof, the curtains to sag and shred. But it felt good, for the first time in a long time, to relinquish control, to let the answers, and the money, come from outside herself. She felt a tiny bit less lonely. Yes, that was the true victory of the day. Loss or gain, she was not alone in it.

She went into the kitchen, where Gibby was eating a ham biscuit, another one in his hand. "What are we going to do until Lucius the Librarian gets here?" he asked, embarrassed.

"Why don't you go shoot something for supper, darling?"

Ash appeared out of nowhere. "Do you call everybody darling, Mother? People you're known for less than twelve hours?" He was clearly irritated.

"Well, I guess I do."

"I find it extremely distasteful. He's not a friend, and not even a distant distant relative. It's pretentious and flirtatious and unbecoming."

"Aren't you the prude?"

"Please don't fight on my account. I just want to know how we could spend a few idle hours, friend," Gibby said.

"Just don't shoot somebody's cow!" Diana laughed, and after a short, hostile silence, the situation was defused.

Turning to his mother, Ash said, "Rose is on her way. Here by morning. She has a list of demands a mile long. So, no shooting. It'll take hours just to get things to her liking.

"Another thing. Priscilla and I were talking about staffing. How many do we need? Do you think eight?"

"Eight is far too many. What would they all do?"

"A proper chef—apologies, Priscilla, but you could use a rest after all this time. People to clean, men to help Clarence—I want there to be cattle again at Saratoga, Daddy would have wanted that—a lady's maid for you . . ."

Diana laughed. "Ash, darling. Those days are long dead. I think four is enough. And gardeners."

"Okay. We'll see."

"As of today, you and Priscilla get your old salaries back. And then get two strong cattlemen to help with the herd. I want to start with seventy-five head of Herefords and Charolais. And then our decorator friend will come and make every room the most famous room in Virginia. It will be the most splendid house in the state."

"And what do I do?" Diana's head was spinning.

"You give orders," said Ash.

"To whom?" he asked.

"To everybody."

"All right, then. My first decision is to put that librarian person in the black-and-white room. Monkish, almost bookish, in its way, and of course, a divine view."

"And far away from everybody else."

"Exactly. It's important to separate the guests from the help. And Lucius Walter is definitely help."

It was almost three o'clock. "Well," said Ash. "No shooting today. I've had almost no sleep, and I'm going to take a nap before dinner. Mother, Gibby, I suggest you do the same."

Gibby said, "I never nap. I get under the covers and think deep, salacious thoughts, then I spend some private gentleman time, and suddenly I feel completely rested."

"How's your eyesight?" Ash laughed at the old locker-room joke, while Diana just looked on, bemused.

"So far, so good. Twenty-twenty, although I realize in constant danger. Then I do a hundred push-ups and a hundred sit-ups, after which I have totally forgotten my dirty, dirty thoughts."

He suddenly blushed and looked shyly at Diana. "Excuse the vulgarity, ma'am. Ash and I have been together for so many years. We think we're funny when we're really not. Forgive me."

Diana just laughed and said, "God, boys are so ridiculous."

"Well, I'm going up for a bit," Ash said. "Clarence, would you wake me when Lucius the Librarian arrives?"

"Yes, Mr. Ashton."

Ashton looked to his mother.

"A nap does sound nice," she said.

"Dinner's at eight. Black tie," said Ashton.

"What? Where do you get these ideas? I don't . . ." Diana hadn't worn evening clothes in the last lifetime.

"Of course you do. Even Lucius is bringing his dinner clothes.

God, I can only imagine. And do me a special favor. Wear that gold dress with the beads all over it, the one you wore the night I stayed up all night watching you dancing."

"That's a scandalous dress. You can practically see through it." She thought of the long shimmering dress hanging in its bag in her closet for all these years. Thanks to a rigid regime of exercise, the fifty sit-ups and leg raises she did religiously every morning, she had no worries about whether it would fit her still, and it was extravagantly beautiful, but, but—there were so many reasons . . . "Lucius the Librarian will run for his life."

"He will fall at your feet and worship your being."

She yawned.

"That dress weighs forty pounds. We'll see how much strength I have left." And she went up to a deep and untroubled sleep in which she dreamed that she was dancing, dancing until the sun came up and blossomed in the darkness.

14

AT SIX THIRTY Diana was sitting at her dressing table in a navy gabardine dressing gown, fastened with a single button at the waist, piped in white, monogrammed, still damp beneath the bathrobe, her hair wild from the bath, held back, but only just, with pins, looking at the reflection in the dying light, at her splendid view of acres and acres of the finest riverfront in Virginia, hers now, irrevocably, without strings, or so he said. She smelled fresh as a baby. She smelled like her Roger & Gallet lily of the valley soap, Muguet, and she was at peace. She had plenty of time to dress. The golden dress hung on the back of her closet door. What a beautiful thing it was, and how she had missed it, and, she was ashamed to say, things like it.

She moved to the dress, held it in her hand, and felt the weight of the silk studded with beading from Lesage, a masterpiece really, but the landscape out the window caught her eye, and she just stood there for moments, imagining the herd of cows that would soon ornament the green, the listless way cows had of seeming to do nothing, nothing at all. She would like some sheep, too, equally listless and then suddenly not, suddenly animated as though struck by a lightning bolt, erupting into action, dancing through the rocky green of the land. And beyond that the town, where the lights were beginning to come on now, even though the stores were closing and people were going home, the lights that would give a soft glow as a backdrop to the farm that was now hers again.

She thought of her father in his grave, of how happy this turn of events would make him, of how pleased that his grandson had turned out to be a deeply decent man, giving up Yale and future to take it all on, to bring it back to the way it was before the Crash wiped him out and the great losing began, the selling off from which Copperton had saved them, but at the price of her body and her youth and her life. She had been a slave to this house ever since. Liberation had yet to sink in, and she didn't believe it, wholly, but she would trust, trust enough, at least, to do her hair and her face, to varnish her nails and put on the dress Ashton remembered, for years wrapped in tissue in its own dark exile.

She had once had herself photographed in each of her dresses, and on the back of each photograph had written, in her fine hand, the times she had worn it, so that she wouldn't wear it again in the company of the same people. But it was always the same people, so it was rarely worn, perhaps two or three times, so small and constant was their social circle.

She sat again at her table, and continued applying carmine lacquer to her nails. She was halfway done when a knock came on the door. The knock that was to change everything, that was to set a seal on everything for the rest of time. She hastily pulled the pins from her hair and opened the massive door. Gibby stood there, half dressed in his evening clothes, a grosgrain bow tie in his hands.

"I . . . I can't. I was wondering if . . ." He stood awkwardly, red-faced, trembling.

"I can try. It's been forever."

He stepped into the room and closed the door behind him. She hadn't been alone with a man in this room for almost fifteen years. "The best way is to do it from the back," she said. "Stand in front of my dressing mirror." She maneuvered him to stand in front of the tall glass, once her father's. They were almost the same height. She deftly tied the tie, got it wrong, had just done it again perfectly when suddenly Gibby turned around and pulled her to him.

Kissing Gibby was like raising the past from the dead—his mouth, his tongue so fresh, all the sweetness of youth, the parties, the night air on the yacht as they sailed up the river past Port Royal, going to sleep at dawn drunk and happy, the bed rising up to catch her before she could fall, the making love to the Captain, those moments recaptured when she could believe again that she loved him and their life was fun.

It was quick, a *coup de foudre,* the way youth is quick about everything. Like all athletes, he was expert at getting in and out of his clothes in a second, and her dressing gown had only the one button and then they were naked on the bed and he was on her, in her, and he had done this before, many times, this was no wiser older woman teaching youth, rather the educated, giving lover leading the unloved back to life, the untouched back to the sea of sensuality.

His body was so profoundly taut and thick yet limber, hers still willowy and pliant, her breasts full and high, her skin smooth as the sheets Priscilla sprinkled lavender talc on in the summer to keep them cool and dry on hot nights, his entirely covered in a soft rust-colored down, so different from the Captain's rough, unthinkable bristle, like being scraped by a hairbrush. Her girlfriends had told her it was sexy. It wasn't. Touching Gibby was like a woman's first touch of a sable coat, so soft, so light.

And then, with a heave she thought would kill her with pleasure, it was over. He was slightly damp, and she rubbed him dry with her dressing gown, noticing a small carmine streak of lacquer on his cheek, which she rubbed with polish remover, the lace handkerchief crumpled in her hand as though covered with blood. Standing naked, his skin glistening red as a plum, she helped him dress again, the studs, the suspenders, the tie, her naked body pressed against his back, her thin arms around his massive shoulders, her adorable face on his shoulder in the looking glass, his funny face with his green eyes only on her. Dressed, she sent him off, not even a kiss.

At the door he turned. "Tonight, after everybody is asleep, at three, I'll come back. And every night after that. If you'll have me."

Not looking at him, staring at her face in her mirror, she whispered, "Yes. Yes. Yes." And then she heard the door close behind him.

She repaired the damage to her makeup and slipped the scandalous dress over her naked body, heavy, liking the weight because it reminded her of him, of Gibby, the way he rode her, like the ducks on the river, and she slipped out of the room, the disarray, the faint but unmistakable smell a man and a woman leave behind, the stains on the sheets, knowing Priscilla would know everything and say nothing. Diana moved to the top of the stairs, where she waited until she had caught their attention, drinking cocktails in the downstairs hall, a third man with them now, and then she moved down, step by step, stately, as though nothing had happened.

As though her whole life had not been pulled apart and put back together as a crazy quilt.

As though his cologne could not still be smelled on her skin.

As though that damned button had not been unbuttoned.

As though.

As though.

Dear God.

As though.

15

WHEN SHE CAME downstairs, she realized Lucius the Librarian had arrived. He was short and portly, bearded, perhaps twenty-seven, and his girth strained the material of his shabby evening clothes, yet he wore them well, as though everybody should look like that, as though he were to be envied his obesity, so well matched by his jocularity.

From his first words—"Mrs. Copperton, there are many, many things Lucius Walter can't do. I can't play tennis or catch butterflies in a net. I can't solve the problems of the world. But give me a damaged book, and I will give it back to you good as new. I have two talents, and that is one of them"—all the anxiety slipped away. He stood in the great front hall, surrounded by many and massive pieces of luggage, and followed his opening remark by saying, "I'd like a view of the river, and do you have a large freezer?"

"A freezer?" asked Diana, amazed.

"Yes, the books cannot be saved without a freezer. How many are there?"

"Freezers?"

"No, ma'am. Books."

"Thousands. Well over two thousand. Not all are damaged."

"Well, then, a very, very large freezer."

"We have a walk-in freezer from when . . . yes. And two other, smaller ones, I think. I hope they still work."

"Let's hope they do. Show me the library."

She led him down the long hall, the two boys following, and opened the high double doors. Lucius stood in shock for a second.

"Great God in heaven. What the hell happened?"

"A tree fell through the windows."

"Yes, yes, I see now. This is a great tragedy. *Would* have been a great tragedy, had you not called me so quickly. Get me every dishcloth in the house. Tear up any sheets you don't want anymore. I need fabric. Lots of fabric." He took off his jacket. He turned to Gibby and Ashton. "Well? Are you going to help or watch?"

"You have to tell us what to do," said Ash a bit sullenly, jealous of any man who took his mother's attention away from him, even for a good reason. "These books are my mother's dearest possession. This has to work. This isn't some crackpot magic trick, is it?"

"The University of Virginia does not teach, nor does it practice, voodoo or witchcraft. If you'd like me to leave, the last I heard, trains go both ways."

"Sorry. Truly sorry. I meant . . ."

"I know. It seems strange. But it's how it's done. At the moment, this is a lost world, Atlantis. We're going to raise it from the bottom of the sea."

Diana and Priscilla appeared at the door, their arms loaded with cloths.

"Good," said Lucius. "First, pick up each book by its spine, gently, and let any excess water drip out, just like this—" He picked up a leather-bound volume and watched as the water dripped and dripped from the pages. When the dripping had stopped, he grabbed one of the cloths. "Next, the book is wrapped very gently, with a clean piece of cloth inserted every twenty pages or so." He showed them. "And then it goes into the freezer, upright, as close to each other as you can get them without touching."

He busied himself, book after book.

"And then?" Ashton awkwardly mimicked Lucius's actions.

"Then we wait. The water freezes and contracts like an ice cube in a tray and cracks off the pages, leaving the pages pristine. Voila!" he said, pulling a silk handkerchief from his pocket. "Mr. Mephisto has spoken. Do we ever eat around here?"

Priscilla raised her head from watching water drip from a book. "Dinner will be at eight."

"Black tie," said Diana. "I see you're already prepared."

"Madame, I am always ready for any eventuality. If you told me it was a Venetian ball, you would not find me lacking."

The twilight passed into darkness, with its labors and its secrets and one slash of nail lacquer on Gibby's cheek, and the gown opening so effortlessly, and her whole life opening like a lotus blossom to bloom for an afternoon, a night, forever, there was no way to tell, and the peculiarities and particularities of new passion passed into the politesse of the long table with its six gleaming candelabra and the golden gown not worn for fifteen years, a boy who sat in the upstairs hall window and kissed her as she twirled by and never lost his love for the woman, and requested that dress because he was still in love with that woman, there had been no other, hers the only kiss good night, and because he dreamed only of her, in the night, in the day, he was sent down from Yale and changed his name, to be with her, to be closer to her, not knowing that she was down the hall in bed with his best friend, his imaginary lover, not knowing what tragedy would come of that for him, for all of them, or the deep pleasure of the body that had come to her at forty-two, she, in a golden gown, now sitting at the head of the long and long unused table, blood rushing through her ears, Gibby, twenty years her junior, still inside her, do not go away, please don't, and sitting among them, straining at his Windsor-blue tuxedo, odd Lucius Walter.

Between courses, when conversation lagged, as though it were the easiest thing in the world to do, Lucius Walter picked up his heavy sterling dessert spoon and deftly hung it from his nose. The laughter that erupted around the table among the four of them was like the sound of a dinner fork hitting the side of an empty crystal water goblet. Lucius was immediately part of this odd family.

"My other talent," said Lucius Walter, the breath from his mouth causing the heavy spoon to sway slightly.

So they all picked up their spoons and tried, but nobody could do it, so that finally the trick became stale, the humor passed, and they sat speechless and bored, waiting for Ash to pour the sauternes.

16

THE NEXT MORNING at ten, Rose de Lisle arrived with the force of a hurricane. She had a look about her that women would kindly call handsome, meaning ugly, but she was ugly in a monumental way: sharp chin, beaked nose, thin fingers covered with enormous rings set with stones that could not always be identified—aquamarine, citrine, topaz. She never appeared without some elaborate turban, always black, on her high forehead, often pinned in place with some ornate Indian jewel. She was never without it.

Ugliness that grandiose had to be respected and admired. There was no saving her, no making her fit in. She was what she was, an ugly woman with impeccable taste, and the most commanding person in any room. Rose de Lisle, however you felt about beauty, was imperial. She was tall, threatening to everybody in the house, with the possible exception of Ash, who like his mother wanted grandeur, a return to the simplicity and elegance remembered from childhood, an elegance that in fact might never actually have existed. But he wanted order. He wanted beauty. Everybody he consulted—college chums, actually the mothers of college chums, who dotted Park Avenue like bees in a hive—said that Rose could do magic for him as she had done for them. Just look, they would say. See how the light catches the Turner. See how the sofa harmonizes with the rug.

And yes, there is a smoking room for the men, with stags' heads and a pool table and silver humidors. Rose knew both the lives of women and the lives of men.

Men. She had probably slept alone for all of her fifty-some years, and it only made her backbone straighter, her smile less frequent, her judgments more immutable. How did she know so absolutely what men wanted? Intuition mixed with bitterness and envy. It was rumored that in her own apartment on Park Avenue, she had a room just like this, and here her tuxedo-clad lady guests would retire after dinner to smoke her robustos and shoot pool until the birds began to sing, when they would rush home to put on their dresses and their low-heeled shoes. So many people in so many prisons.

So Ash was included in every discussion of what was to be done. Diana cherished these sessions, and Ash loved working on a project with his mother. It drew them together in a way they had never been together before, and finally they felt like mother and son again, completely and entirely, bonded by an affection beyond blood, two minds set on the same quest, under Rose's guidance.

"I know everything about this house," said Rose at their first sit-down, after her sixteen bags were put into her room and her tiny dog, a papillon named Butch, had been fed and had peed on the first of the many rugs he was to defile in his long stay. "Designed by John Ariss in 1787, it was at the time the biggest house in America. Ariss also designed Mount Airy, just up the river, ancestral home of the Tayloe family. It is said he helped George Washington design Mount Vernon. The examples of his work are few but choice. Saratoga is still one of the most perfect examples of Georgian architecture in the country. And by far the biggest. It is a tragedy, my babies, what it has fallen into, the disrepair, the rot, the lack of love. I did a lot of reading with all these vulgar, fat, horrifying people snoring and belching and farting all night long on the train, up and down the corridor. I had to open the window of my compartment, so I froze to death all night, even in my sable coat.

"Poor people have a terrible time trying to be grand." Rose spoke with just a hint of sympathy and more than a touch of disdain. "It's all desire without means. But have no fear. Ashton has buckets of money—I've done my homework, sitting up all night in my freezing compartment, a sleeper they laughingly call it—the books, the pictures, the debutante balls, the engagement ring, the faux captain, unhappiness piled on unhappiness and then, and then nothing for all these years, until Ashton's friend in New York"—she raised one eyebrow knowingly—"called me and the ticket arrived and here I am, driven at breakneck speed by some Neanderthal through the lovely dawn until the house came into view. Butch shat in the car, which made me enormously happy. Where was I?"

"Excuse me," said Diana. "I don't mean to be rude. But who are you?

"I am Rose de Lisle. Most people of taste know who I am. Generally I need no introduction."

Ashton broke into a conversation that was clearly taking a turn for the worse. "I told you about her. I knew she had to come as quickly as possible. I had my friend buy her a ticket on the night train—"

"Disgusting," said Rose, lighting a cigarette.

"—and she's going to stay and help us put the house back together. I hope . . . I mean, I meant to surprise you. I'm sorry. I should have—"

"No. It's perfect," said Diana. "Forgive my rudeness. I was just confused. You're most welcome here, Miss de Lisle."

"Madame, but call me Rose. It's more *intime*." She had a low, sultry voice, entirely masculine, and a way of drawing out her vowels that made it seem as though she were speaking a foreign language, although she clearly wasn't.

"So we're five for dinner now. I'll tell Priscilla."

"Don't go to any trouble for me," Rose said. "I hardly eat anything."

Gibby chafed under his exclusion from these meetings, realizing that there was a bond between Ash and his mother that he could not, would not, ever be a part of. Soon Ash was rising early to look at paint and wallpaper swatches with Rose and his mother while Gibby rode alone through the forest trails and did his daily exercises on the rings and bars he had set up, keeping up his remarkable prowess in gymnastics, the strength and grace that had made him captain of the Yale team, smiling front and center in the team picture, medals around his neck, while Ash stood in the second row, sheepishly too tall, unnoticed. He could tell Diana's mind was elsewhere, and that Ash had a place in his mother's heart that he could never hope to enter.

Rose had put her stamp on Park Avenue from Seventy-Second to Fifty-Ninth, and sad was the couple who couldn't afford her outrageous fees, or stand her imperious manner. Many, many people found her repellant, a mannish lonely lady with a pushy way and a mysterious background. Her relations with these people always ended badly and quickly.

However. She had done the residence at the White House, taking always into account that FDR was in his wicker chair. "Lovely people," was all she would say. "Eleanor wanted everything green. Every shade of green you can imagine. So it's not all tea and crumpets, you see. And if you should ever hear that she and I had a little fling, well, my lips are sealed unto the grave."

Coming from the train, she wore a fuchsia suit, with an enormous black silk rose at her neck, covered with a long and elaborate Chinese court robe. A huge turban was held on her head with dozens of Chinese cloisonné stickpins. Her dark eyes, lined heavily with kohl, roved everywhere before she took off her dove-gray opera-length kid gloves. And she brought her wretched dog, the fat papillon Butch, to whom she gave hundreds of treats and spoke as if it were a person.

The first thing she said was, "Babies, give me half an hour alone to poke around, see what I'm up against, then we'll have a short talk, then I'm going to bed for three days to rest from that ghastly train ride and think about what the next steps are. First to go are the rats, I can tell you that."

Diana, startled, said, "We don't have rats."

"Of course you do, baby. All these old piles do. I've already called Harry the Rat Man in Richmond. I called him from a pay phone in the train station. He'll be here tomorrow."

Ash and Diana and Gibby sat in the kitchen, listening as Rose paraded through the house, occasionally lifting this or that, to look at the marks on the bottom, presumably, and then finally she rushed into the kitchen, breathless, as though the house were on fire. She came to an abrupt halt in front of Diana and stared at her for a long time.

"Ghastly," she said. "A desecration."

There was no answer sought, and none was given. She turned to Priscilla. "I would like breakfast on a tray at seven. Two coddled eggs, and black black coffee. No milk or sugar. Do you have a toast rack? Well, polish it up. And a rack of very well-done toast. At lunch, a chicken sandwich on homemade bread, the chicken sliced very thin, and whatever is being served downstairs for dinner, very hot, very hot. I will join you at table. We have a lot to discuss, but not now. I'm too devastated. Ashton, did you put a telephone in my room, as I asked? Good. I have many calls to make."

And so it started. Rose wasn't satisfied with the first guest room she was offered, so another was made up for her, more to her liking, and she specifically asked that the big four-poster be removed and replaced with a single iron bed, actually Diana's childhood bed. The finest sheets were put down on this, and out of one of her sixteen trunks, Rose pulled fantastic embroidered silk Chinese coverlets, three or four of them, and she asked for six pillows, and for the bed to be placed so that she had a direct view of the river. Beside the bed went Butch's gigantic canopied silk dog bed, and after all this, Rose disappeared as she had said she would, although every now and then she could be seen sweeping the halls in one of several magnificent embroidered silk robes she had in her trunks, going to the kitchen to ask for a little nibble, a peach, an avocado, a bunch of grapes, all of which were out of season, but Priscilla went down to Tapphannock and came home with whatever was rare, cheeses, fruits, little *amuse-bouche* that she thought Rose might like. Rose liked none of it. Everything she wanted was completely unobtainable in the tiny river town. She existed on coddled eggs at seven, fried egg and bacon sandwiches with the edges cut off, which she had never had and which she adored, at one, and tea and what she called bikkies at four. Somehow, out of this, a strange friendship between Rose and Priscilla was formed, as if they were going to get dressed up and go to church together.

Rose was something Priscilla had never seen before, kind of like a freak in a boardwalk circus. Rose would babble on about Noël Coward and Cecil Beaton and those Mitford girls, people Priscilla had never heard of, as though they were Priscilla's friends too. But at least Rose was providing Priscilla with amusing anecdotes to tell Clarence when they lay in their big bed together at night.

Finally, after a week, Rose's bedroom door opened, and she

emerged in full fig. She hadn't yet begun her work, preferring to lie in her single bed, smoking the black cigarettes that Nat Sherman made only for her and which she smoked with a voluptuousness unseen since the great seraglios of the sultans. When she emerged, it was in a magnificent embroidered silk dressing gown over black silk harem pants, a black velvet turban on her head, wearing an enormous aquamarine ring that, like a good portrait, appeared to look at you from any angle.

"How magnificent," said Diana, overcome not just by the ring but by the whole, unlike anything she had ever seen in her life.

"A present from the duke of Naples," said Rose. "Heavens, could that man get you out of your clothes in a biblical minute and lay you out flatter than a salmon filet."

For her first night downstairs, Priscilla had pulled out all the stops, covering the table with the best food the South had to offer: a real ham, smoked, soaked for days, then cooked and glazed; yams, and collard greens, and Sally Lunn, and for dessert, a plum pudding with hard sauce.

Rose took one tentative bite of the ham and then pushed her plate away. "This is beyond awful," she stated, both beginning and ending the conversation on the subject of ham. She called in Priscilla. "Priscilla, dear, would you make me some of those divine fried oysters? I'll just have that, and some of that mysterious bread."

After dinner, Rose and Diana and Ash and Gibby took a walk through the house. It took a long time. They didn't argue, but every now and then Diana put her foot down when Diana felt that something Rose thought should go should definitely stay. There was, on one of the many mantels, a tall vase, broken and jagged at the top, that her mother had picked up at a yard sale in the twenties. Rose immediately consigned it to the trash pile. Diana said, "That is one of the most treasured things in the house. I don't know why, but it is. If you asked any of the living relatives what they wanted after my death, that would be the first thing to go. It will never leave, or even move from where it is, at least in my lifetime."

Rose shook her head, as though she had just realized she was dealing with a crazy woman. She turned on her heel, simply saying, "Well, sadly, it's your house."

When they got to the dining room, with its peeling wallpaper, Diana said, "Well, I guess this has to come down."

This time it was Rose's turn to play her card. "Are you a madwoman? This is eighteenth-century Zuber wallpaper, the most precious wallpaper in the world, hand-painted. It has to be restored, not taken down. It is rare as rubies, a piece of history. I know a man . . . well, never mind, I've called him already. He'll be here tomorrow."

"What is all this costing?"

"I knew that question would come up, and your son, Ashton, expressly told me not to answer."

One day followed another. Rose had Clarence bring in a large wheelbarrow from the barn and, followed by Ash and Gibby and an increasing entourage of strong village boys, prowled the house, pointing with her long, thin fingers at this thing or that, picking furniture and having it moved, some to the barn, some to be given to less fortunate relatives who then spent their lives saying, "This came from Saratoga," and some to be crated and sent to New York to be put up for auction. Diana trailed her everywhere, sometimes weeping as she saw this or that go onto the trash pile.

One day, as it was getting dark outside and they were alone in the library, Rose suddenly turned to Diana and said, "Tell me about your life. There's a sadness lurking in those eyes."

"I . . . well, it's nothing, I guess. Nothing I would tell. We don't much discuss our private lives down here."

"Bull. There's no such thing as a private life, unless you live in a nunnery. You don't. I see it. I see it in your eyes, in your face at dinner, a sadness, a great weariness, a great effort to keep up. I see it as though a dark brush had painted over your calm face.

"Look at me. The Chinese coat, the rings, the turbans. Am I beautiful? No. Am I ruthless? In my own way, yes. But I have a heart of pure gold. My heart is worth more than any maharajah's jewel."

"And so . . . ?"

"Just because you're tormented, that doesn't mean you can't have a glorious life. People stare at me in the street, which I avoid as much as possible, except to walk from my door to the limousine, and I do not give a damn what they think. But I know what I see. And what I see is a woman with secrets. So if you ever want to reveal them, if you ever want to talk—and you do—every minute of every day, I will probably still be here."

They had begun to leave the library when Rose suddenly clutched Diana's arm. "But make no mistake. When you tell me—and you will, you will have to—there will be no violins, no sisterly hugs, no melodramatic tears on silk, like out of some cheap romance novel. You will talk, I will listen, and, if, *if*, I have something to say, I'll say it. Then we'll part, and it won't be brought up again."

"Understood," said Diana, taken aback. "And I'm not here to pour my heart out for your amusement."

"So we're clear."

"I understand," said Diana, wanting to be somewhere, anywhere, else but in this darkening library with this bejeweled crazy woman at this moment.

Just then the bell rang for dinner. Priscilla had slyly introduced Rose to crab cakes, famous on the Rappahannock. And Rose was as desperate for crab as she had been for oysters, of which she was beginning to tire. Now she wanted crab cakes all the time, and crab salad for lunch. Priscilla was a genius with a crab.

THEY WENT INTO the dining room and took their places at the table, which had been made much smaller, because Rose believed it encouraged intimacy and conversation to be jammed together like sardines in a can. Besides, she'd taken a shine to Ash and was determined to have him, so any chance to be near him was an opportunity not to be missed, although she knew more about him than he knew she knew. The wallpaper man had come from New York. He opened his paint box, and a brand-new set of tiny sable brushes. And then he went to work, patiently, patiently, magnifying glasses slipping down his nose. The Zuber wallpaper was almost finished, and it looked magnificent. He had washed what was left of the original, rinsing away centuries of cigarette and wood smoke, so the colors were rich and true, and then, with tiny bottles of paint and the tiny sable brushes, he filled in the gaps. A Chinese woman with a parasol crossing an arched bridge to go into a lush garden to meet her lover, who lingered in a field of pale peonies, over and over, all the way up to the fifteen-foot ceiling. Even in the lowered light from the Murano chandelier, the light dimmed at Rose's insistence—"One doesn't want to feel as though one is dining on a baseball field at night"—it was incredible, a word her father had taught her never to use. If it's there, he had said, it can't be incredible. It simply is.

Behind them, on the far wall, a fire blazed in the fireplace so large you could walk into it to scoop out the ashes without bending over.

Rose still took her coddled eggs in bed on a tray. On her first day, she had taken care of Priscilla and Clarence by slipping them a handsome amount of money for services not yet rendered; she knew she was going to be difficult, she said, and they deserved something extra for the work she was going to require of them. There were now many servants in the house, and Priscilla and Clarence rarely left the kitchen or the garage, but Rose knew that, as in most great houses, the servants were the ones who ran everything. Harry the Rat Man seldom went home. "You have a serious infestation problem," he had said when he arrived, and after that he kept his own counsel, putting his odd little black boxes in every corner, coming into the kitchen every morning with another rodent by the tail, as though he had won a blue ribbon at Ascot. He ate in the kitchen with the servants and slept in the gatehouse, although he considered himself a professional and not a servant. The other new servants were good-looking but inefficient young men and women from the village, in training under the watchful eye of Priscilla, who taught them everything—how to iron a blouse, how to iron a tablecloth after it had been put on the table so there was no sign of a single wrinkle, how to serve from the left and remove from the right. Most of all, she taught them that invisibility the best servants have. How to walk silently when the lady of the house nods her head, indicating they should clear the table, which they should do without making the slightest noise, no clinking of spoons, nothing that would interfere with the conversation.

They had been lucky. In an old trunk in the attic, they had found the original plans for the house, drawn by John Arris himself and obviously done again and again, to suit the wish of some very particular and difficult man who was paying for the building. And obviously, with each drawing, the house had gotten bigger and bigger and bigger and grander and grander, until it seems the plans had been hidden away in this trunk so the busy builder could fiddle no more. They were signed and dated by him and noted in a fine hand, "FINAL."

"I need the big wheelbarrow. And two of the strongest boys around."

"That would be us," said Gibby, putting his arm around Ash.

"How darling of you," said Rose. "Are you really that strong?"

"God, we're so strong, women faint at our touch."

"I would ask for a demonstration, but we haven't the time. Besides, women and Chesterfield sofas are two very different animals. But any help will be a blessing."

And she got it. In one of her morning calls, she called the director of Colonial Williamsburg, the restoration of which had been finished about ten years before. Many of the craftsmen, the best in America, had lingered on, retiring to live near their masterpiece and with easy access to the glittering and endlessly fascinating water. They loved it when their grandchildren came to visit, and they could walk them through the magnificent but ultimately fake village and say, "I did that." "I hung that wallpaper." Or "I did all that plasterwork." Rose got every one of them, whoever was left, to take the trip up the river and join them in the work. She paid them enormous amounts, but Ash didn't care.

Diana and Rose gave them the tour, pointing out every flaw, and the workers pointed out flaws that even her eagle eye had missed, and so they were ready to go to work.

The men were too old to go to the war, which came closer and closer every day. The boys could be called up at any time, and Gibby faced it bravely and eagerly while Ash looked through his law books for ways to avoid it. Gibby wanted to fly planes, a call to death. Ash explained to anyone who would listen that he was the sole support of his mother, which was actually, now that he had fixed things, the reverse of the truth.

The war and the renovation. They talked of nothing else.

As Paris burned, as Europe fell, Diana chose wallpaper; she chose silks and brocades for curtains and hangings for the beds. Rose felt there were certain rooms meant for men, but that guest rooms were mostly feminine, so Diana spent hours looking through books of wallpaper, toile de Jouy, Zuber, cabbage roses, endless patterns. In her room, she didn't want wallpaper. She knew that her bedroom was also her tomb, so she wanted a room to die in, and so she chose a silvery gray, on which there were to be painted silver medallions, and the curtains and hanging of pale silver dupioni silk shot with gold.

The Zuber wallpaper was finished. The little man came down off the high ladder with his pots of paint and his tiny brushes, and even Ash, who knew that it would have been far cheaper just to pull it all down and replace it, had to admit it was perfect. Then Rose decided that the undistinguished woodwork that went from wallpaper to the floor, the dado, and all around the windows had to be painted. She looked through her book, and there were six books, and she finally said, "Oh, fuck it, let's just paint it bloodred. So red it's almost black. And then, my babies, my big gift to you: a decorator's secret. We're going to lacquer all the red. Just ordinary shellac. Don't get scared. The beauty of paint is, it's cheap and you can always paint over it."

When one of the Williamsburg men, a master painter, had finished, it was spectacular in any light. It glowed like a Fabergé egg, and made the wallpaper the only thing that captivated the eye.

Now it was time to clean house. Rose and Clarence got out her wheelbarrow again, Rose dressed somewhere between an Oriental queen and an Iowa farm woman, Chinese court skirts over denim overalls. Diana stood by her side, both excited and afraid. Nothing had been touched at Saratoga for two decades. She suddenly found its haphazard decay endearing beyond words. That was where her father sat to enjoy his Cubano after dinner. By the window, there, that was where her mother sat to read, catching the last light, although, in fact, she spent more time looking at her beloved river than at her book. It wasn't about moving furniture. It was about upsetting the apple cart of her childhood memories, the whole memory of a family life, and the life before that, the ghosts of the men and women who had always sat in that crewelwork chair.

And the river flowed. It flowed endlessly, different at any hour of the day. At sunset, it burst into a palette of color that, if it were painted exactly, would look cheesy and tasteless. But, looking at it, as her mother could do all day long, it was a world of wonder. Calm, she watched for the leaping of the fish, disturbing the quietude of the deep deep blue of the deepest water, thinner at the shore, becoming sandy and almost brown, ripe with oysters and crabs. And at sunset it was as if a giant card trick were being played. The blue turned purple, then mauve shot with streaks of pink, until the whole of it, the great wide whole, burst into pink streaked with a pale gray. When the water was rough, even in the slightest way, it all broke up into a crown of jewels, the cerise at the top of each wavelet so bright it burned the eyes, falling off to black at the bottom of the trough.

And when the sun had finally set, the whole sky caught fire, sucking the color from the water, the gentlest wave a roar of light, raging against the darkness to come. The color drained, twilight set in, and the brightness of the sky turned orange and one felt as if one's lover were leaving. It didn't matter that the sun would rise in the morning and it would all happen all over again.

Once Diana and Gibby and Ash found themselves down on the dock at sunset, watching the whole miraculous show. Ash turned to his mother. "You look so beautiful. At this exact moment, you are the most beautiful woman in the world."

She laughed and ran her hand through his hair. "Sweetheart, everybody looks beautiful in this light. You and Gibby are, at this very moment, the handsomest men on the planet." And they all locked elbows, in love with each other, in love with themselves, and stood transfixed at all this beauty until it was dark and they had to make their way back to the house, that great glimmering ship, the lights coming on all over the house. Home. Her whole life in those walls. She had slept in the same bed for twenty years, and woken every morning in the darkness, her first sight the river, her timekeeper, her heart, the door that opened to everything else.

And at that moment, she knew what was to be the idea for the decoration of the house. The house must reflect the grandeur and the color of the river.

She told it all to Rose, who sat with her for several days through a whole sunset. Rose looked and looked hard. "In England, those snotty people always say red and green must never be seen, and I say, fuck them. I can picture it now, like a jewel box. Tomorrow, in the light, we'll go through the color book from Farrow & Ball, and we'll pick all the colors and then we'll have some local genius at Benny Moore copy them all, room by room. You will be the jewel of the Tidewater. Unconventional, but who wants one of those sad Williamsburg lookalikes? Everything dark. Everything proper. Everything dead as Tut."

Then they just sat, Rose sipping the last of her Manhattan, silent, happy. Rose reached out and took Diana's hand and they just sat there, hand in hand, until it was completely dark, the moon rising over the river, orange at the horizon, then pale gold then white as it rose full into the night sky, glimmering with stars. One of the town girls in her crisp uniform turned on the lights, one by one, until the house glowed on the water.

And now it was all going to go, and part of her couldn't wait to see what Rose would do, and part of her wept for the first chair that was moved so much as an inch from where it always sat. Ash stood tall by her side, and helped her through something that Gibby would never, could never, understand. Both felt the same wrenching feeling in the gut, and while they both were committed and excited by Rose's plans, neither one knew quite why they were doing it.

The South is littered with big piles like Saratoga, mostly falling apart, through lethargy or destitution, and objects like Uncle Harry's leather club chair, cracking and tattered as it may be, take on the aura of religious relic. Time ravages them, and generations go on not noticing.

Rose de Lisle noticed everything. She got up in the dark, watched the river, the glitter of the moon on the slate-black water, until the sun came up. When she came out of her bedroom door, it was as if lightning had struck the house, or like Pallas Athene had appeared, fully armed and ready for work.

Followed by Clarence and his wheelbarrow and the two boys, followed everywhere by Diana, she would stop in front of an ormolu clock, or a sideboard missing its back leg, held up by books, and she would hmmm and scratch her chin and then she would point her regal finger, and into the wheelbarrow it would go. She didn't even have to say anything. When the pause came, and the finger pointed, they just knew. "God. I'm beginning to breathe again," she would say, and they would continue with the march of devastation. Down came the velvet curtains, which had hung in the dining room since 1887; they looked exactly like

Scarlett's dress, fringed in gold bullion, and so old the velvet was shiny. Up came the needlepoint rug Aunt Sally had brought back from China, ten by twelve, not counting the holes where the diminishing rat population had eaten it.

They opened a closet, and there was china, God, china everywhere, settings for forty-eight of Canton Willow, Rose Medallion, settings for twenty-four, a setting for twelve, French, dark green, decorated entirely with playing cards, odd, must have been for card parties, and more, roses, and deities; apparently near nakedness, offensive in art and statuary, was acceptable when it was covered with asparagus hollandaise.

Diana thought of Sherman's march through Atlanta. Nothing was left unscathed. Nobody understood the South. Nobody realized how dear Aunt Lucia's cracked vase was. Nobody understood the sorrow of the irreplaceable, however battered. Jeb Stuart had sat in that chair, and tatty as it was, it would never leave where it stood. His muddy boots on the bottom rung, Stratford Hall just up and across the river. People of distinction had dropped their coffee cups on the floor, just there, and the pieces had been swept up and glued back together and put into a cabinet and never used again, and whoever had remarked on the brilliant painting on the porcelain, or on the obvious, jagged cup, had been told, simply, "That was the General's cup," thus ending the discussion because everybody knew, everybody knew it had a value beyond its lost usefulness as a drinking vessel.

Rose pointed her imperious finger at the battered wicker wheelchair next to the drinks table and said "Gone." Diana stood before it as though she were the last soldier at the Alamo. "My father sat in this chair for over fifty years," she said. "It will not ever be gone, or even moved. That's where he watched the river, day after day, the calm, the tides, the whitecaps when the wind was up. Noël Coward got up from the table outside and came indoors and took his lunch with him, right there. Isadora Duncan danced for him in that hallway. No. Not ever."

Diana had spoken.

17

THE HEART IN love has its bright places and its dark places. This is the price you pay for the stilling of the monotony of the endless gong of the lonely years, the nights spent alone, the sheets changed with the humiliation of only having been half slept in, the mournful eye of Priscilla, who believed woman was not meant to be alone, Priscilla who had slept lovingly beside her husband for twenty-seven years and knew every inch of his body as well as she knew her own, who believed when the horse collapses under you, you get up and get right back on another one. The memory never leaves you, the expectation of return, corners of your lonely heart that cannot be illuminated, no matter how fiercely you may love. And you do not forgive for this, not your dead husband, not your limber lover who tells you again and again that he loves you, as though he knows what love is. You do not forgive because there is no forgiveness in your heart. You accept, accept even with gladness, but you do not forgive.

So, however much you love, the heart remains both enraged and enraptured. And you wish it were not so; you look at the funny face of your lover, who looks back at you with adoration, and you wish to accept, to worship in return, but you suddenly find you can't, you won't, and the worst, most infuriating thing is that he understands all this, so much so that you don't even have to talk about it, understands it with a patience that would shake Job. He understands, and he meets you for two minutes or five or half an hour, or at four in the morning if that's the only time you feel safe. Whenever, he looks at you with an unbidden adoration that anybody can see; your own son, who grows more jealous by the day, becomes a seething ball of jealousy, because although he doesn't know what's happening, time and place, caress and kiss and penetration, he knows the essence, the adoration and the gladness in your heart. He might have accepted, even welcomed a stepfather, an athletic, duck-shooting ruddy man he could ride to hounds with, smoke cigars with, but this, this that he knows without knowing a single detail of time or place, this tears him apart. Gibby has been his for eight years, both at Exeter and Yale; he meant in his dreamy heart that it would be so forever. Now he feels a seismic shift, and his heart is slowly breaking.

SHE WAS BRUSHING his hair, still wet from the shower, and she thought he had gone to sleep. But he opened his eyes and spoke like a sleepy four-year-old.

"Mama?"

"Yes, darling?"

"I've always wondered . . ."

"Wondered what, baby?"

She had a way of saying it that was so endearing, it wasn't infantile at all, there was nothing childish about it; she only used it when she was deeply affectionate, and the only one she ever used it with was her son. It was something between them that meant they were bonded by an affection so intense that they only used this in private, only alone, usually in the dim rose-colored light of her vast bedroom.

"Well, this is hard. Why did you never . . . never pick me up?"

"Who told you that?"

"Mammy Evelyn, before she left."

"I was afraid."

"I was a baby!"

"You were the most beautiful baby I had ever seen. That anybody had ever seen. And you have to remember, I was only twenty. I couldn't get close to you. You were a very small baby, you know. Fine-boned. Very fragile. I had your portrait painted and hung in my bedroom so I could see you day and night, or at least the thin veneer of what some painter thought you looked like. I had you photographed by all the famous photographers. The photographs, a dozen or so, sat on my night table and I kissed each one before I went to bed at night. I'll show them to you.

"I took to creeping into your room very late at night when you were deep asleep, and Mammy Evelyn was sleeping on her cot in the corner, and I would sneak in and I would pick you up, and nobody knew, until you opened your eyes and howled, and Mammy Evelyn would wake up instantly and take you from me and you would calm down and go back to sleep and I would go back to my bedroom and go to sleep. Then you started getting the rash, and nobody could tell why, until we took you to a very learned pediatrician and he said it was because you were always being woken up in the night by the total stranger, and it scared the wits out of you. You literally didn't know who I was.

"They had no idea what to do about it. The smartest doctors in the country, totally stumped. But Mammy Evelyn did. She taught me how to be your mother. She taught me how to change your diapers, and feed you, and hold you when you were afraid, and tell you stories to pass the time until the storm was over, as you clutched my skirt.

"And one day, I remember it exactly, you got up, we were at

breakfast, and you threw your arms open and you said, 'Mama!!' and I knew we had won, Evelyn and I. I knew I had a son—and that my son had a mother."

"I remember that, too. And then Mammy Evelyn packed her bags and went away somewhere. Did we ever know?"

"She cried so hard when she left. But she said her work was done. I told her she could stay here for the rest of her life, but she said it would hurt her inside too much and she had to move on. I drove her to the bus."

"But where did she go?"

"Cleveland. Cards came at Christmas."

"Is she still living?"

"I suppose so. The cards stopped coming when . . . when everything changed."

His hair was long dry, but she kept running her fingers through the curls, so soft, so shiny. He was almost asleep.

Gibby would be here in an hour. Throughout the whole conversation, she had kept her eye on the clock, ticking the minutes away.

At the door, Ash stopped. "Will you come rub my feet, at least?"

She was about to say no, to say how ridiculous it was, Ash a grown man, but then she remembered all the times, all the party nights, when he couldn't sleep, and he had sent Mammy Evelyn down to ask if she would come up and tuck him in, rub his feet until he fell asleep, and she had refused, caught up in the fun, the dancing and the drinking, refused, and left him to his sleepless bed, so that he wandered the halls and kissed her image through the diamond panes of the bay windows, and she owed it to him, she had a debt, and she hesitated but she said yes, trembling, and followed him down the hall to his room, and stood awkwardly as he took off his silk dressing gown and dropped it on the floor, and got into bed, his cotton pajamas so perfectly pressed, Priscilla must iron them every day for him, and she sat at the foot of his bed, and he stuck his feet out from under the covers and she massaged them, and watched as he calmed.

"Do you remember? Do you remember the prayer we used to say every night?"

"Of course. I still say it."

Together they said the prayer, straight from the prayer book, from the prayers for children:

> Oh Lord support us
> All the day long
> Till the shadows lengthen
> And the evening comes
> And the busy world is hushed
> And the fever of life is over
> And our work is done.
> Then in thy mercy
> Grant us a safe lodging
> A holy rest
> And peace at the last.
> Amen.

His voice left hers. She was softly speaking alone. He was already asleep. She put his feet under the covers, and tucked him in tightly, and smoothed back his silky hair, and kissed him on the forehead, leaving the nightlight on because he was afraid of the dark, and quietly left, closing the door softly, and returned to her own room to wait.

18

DOWNSTAIRS, IN THE kitchen, Lucius Walter carefully removed the sheets of paper he had put in the now-thawed book before him and began to iron each page, pushing away the troubling thoughts of handsome men that haunted him constantly, particularly in the dark, at three o'clock, when everybody was asleep in their beds and he was alone. He was happiest then, saving the books, one by one, but still the thoughts darted in and out of his mind, like a goldfish in a bowl. The man, in this instance, in the dead of this particular night, looked surprisingly like Gibby Cavenaugh. He heard, or thought he heard from upstairs, a door open and close, but he wasn't sure. Old houses make noises at night. You don't even have to listen very hard. A creak here, a crack there, floorboards rising and falling. History meeting itself on the stairs, each tread a moment in time, a dark second in a long history.

Then he cocked his head. Another door opened and closed. There was no mistaking it. So. There were only so many options. Somebody had gone into somebody else's bedroom. And at three o'clock in the morning, there could only be one reason for that kind of behavior. Lucius, ironing, reviewed the possibilities. The two boys? Such a dazzling prospect that he burned the page he was pressing. Unprofessional and tragic, but there were so many books, and probably nobody ever read them anyway, nobody would ever know. He stopped pressing and gave himself over fully to imagining the scene of Ash and Gibby alone in the high-ceilinged bedroom, naked, muscular, in the dark, the moon flecking their bodies with light as they twisted and turned for possession one of the other. Because wasn't it a war? thought Lucius. Wasn't there, finally, a winner and a loser?

As much as Lucius would like to dwell on that scene, he realized there were other possibilities. There were Ash and his mother. Lucius had seen the way he looked at her, his eyes never leaving hers, following her every move like a puppy with its new owner. It was clear the boy was in love with her. Rich people. They were capable of anything, thought Lucius, who had his clothes and not much else. It might have been going on for years, since the death of the husband or even before.

But, no. That couldn't be it. Too gothic. Too perverse. So that left the gymnast boy. He lifted his iron from the page and sat down in one of the kitchen chairs, trembling with longing. A shiver went up his spine. He could see it all. The silken clothes slipping off, left to lie carelessly on the floor. Her waist as slender as a schoolgirl's; her hair still damp from the bath, for surely she would have bathed for her lover. This would be no surprise visit, and it was not, Lucius was sure, the first time. His legs like tree trunks, the muscles in his arms hardly straining as he picked her up, called her mother, and put his mouth to hers, her expensive scent filling the air around them. Jicky, she wore; it smelled of citrus and lavender and hay, both feminine and masculine. Her skin was smooth as silk, touched with rare oils, his rougher, but clean. He was so young, so young, and his skin had not yet acquired that leathery quality that an older man had, but years of gymnastics had given him rough and callused hands, no matter how much cream he put on them every night, and he was careful, when he touched her, to use his hands gently, to caress with a sweetness and a graciousness that showed his love and his desire. "Diana," he might say. "Diana, are you happy now?" He smelled like a baby. "I love you." And she knew it before he said it and wondered what was to be done with all that, that world of information.

And she would look at him with her glittering eyes and say "Completely and divinely happy," and she would think she meant it, would mean it, if only for that exact moment.

He would carry her to the bed and draw back the covers, Lucius could see it, sitting in the half-dark kitchen in his plain, threadbare terry robe, his monogram almost worn away, could hear the sigh that came from Diana as he laid her gently down on the pristine sheets, embroidered with hyacinths. Gibby wouldn't so much lie on top of her as float above her like a cloud, hover like a hummingbird, darting here and there, drinking the nectar of her body. A hummingbird has to keep moving, darting into flower after flower. Its heart beats so fast that if it stops to rest, its heart may not start again, and so it stays on its relentless quest for the sweetness of the floral world. And she, in turn, would open like a flower, so that he might drink his fill wherever he landed, before he moved on, each place a surprise to her, a revelation. She had largely, in the years since the Captain died, forgotten her body, taken it for granted, carried it around like a satchel packed for a weekend with friends. Now she possessed it again, owned it fully so that she might give it away to this boy, who had taken possession of her the instant their eyes met, twenty years her junior, now making love to her while her own beloved son slept not forty feet away, her son who was afraid of the dark.

Lucius was trapped in the kitchen. He couldn't go back upstairs until he heard the opening and closing of one door and the opening and closing of another, and so he waited, too stimulated to iron anymore, too bereft to move, even though he was cold, his feet were cold, and he waited a long time, shut out of love, the way he always had been, the way he probably always would be. All that happened upstairs happened only in his imagination, his vivid imagination, calling to mind the gut-wrenching image of what it must be like to be naked with another person, skin on skin, to have sex, to say I love you, to be loved in return, that moment when your heart flies over the cliff into the great and tender abyss. As for the rest of it, the penetration, the heaving, the film of sweat, the ultimate climax, his imagination did not run that far. The rest was lost to him, like a novel he put down somewhere and couldn't find again to see how it all turned out. Tears came to his eyes and flowed down his face, catching in the stubble on his cheeks. Where was he to go, frozen, as he was, on the other side of the plate-glass window that descended when two people locked themselves in the embrace of the night? The same stars shone on Lucius Walter. Stupid. A grown man crying in a strange kitchen at three in the morning, a hot iron on the table and a dozen sodden books. He felt a sudden rage and despair deep as a well. Where was he to go? Love, for him, was archaeological, a dig for a treasure he would never find. He wept. Goddamned books. He carefully turned off the iron and sat, weeping, until he heard the heavy door upstairs open, then a pause, and then close, then bare feet creaking on the wide planks of the hall, another door opening and closing softly.

There he was, a grown man crying in the cold kitchen, the fires out, in a grand house on the Rappahannock River. Finally he felt he had waited long enough, and he rose with effort and left the kitchen, leaving the one light on, and made his way up the grand staircase. At the landing he sat in the big window and wept, as the millions of stars blurred in his vision until the whole night sky was a sheen of light, a brilliance without any pinpoints of particularity. He sat until the sky began to lighten and the moon began to pale over the river, and then he made his way to his cold bed, and slept as though dead, his pillow wet with tears.

19

LUCIUS WALTER DID not appear at breakfast. The evidence of his work was spread all over the kitchen table, the books upright, the cold iron; there was no space, so they ate in the huge dining room. Now that the house was peopled again, Priscilla and Clarence no longer ate with Diana. They had returned to their customary roles of mistress and servant, and Diana, while sad, realized the rightness of it, the inevitability.

Diana, at the head of the table, looked tired but luminous. Her skin had taken on a transparency that brought out her bones, generation after generation of selective breeding carrying her through her exhaustion and wonderment and confusion about the events of the night. "I love you," he had whispered in her ear. "I love you forever and ever and ever." These romantic boys with their far-fetched notions, their bravery with their heart's undertakings, their willingness to step off the cliff and into the vast abyss of love's explosive rule.

She had believed him. Hadn't she? There was no doubt about it.

Looking at him now, fresh, shaved, exuberant, did she believe him still, in his corduroys and his white shirt and his sweater thrown over his shoulders, did she believe him still? And did it matter, in the face of his torrential love for her?

And how was this going to be? How, under Ash's watchful

eye, could they even meet? Because after all, once the first rush of passion had raced through them, it was all plans and assignations, and plots to find half an hour here or there where they might reasonably be absent, be alone.

Gibby loved her, and yet at breakfast he largely ignored her, talking with Ash about plans for the day, fishing, riding, and she was not the woman who had given herself to the redheaded gymnast only a few hours before. She was the mistress of a great house, five at table, the Canton china, already planning dinner, a standing rib, a charlotte russe for dessert, and all that that entailed, the glasses, the linens, the work. Always the work.

How did people stand it? How did they bear to lie naked in each other's arms in the dark, the outlines of their bodies written only by the moon, to kiss, to swoon, to go into one another's bodies, and emerge to find themselves at the breakfast table planning dessert and picking wines from the cellar?

"Ash, excuse me," she said, stopping for one minute their excited conversation. "Could you pick the wines for tonight? A Pommard, I think. I haven't been down there in ages. I don't know what's left." She told him the menu. "And a tokay. I don't want Rose to think we're just country bumpkins."

"Of course, Mama. Champagne, I'm assuming. Could be fun," Ash said, a wide smile on his face.

"For whom?" Diana answered, laughing.

"For one and all." Gibby laughed too. "We're the Three Musketeers, and d'Artagnan has arrived. Not to mention little Sancho Panza, not to mix my literary tropes."

How could all this be happening, this normal life, the general run of things, after last night? Did men forget? He called her love, he called her darling, all this not five hours ago. Who was this redheaded boy who crept into her room in the moonlight and took her wholly, possessed her entirely, and then sat across the breakfast table from her now, putting strawberry jam on a piece of toast? How was this possible? She yearned for him. Let the world go away. Let the books rot. Let Rose go back to New York. Let the house fall down. She had never said "I love you" before. Did he think she didn't mean it? Had he heard it so often it had become a commonplace of speech to him? How deep in the forest was she, and would she find her way out? She wanted nothing but his body. Perhaps, in this way, men and women were truly different. For a woman, once the fire was lit, it burned forever. Hotter and hotter the longer it was ignored or denied. For a man, it went on and off, like the heater in a London flat you slipped a shilling into so it gave off only so many minutes of heat, no more.

Lucius Walter joined them, unshaven, wild-haired, his eyeglasses bent as though he had slept in them, with lowered eyes and shy apologies. The rest of them were finished, and had things to do, so with apologies of their own, they left him sitting alone at the vast table, drinking the hot coffee Priscilla kindly brought immediately and eating cold buckwheat cakes. He was dying for some soft-boiled eggs, but when Priscilla asked, he was too shy to ask for anything. He didn't want to cause trouble. There was trouble enough coming to this house.

So he sat alone, in the way he had realized in the night last night he would always be the last to arrive and would always sit alone. Stop it, he thought. No more self-pity. There was plenty of work to do. He was surrounded by pretty people, in a grand house. Buck up. The iron waited. Not a grand piano, a Bösendorfer. Not paints and brushes, or the shoes of a ballet dancer. An iron. The most mundane of household items. The tool of his trade. The tiresome monotony of it. Let them have their liaisons and their lust and their perversions. It had nothing to do with him. Let them wear their silk dressing gowns while his was fifteen-year-old terry from Brooks, the monogram washed so many times it had unraveled to the point of illegibility. Let her stay up all night and appear at eight fresh and shining like the tower on the hill, her body once again her own secret possession. He had a skill. They needed him more than he needed them. As soon as the thought entered his mind, he knew it wasn't true. He needed them desperately, a secret he must never show.

The point was, it was hard not to get mad, mad at all the things he didn't have that they took for granted. Wine cellars and docks and sloops and brightwork. And love.

So what he really wanted in his heart was to go back to bed and stay there all day, all year, forever. Why should he try to move in this world he wasn't born to, and would never, ever enter? And what would he do with his own fearsome desires? What—and this was the eternal question, what would become of Lucius William Walter? What love awaited? What heroism? What beauty? What encompassing act of kindness?

The future, as he saw it through the steam of his coffee, was as vague as the sheen of the night sky only hours ago, seen through his secret tears. He had scanned both the vast horizon and his coffee spoon, and there was nothing there.

At breakfast they all acted as though nothing had happened in the night. The world had shattered into a million bits. There was no putting it back together and they didn't even notice. Didn't even notice.

But he did. Lucius William Walter, in his threadbare robe, saw everything.

20

THE BOYS ASKED her to unlock the gun cabinet. For the first time in years, she got the key from her jewel box, and there they all were, hunting rifles from Holland & Holland, exquisite, shiny, well used, from the days when twenty or thirty of Virginia's finest got together to shoot duck on autumn weekends. They looked in admiration for a long time before they chose. She told them the provenance of each gun. The duck hunts in the fall. The governor shooting, drunk, and bringing down a fine mallard, on the table by suppertime. The look and smell of twenty ducks hanging on the back porch, draining and waiting to be eaten. All of them drunk at dawn when they went out. This gun had misfired, and blinded the first son of one of Virginia's finest families. It was not play, she reminded them. It was sport. Fall sport.

"Did you ever shoot?" Gibby asked.

"My mother could shoot out a turkey's eye at a hundred paces," Ash said.

"Be careful, Gibby. I'm a natural-born killer." She paused, looking out over her fields to the river. "How I loved it. Getting up at dawn. Putting on the shooting clothes that would seem ridiculous to me now. Tweed everything. Enormous knickers. Argyle socks. Brogues. Father would let me have a sip of brandy. And then we would go out into the dawn with our hunting dogs, Preacher and Judge, spaniels, bird dogs who got so excited, perfectly trained, me beside the governor or some senator or titan.

"At first they babied me, pretended I was one of them but snickered behind my back. They babied until I yelled out, 'I got it!' and brought down a twenty-eight-pound turkey, the hardest of all the birds. After that, I was just one of them. How I loved it. The kick of the butt of the gun against my shoulder when I knew my shot was sure. Waiting for the sound, the raising of a covey of pheasant or a brace of ducks on the river, and the dogs would race to raise the birds, and then twenty men would shoot to kill, and birds would fall, and everyone would shout, 'It's mine! I got one!' and the dogs would swim out and bring them in in their soft mouths. It was thrilling. Then they all looked at me, but I didn't say anything, just smiled, because what did it matter? Let the governor have his day. Then more brandy out of sterling flasks all around. You two go out and play. When fall comes, I'll show you how to hunt for real."

She remembered it all so well, the smell of gunsmoke, the camaraderie of men, hitting a turkey dead-on, in the head, the hardest bird to shoot, and after that there was no condescension, no smirk on a single face when she joined them and accepted the swig of brandy that was offered. And after, while the men ate the huge breakfast that was always waiting for them when they came back to the house just after dawn, hands freezing, each man carrying a brace of ducks over his shoulder, then came the cleaning, her particular task, the wadding and the rod, the black on the cotton, the patience it took, herself as ravenous as the men, but not willing to leave one rifle uncleaned.

Now Gibby and Ash were moving out on a perfect spring day. Totally unschooled, with lethal weapons in their hands. What game did they hope for? A rabbit, at best. They knew enough not to shoot one of the eagles that perched in the black pines along the shoreline. But off they went, eager for the pop of the finest rifles in the world,

Lucius had been given a room away from the action, with his books, which he took day after day from the dozens in the freezer, and he spent the days ironing and listening to the jazz in his head. Once he started working, the torment of the breakfast table left him alone, and there were only the pages, one after another, the steam from the iron, the books coming back to life and being put back carefully in order on the mahogany shelves.

Ironing books, in a room as far removed from the life of the house as possible, with the incessant noise of the builders who were putting the room back together, repairing the damage, first removing the giant limb, cutting it up for firewood with a chain saw that roared into life exactly at nine, the moment they rose from the breakfast table.

Or in the kitchen at night, one light on, cold, in his bathrobe, everybody long upstairs and in their beds but secretly not. Alone in both places, unnoticed, the invisible laborer with his single skill, his other being exhausted.

He pictured a dinner party, some dinner party somewhere, the horsey beauty on his right, immaculate breeding in blue silk and pearls, big pearls, the handsome man on his left, asking the inevitable American question, the man sleek in his custom-made tuxedo, Lucius in his threadbare thrift-shop find: "So, what do you do?" And Lucius's face reddening with embarrassment: "I iron books." And the man looking at him blankly and turning away, never to look back, when he might have said "restore books," or "curate libraries," anything to make it more glamorous, to keep the conversation going, so the man might have said, "Oh, really? How fascinating," and then they might have launched into a conversation and the man might have lit his cigarette, lit both their cigarettes with his gold lighter, and the man might have looked into Lucius's eyes and seen possibilities, the churning fire of passion. But that's not what he said. He extinguished that fire before it was lit, as he always did. And the affair with the handsome stranger was unbegun before it had the slightest chance of starting.

Lucius the dependable extra man. Lucius who could be counted on to cover his despair by hanging a spoon from his nose. Lucius the court jester. Lucius whose big trick, unseen so far at Saratoga, was that he could walk on his hands up and down a flight of stairs, his eyeglasses and change falling and tinkling as they bounced down the stairs. Lucius who could pick any lock with a paper clip. Who could make an egg stand on its end. Lucius who slept alone, who would gladly give the other half of the bed to any man who asked him, for warmth, for sex, for comfort, for the sheer pleasure of not having to wake up alone. Lucius, who would surprise and dazzle the world one day.

He tried to imagine another man's skin against his. It felt like a well-ironed book, crisp, flat, perfect. He remembered the dark trysts he had had in movie theaters, in the back room of bars that only some men knew about, and they felt crumpled and useless, ready to be thrown in the bin. And here he stopped. He had never had sex in a bed. He had never had sex naked. He didn't know their names or remember their faces. Sad Lucius. Sad, self-pitying Lucius, who could hang a spoon from his nose, who could do many things, with cards, with hard-boiled eggs, silly tricks to say to the world, *It's all right. I'm fine. I'm perfectly fine,* while inside, empires crumbled, and there was no end to the desolation. He was forty-two, half over. If not now, when? Ever? Never? Never was unacceptable, a bottomless pool in which he drowned again and again. There were five of them in the house.

Two of them were having sex, he was sure of that. That left one, and he thought he knew which one. The weeks had gone by, and would continue to pass. He would make this happen. He would make one man love him, and if not love, accept him for a night. We all need encouragement. Without it, we wilt, like roses left in an empty glass when the water evaporates.

It was ridiculous, he knew. This would not happen. But even the thought of it made the blood course faster in his veins. Lucius the invisible one. Please, please stop and see me. Look at my face, my eyes. Let me touch you, here, and here. Please, I am begging. Without it, I will die.

How long *had* he been here? The days were infused with such a sameness, it was hard to tell. The iron, the book put back on the shelf. The reconstruction of the library was now done. They had dressed and gone to church at least three times.

He must have been here two months. It was hard to tell, but that's what it must be. The boys seemed never to run out of amusements, Diana out of chores. She had written to the dressmakers of Paris, and the boxes had already begun to arrive, marvelous things, perfectly au courant. She wore them at dinner. Time had passed. He had arrived with the storms of late winter, and now the halcyon days of spring were on them like a whisper.

Did he go to her every night? Did they find ways to get away from the other boy and meet in the daylight? Suddenly, without his noticing, there now seemed to be no end to the money. The house was filled with servants, the girls in starched white aprons over black skirts, with white cotton blouses and equally starched white caps on their heads, polishing and dusting the entire day. Rooms that had been closed were opened and aired out, everything taken out and dusted and polished and put back. Now that the weather was nice, the gigantic rugs were taken out into the yard and beaten and aired for the first time in years.

And there were men as well, handsome boys from the village in black pants and white shirts, with jackets they wore if company ever came, although none had arrived yet.

He lay on his bed all afternoon and pondered these events. Every once in a while the pop of a shotgun brought him out of his half sleep, the boys out shooting at rabbits or what birds Preacher and Judge could raise. Whatever they would bring home would be so infested with buckshot it would be inedible, but he guessed they were having what most men considered to be fun.

That was the problem in a nutshell. As hard as he tried. Lucius William Walter was not most men, and he never would be. Lying down into the comfort of a twenty-five-year marriage, the dandling of a small grandchild on his knee, the papery, geriatric kiss of old age—these were not to be his. Unless he accepted the niceties of a crisply pressed page as a reason, there was no reason to live.

He tried.

He tried very hard,

He could not accept that that was all.

He drew the bloodred damask curtains and turned out the lights in the middle of the day and slept. If he could have slept forever, that would have suited him just fine.

21

THE STARS RAVISHED the night sky. The black pines and oaks reached high to caress the skin of night. Gathered by the river, they stood just letting everything go for this one moment, this one gift from the hand of God.

It had been the custom, in the old days, the days of her grandfather and all her grandfathers and grandmothers before her, to give a picnic down by the river every Fourth of July for all the servants and field hands and stable boys and all their children. The custom had fallen into disuse during the long years when there were no servants and no money, but Diana revived it, and there they all were to watch the fireworks from across the river, the children in their best clothes, racing back and forth as though their own short fuses had been lit.

The men and women stood around, their overalls and flowered cotton dresses scrubbed on washboards to a paper thinness and smelling of hand soap and river air, mostly awkward in the presence of their mistress, even though many of them had known her since she was a child, working for other people during her years of Saratoga's desuetude. They shyly drank beer from bottles nestled in tin washtubs filled with shaved ice—Priscilla had made it clear to everybody that two beers was the limit, though many of the men had stashed Mason jars full of moonshine in the woods to which they frequently retired—

and ate from the vast picnic she and Diana had worked days to prepare. Deviled eggs and ham biscuits and barbecue and griddle cakes and potato salad and tomato aspic and caramel cake, devilishly hard to make but child's play for Priscilla—practically the entire history of southern cooking. Of course there was Priscilla's secret fried chicken. Bernard had killed sixteen chickens, snapping their necks like matchsticks, and she had plucked them and fried them. She believed that good fried chicken started with a plain brown bag from the grocery store, half filled with flour and spices. "If it ain't no paper bag," she said, "it can't make no fried chicken." It was done to a brilliant gold; as each bite was taken there was a crunch, and flakes of the crispy coating would fall down onto the pristine starched dresses and be brushed away.

There were big pots of steamed crabs from the river, bright red and dusted with a liberal coating of Old Bay spice. There was roast croaker and rockfish and sugar toads, a sweet fish all but unknown outside these few counties, all served on the best china, brought down in a wagon behind the tractor. Some of the men had spent days making crude picnic tables, and there they sat, on their best behavior, while Diana and the rest gathered around a bonfire, even though it was a warm night.

Some of these people had only worked here two months. Some were the sons and daughters of men and women who had spent their whole lives on this farm.

Rose was carried down, looking like a brilliant, sparkling Roman candle herself, all bangles and sequins, sitting regally in a velvet armchair that unfortunately kept sinking in the sand, tilting her dangerously forward, until some of the men put boards under the chair's legs to put her on almost solid ground.

The swimming pool was open and the children played and splashed in the sunset, their faces glowing with happiness as

Gibby and Ash waded in and threw them up in the air to make cannonball splashes, coming up laughing with delight. The more daring stood on Gibby's shoulders as he held their ankles, and then dove in, seeing how far they could travel underwater before breath ran out and they rose gasping into the rosy light that slanted across the river and the beach. Diana was touched almost to tears to see her lover and her son take such care of the young ones, many of whom, like so many river people, couldn't swim.

It hit her suddenly like a bolt of lightning, a pang in her heart—her lover, her son. Her lover and her son together, her son and her lover, playing with golden children in a rippling pool, the water slick on their broad brown backs, their hair throwing up a fountain of starlike droplets each time they emerged from under the aqua surface and tossed their hair back to shake off the water. Her lover. Her son. Haloed by the setting sun, they hardly seemed like separate beings to her anymore. Instead, they seemed to be a single continuum of youth and beauty and desire, and the sight was so unbearably beautiful, she turned her head away.

She felt a grace fall over her, unearned but given, a peace and comfort falling like the roseate light from the setting sun. And she felt, although she tried to push it away, an enormous and deeply erotic longing for the single godlike creature her two men had become in her misted eyes. Her youth was fading, and she knew it. She stood on the precipice of whatever leap the next years would bring, but the boys would stay like that in her mind forever, beautiful, young, conjoined in their affections for each other and her need for them both.

From the trees she and the boys had hung poles to hold the two flags she put up, both American and Confederate, the flag her grandfather had carried into the Battle of Fredericksburg, now worn and shredding but showing still the powder-singed bullet holes from that conflict.

The house servants stood slightly apart from the farm workers, to whom they felt slightly superior, and made small talk as night fell, the men darting into the woods to take swigs of the moonshine they had hidden there.

The black men and women stood back, silent, wary-looking. "Come and have some supper," Diana called out to them, but still nobody moved.

Priscilla walked up to her and asked quietly if she could speak to her, and Diana took her hand and rose, and they walked slightly apart from the others.

"Why aren't they eating?" Diana asked quietly.

Priscilla looked at her in the eye and seemed not to know what to say until Diana prodded her.

"Miss D., please don't take this the wrong way."

"You're like my mother, Miss Pricilla—tell me."

Priscilla said nothing, but instead averted her gaze over Diana's shoulder, and stared for so long that Diana turned too, and then she saw it. The flag. For her, a flag of pride, for many, the flag of slavery, a long history of nothing but bad things, chains, intrusions in the night, terrible, grotesque scars that would not, could not, go away. Ever. Not in a century. Not in a hundred centuries.

Diana turned back and buried her head in Priscilla's bosom, as she had so often as a child.

"Oh, Priscilla, how stupid. I hadn't thought—"

"No reason you should. But they do. Of course they do. How could they ever forget? How could their children's children's children forget? And it hurts their hearts. That's why they ain't eating."

Diana turned and called out to Ash, who was playing leapfrog with the little ones. He came running over.

"What, Ma?"

Diana stared at her grandfather's flag, a whole history waving in the breeze, and then said to Ash, "Take it down. Take it down right away and bring it to me."

Everybody watched; even the children stopped playing and stared as Ash clambered up the tree and grabbed the flag and ripped it from its pole. Already fragile, it came away easily in his hands, and he ran to his mother with it. She took it, folded it carefully, and then walked to the bonfire, with everybody still silent and mute, and threw it in. She stood watching the banner go up in flames, the way everything had, remembering the sad, romantic tales her grandfather used to tell her as she sat on his lap, his eyes misted by a rheumy film. The cabins that lined the dirt road down to the fields empty, a muslin curtain here and there lifted by a breeze from the river. The linens unironed, the fields gone to seed. Then she turned to her workers and friends as her grandfather's flag burned into ashes that blew up on the draft of the heat into the darkening sky. They looked sideways at each other, in hostility, alarm, and admiration.

"Please," she called out to them. "Tom? Edna?" She walked up and took the callused hand of an enormous black man who had shod her horses since her first pony. "Big Willy? Everybody—you're my family, my whole family, and I would be most grateful if you would join me now for supper. Priscilla and I made it for you. Please come." And they did.

Plates heaped full, they all sat down and ate heartily, as Priscilla walked among them, asking if they wanted more of this or that. "I'm telling you now," she said to them all, "what you don't eat now you're taking home. We have baskets for every family.

Miss Diana and I done worked for a week. I'm not carrying all this good food back up to the house, so don't hold back. There's plenty more."

Already, across the river, they could see occasional fireworks, Roman candles and skyrockets going off. Except for the clinking of forks and knives, the ancient, honorable silver brought from the house, polished until it gleamed in the sunset, they all sat silent while an eight-year-old boy played the fiddle and his uncle the banjo—Virginia reels and other old songs like "Devil's Dream." The child's face was somber, the country custom, and the fiddle was lively. As the fireworks began in earnest, they played "Amazing Grace," followed by President Wilson's national anthem,

Without warning, there was suddenly an enormous bang in the skies above the river. Some of the younger children screamed and hid in their mothers' arms, but the retort was followed instantly by a gigantic purple flower in the sky, and then a green and a gold, and shimmering silver balls that fell into gentle branches like a silvery willow tree.

Gibby delighted in sitting with the children and explaining each brilliant explosion, telling them how fireworks came all the way from China, and how nobody in Europe could figure out how to make them until two missionaries brought back the recipe, and afterward they took the world by storm. "There are only five colors," he said. "Nobody has ever figured out how to make another one. Not even me." He laughed as the children's eyes widened.

For half an hour nobody moved a muscle, just stared in wonder at the sky and the beautiful colors and shapes reflected in the dark river water, itself covered with summer phosphorescence, so that when a fish jumped, beautiful green sparkles fell from its arching back.

Then, with a final loud bang, it was over. A fog of smoke, acrid but pleasant in a way, hung over the river as it began to drizzle very slightly, cooling the night air and bringing a rush of fresh cooling breeze. Then each family began to gather itself, calling out for the little ones, one of whom ran back and kissed Gibby on the cheek, and he hugged her back as if she were the last person he would see on this earth.

Then the workers picked their way back into the darkness, carrying kerosene lanterns, and they were alone, rimmed in gold by the light of the bonfire. "Priscilla? Clarence? Did you get anything to eat? You never stopped moving."

"I got us some plates covered with wax paper in the truck. We'll eat back at the house."

They all pitched in cleaning up, putting the scraps into a big trash can and the plates and the silver into baskets lined with towels. It took a long time, and everybody was tired, but happy, too. It had gone well.

Diana herself felt an enormous exhaustion, having worked in the kitchen beside Priscilla for days, helping her with what little things Priscilla would entrust into her hands. "Ash? Gibby? We're going back up to the house now. I'm so tired. Are you coming?"

"I definitely am," said Rose, waking from one of her little naps, only barely interrupted by the fireworks. Her only words during the picnic had been at the sight of the sugar toads. "You don't seriously expect people to eat these things, do you? Are they rats or fish? Either way, remove them from my sight immediately." She didn't like being out among "the people."

Ash rose to kiss his mother good night. "We're going to sit down on the beach for a while and talk, Ma," he said.

"And get drunk and be romantically mournful." She laughed.

"Very possibly," Gibby called over his shoulder. "Thank you for a lovely evening, Miss Cooke, ma'am."

Slightly stung, she bowed slightly from the waist, and then went all out and did her famous curtsy. "The pleasure's mine," she called out. Clarence lifted Rose, still in her chair, onto the flatbed. Then Diana and Priscilla climbed onto the tailgate and Clarence began to slowly pull away toward the house, Rose screaming in agony at each jolt in the road. There were many jolts. Diana grabbed on to Priscilla as the truck hit the first of the deep ruts that furrowed the road.

"Don't be too late," she called out. But the boys had already turned away, and she didn't know if they had heard her.

The truck rattled up the dirt road, Rose screaming as though she were being jabbed with spears, Priscilla and Diana sitting on the tailgate, singing "Aura Lee," a song Diana had made Priscilla sing to her as a child, Priscilla hardly more than a child herself, in her rich voice, over and over, until it became their secret anthem. They would turn to it in times of special joy or trouble—sometimes just humming it was enough, but at this minute it seemed fitting and right to give full-throated cry for this star-spangled night.

Take my golden ring;
Love and light return with thee
And swallows with the spring

By the time Priscilla had finished singing, and more and more softly she sang, Diana was nodding on her shoulder. Behind her eyes, she still saw the magical Chinese lights in the sky, reflected in the water, and in the pupils of every wide-eyed watcher. All mixed in with Priscilla, from far, far away, she heard the miniature fiddler and his proud country choirboy, singing, "Oh, say, can you see, by the dawn's early light," his hair plastered back, his voice screeching as he reached the high part, and everybody standing and cheering, drowning him out. Sweet-faced American boy. Sweet. Sweet. Sweet.

Back at the house, Clarence and Priscilla lifted Rose, who mercifully had fallen asleep again, silver flask in hand, from the truck, and carried her up to her bedroom, and left her, still in her canopied chair. Then they unloaded the truck, the dishes, the silver, the detritus, into the sprawling kitchen. Diana tried to help Priscilla as Clarence brought basket after basket of dirty dishes in from the truck, but Priscilla shooed her away, saying, "You too tired, little lamb. Now you get upstairs and get into your bed."

"I'll do that. Thank you both so much."

"Say your prayers, missy," said Priscilla.

"I always do." Diana smiled and was gone.

She walked through the quiet house, leaving the lights on for Priscilla to take care of. She thought of the waste, and felt again her father's disapproval. And she thought of all the fathers, stretching back generations, the children growing up to have children of their own, to take on the burden of Saratoga, to carry on the line, and the vast house suddenly seemed heavy in her heart and on her shoulders, like a millstone around her neck, dragging her back through time and history.

On her way up the stairs, she stopped and looked out the window at the river, that river that had flowed through her life and her heart since she first drew breath. The smoke had lifted; the night was clear, the water calm, a white three-quarter moon brightening even the darkest places, the tide flowing out toward the Chesapeake Bay and the sea, interrupted only by the occasional leap of fish, the summer phosphorescence throwing magical sparks of brilliant green into the night.

The boys had added more wood to the bonfire, and it blazed high. They sat beside it, passing a flask back and forth, laughing in a way that filled her heart with tenderness and, again, longing.

Suddenly they jumped up and quickly stripped out of their clothes. They stumbled naked and drunk into the river, wading into the shallow water near the shore and then diving, their bodies cutting through the water as smoothly as the moonbeams on the tide.

When they surfaced, they seemed no longer human but piscine, fish without scales, the water running down their backs, slick and sparkling with that green that quickly disappeared. They were gods, they were the most beautiful thing she had ever seen, and she was suddenly wide awake, her eyes locked on her son and her lover, now unrecognizable, citizens no longer of the land but of the tides. Her twin Poseidons.

She ran to get the binoculars on her father's desk, the ones he had used to watch the blue herons nesting, to catch the flight of the bald eagles, so plentiful then, fewer now. She ran back up to the landing to see them glide through the water like green glistening dolphins, smooth, reckless. And drunk. She was scared they would drown; she couldn't turn her eyes away until they were safe again on land.

They swam toward each other, and in the shallows they embraced, holding gently on to each other as they stood quietly, water only to their waists, swaying slightly, dreamily.

An electric current ran down her spine, from her brain to her vagina, and she gasped in shock. She trembled on the landing. Her light clothes suddenly seemed to be strangling her as she looked as if through a magnifying lens at something so illicit, so private.

As she watched, Ash suddenly took Gibby's face in his hands and turned his face up and kissed him full on the mouth. Tears began to run down her face as she stood, solid as stone, wanting to turn away but unable to, lacking in will and wish.

She hadn't thought. Not since they walked through the door

that first night, now so long ago, all camel hair and laughter. She just had not thought. There was a sharp intake of breath as her knees trembled in fear.

Gibby suddenly put his hands on Ash's chest and violently pushed him away. Ash pulled him back, tried awkwardly to kiss him again. Gibby pulled back his arms and punched twice, a brutal left to the side of his head, then a killing right to his face, punched him so hard that Ash went down instantly, unconscious, under the water. He did not come up. Diana screamed. In seconds, the endless seconds Ash was under the water, Priscilla appeared at the bottom of the stairs. "Missy?" she called out softly.

But Diana didn't answer. Priscilla slowly, reluctantly, turned away. Diana frantically took up the glasses again, to see Gibby desperately trying to find Ash under the black water, scissoring his legs, fanning his arms, diving again and again, throwing green sparks into the black night each time he surfaced, the tide going out so swiftly now, he could be anywhere. The seconds, then minutes, passed, Gibby more and more frantic, diving again and again, finally finding him, already twenty yards downriver, pulling him up by his dark hair, his face streaming with black blood and green phosphorescence, glittering Poseidon dead.

Gibby pulled Ash into his strong arms and slung him over his shoulders, limp and heavy as a corpse, and carried him back upriver, fighting the tide, Ash lifeless, and carried him to the beach. Ash had been unconscious underwater for two minutes. Gibby was screaming, a full-throated cry of fear. Two endless minutes, or hours—what did it matter now—followed by Diana through her binoculars, watching the death of her only son at the hands of her lover.

Gibby laid the lifeless body out on one of the quilts. He put his mouth to Ash's—finally the kiss Ash must have so longed for, the kiss of death, the kiss of life—and blew air into his lungs, then pushed on his chest with sharp, quick jabs, again and again, then more air, mouth to mouth, then more pushing, harder this time, this routine over and over, again and again, it seemed hours. It wouldn't help, and Diana was weeping fully now, unable to go to her beloved son. More air, mouth on mouth, more frantic pushing on Ash's powerful chest.

Finally there was a choking cough, and water spewed from Ash's mouth, and he finally breathed on his own. Gibby wept. He knelt on the beach and wept for his friend. Then he carefully, lovingly, dried him off with his shirt, avoiding Ash's arms, which still reached up to embrace him, trying to pull him close, as a drowning man tries to pull the next man under. He wiped the blood from his face and covered Ash with all the quilts left on the beach, damp now from the dew, wrapping him like a mummy. As though he were folding the flag for a dead soldier. All this tenderly, with great grief, his beloved friend. He knelt over him for a long time, stroking his hair, wiping the tears from his face with the back of his hand, and then he kissed him on the forehead and the mouth, and rose unsteadily to his feet, picked up his clothes, and began to walk naked back to the house. Naked and alone, Ash bundled like a corpse on the beach. Walking away from all that was, from all that was left unsaid, that would never now be said, from the friendship that was now at an end, however they found a means to carry on. Embarrassment trumps forgiveness. Sad, but true, and Gibby walked with sagging shoulders and tenderness in his gait, away from Ash and all that was. It was almost dawn; the sky was beginning to lighten, a fan of rose on the distant shore.

She felt a sudden urge to vomit. She threw open the window and leaned out, her heart churning as the night, the whole night, fell to the ground below her. She wanted to run to Ash, but her legs had turned to stone. Her heart had also turned to stone. Her son, his "friend" in New York, the longing looks he gave as Gibby poured the wine, Rose's arched eyebrow, it all seemed so clear to her now.

Sin, she thought, unspeakable sin.

Her son.

The child of her womb.

Undeniable, brave, young, and strong.

She collapsed softly to the floor, her knees giving way, and then the rest of her, falling to the rug her mother had brought back from China so long ago. Her eyes closed, and she lay as if dead, a wisp of her smoky hair falling over her pale face, rising and falling with her every exhalation.

And she lay there until the pale sunrise slanted through the window, and Gibby, dressed only in his damp khakis, naked from the waist up and smelling of salt and covered with sand, picked her up in his arms and carried her up the stairs, kissing her sleeping face here, and here, and there, and laid her in her bed, his hands caressing every part of her body, and ending the night with a gentle kiss on her forehead, leaving her asleep, a sleep from which she never wished to rise, and then leaving her alone, covered with a light silk coverlet, all the windows open to let in the cool air of dawn.

Independence Day was over. Day would follow on day, and nothing, nothing, nothing would ever be the same again. The snake had eaten its tail; the world had stopped on its axis. The heart that beat faintly in her chest would never ever ever be the same, and she had nothing solid to cling to, ever again. Her boy. Her beloved son. The end of the line.

But, love.

But love.

But always love.

22

IT WAS A house of shadows. Ash, battered and bruised, was silent at the table, drunk almost all the time, and solitary in his ways, avoiding Gibby as much as possible, eyes lowered when they passed in the hall or passed the salt at the table, setting the cellar carefully on the tablecloth, hands never touching, a strict observance of manners, no more. Gibby taking over the role of master of the house. Ash never asked his mother to brush his hair dry, or rub his feet at night, or say his prayers, because he knew, just as she knew when he was having a migraine, that she knew, that she had seen everything. For her part, for the second time in his life, she couldn't approach him, couldn't touch him. Her revulsion had triumphed over her love.

Nobody knew what to say. Only Rose, a peacock in a dying, withered garden, and Lucius, her shabby, paunchy foil, chattered on as though every night were New Year's Eve. It didn't matter to them that nobody responded. They were here to sing for their supper, and sing they did.

Only Rose swooped down on Ash, like a bright cockatoo, again and again, drawing him into the sunroom after dinner, draping the lamps with silk handkerchiefs she pulled from her enormous reticule of Chinese brocade for long conversations from which he often emerged clearly having been crying, Rose holding his hand like an older sister.

Pretending nothing had happened, he claimed he had a lot of business to do, much of it involving trips to his bankers in Richmond, three hours away, where he stayed for days at the Jefferson, unknown, beloved by the waiters and bellmen for his enormous tips, going to his tailor's in the daytime, visiting gentleman's clubs at night, often coming back drunk to the hotel, having lost his gloves or his ebony walking stick, accompanied by a young man like himself, drunk and elegant, a gleam in his catlike eyes, and they would ascend in the elevator, seen once, then gone. His body had lived through a lifetime underwater, but his heart had not. He was dead to the world, dead to opinion. He was surrounded in Richmond by people who knew him, knew the family, and of course word got back to Diana. She turned a deaf ear to the gossip. She wrote him long lavender-scented letters, explaining the complexity and profundity of her love for him, trying to say that nothing had changed without saying nothing had changed—because they both would have known that that was a lie. They both knew that everything had changed.

He hated leaving his mother alone with Gibby. He had seen the glances, the subtle, almost accidental touching of hands, the way she called on Gibby, not Ash, to help her get something off a high shelf—but he had to get away from both of them.

Diana grieved for her departed son, but she could not help herself. Left with her lover for days at a time, she was no longer hesitant about giving herself to him. She no longer thought of the difference in their ages. She became the predator, he the prey. She would find the secret places in the woods she had loved as a child, and in those places she would devour him, frantically tearing at his clothes until he was before her, entire, wholly her lover, his steel legs, his barrel chest, covered with a boy's down, his hands that could grip her so tightly he could break her in half.

She loved sex with Gibby. With the Captain, it had seemed no more than a vulgar exertion in which she was not included. By the end, she would simply wait for him to finish and to leave, and then she would get into the bath and sit there until every trace of him was gone.

With the Captain, she had never been naked. Oh, she had taken her clothes off. But that didn't mean she was naked. She protected herself so fully and with such might that he had access only to that part he desired, and when it was over, and it was over quickly, he had not touched her body, not really. With Gibby, her boy lover, she was entirely nude, every inch of her flesh available to him. Even dressed, she felt naked when he gave her the smallest glance.

Their favorite place, the most dangerous and perhaps favorite because of it, was the loft in the stable, stable boys coming and going just below them, bringing the horses in and out from their exercise, the nearness of discovery, the pricks of the straw on her back, sometimes leaving blood.

Love had no end for them.

Her lover. Her beginning, after so long. Her entrance into the world of sensuality and adoration. After so much sorrow and terror with Copperton, the sweetness of love.

They could never marry. He would leave.

When he was on his deathbed, surrounded by children and grandchildren, he wouldn't even think of her, wouldn't even remember her face.

And that, as she lay with the hay tearing her back and her boy lover devouring her naked body, was all right with her. He had given more than he knew, and she had given all she had, and taken all there was.

This would not end well, Diana knew. She would die alone, or perhaps Ash would emerge from the shadows of his secret life to hold her hand as she whispered Gibby's name so softly he couldn't hear.

And then, suddenly, she stopped herself from painting this lurid deathbed scene, because she knew for certain in her heart one true thing:

She would outlive them all.

23

MEN PERCEIVE LOVE differently in their bodies than women do. When Gibby was walking with her, holding her hand, lying with her in a hayfield, or waiting outside her bedroom door at 3:00 a.m., his desire was complete, the whole world to him.

When he whispered in her ear, "I love you, madame," chuckling, he meant it with an unbridled joy that he felt at the moment would never go away. It was, in its way, grotesque, this husky boy devouring every inch of a woman who was his best friend's mother. Lurid, forbidden in myth and reality. As he made love to her, he said "I love you, I love you" with each penetration, deeper and, along with her, more defenseless. And he really thought he meant it, believed it. He never lied to her, not with his mouth or with his body. He was young. He was strong. These are the things he had to give her, and he gave wholeheartedly. The wisdom of the ages. The freshness of a perfect young body. This belief from the deepest part of his heart, from the oldest myth, that he was at that moment possessing the forbidden fruit, and yes, he knew he was flying too close to the sun, and yes, he was willing to die for it.

In Diana's bedroom, in the dim and blue light of dawn, as they were lying entwined like the snakes of Laocoön, she raised herself from the bed and rested her head on her hand, looking down on her perfect, perfect lover, who was still covered with the sticky sheen of their love. She ran her finger through it and put her finger to her tongue. Sweet and clean. He would be here, and then he would be gone. There are things that age knows and youth does not imagine. She laid her hand softly on his chest. "Darling," she said. "Tell me how this ends well."

"We're only just starting."

"I knew you wouldn't understand. It's not your fault. I won't ask again."

"It ends in joy, or it ends in tragedy. Or it ends in boredom. You grow tired of me. Those are the only outcomes. Are you strong enough for those? However it ends, if it ends. I will never leave your side. I will always be by you. I will always be inside your body. You are the only home I've ever known. And broken animals always follow their instinct and go home. I'm broken. I'm lovesick."

Later in the day, as though nothing had happened, she would sit and go over column after column of numbers with two dour, thin-fingered men from Richmond who tried to explain her finances to her, column by column, but she couldn't pay attention. She was distracted by looking out the window. In the woods, near the house, so she could see him, Gibby had hung a gymnast's rings and put on his leotard, pure white, skintight, and there he was exercising, the moves more and more difficult, finishing with the most difficult of all, the Iron Cross, during which he turned and looked toward the house to make sure that she saw him, until this or that curtain opened and her small hand waved. He wanted to be stronger and stronger for her, the strongest man in the world. Once seen, he would leap to a perfect landing, running with sweat, raising his arms in victory, thinking that he had given her something of worth, when what she wanted was the sweetness of his skin, his tongue against hers, and his penis painlessly inside her, the snake of love.

She wanted him to remember her, to love her in some small way.

"Do you. Do . . ."

"What. Anything."

"Do you love me? Even a little bit?"

"Outrageously. Immortally. Disastrously."

"Don't make fun of me."

He ran his hand along her thigh. He kissed her body at the curve of her hip, laid his head there. "Why would I ever do that?"

"I don't know. Such a melodramatic answer."

"But not insincere. You think, because I'm young, I'm like a toy. But it's true. I love you beyond life. In heaven we are married. Forever, like Mormons. And thinking of this morning, up there on the rings, there is disaster in our future. There is no other way out of this. Secrets will burn a hole in our hearts sooner or later. But now, right now, and for as long as I can, I love you. And that is not the answer of a child or an opportunist. It is the answer of a man in love."

"We're doomed in so many ways."

"But not now. Not tonight. Look at the moon. That is not a punishing moon. It is a loving moon."

"Yes, but not for Ash . . ."

"I don't know what to do with him now. He won't talk to me. It doesn't matter to me where his desires lead him, but I can't be what he wants me to be. He always seemed so hidden . . . but now I understand. We slept in the same room for years. It must have been agony for him. I feel so sorry I couldn't have been the kind of friend he wanted. But I didn't want him. I didn't know it then, but I was waiting for you."

"Kiss me, please."

He kissed her lips. He licked her nipples. He sought her clitoris with his tongue in that way that always makes women both sad and happy.

* * *

AS THE WEEKS wore on, she came to accept it, this deathless love, this love that took her where he led her.

On any given day, they didn't know how much time they had. One wild day, even though the wind was blowing fiercely, and everything was tilting and thrashing, the sky darkening to a thunderstorm, Diana took Gibby down to her secret rock and showed herself to him, as she had to those boys all those years ago. A boat passed. The oystermen, all gathered on the side of the boat, raised their nets and slowed their engines and hooted and yelled and then fell silent as they watched something that most, but not all, of them would never have in their lives, the completeness of taking and giving. The sweet skin, the smooth hands, their own rough and cracked from hauling in the oysters in the coldest weather. The season was months away for them, not until the cold weather set in, a month with an R, but nothing like this awaited, so they watched, Gibby and Diana oblivious.

After they were done, as the rain began to fall, lashing down fiercely, with lightning over the river, Gibby told her to stand very straight and raised her like a board over his head, his strong arms holding her securely, and twirled and twirled her above him as the rain streamed from her body like a water sprinkler.

When he was forty, she would be sixty; when sixty, she would be eighty; with each revolution they aged in her mind, but it was too dangerous to think of the future—she couldn't afford to wither and collapse at this height, this velocity. So she relaxed into it, pulling her arms in and out, watching as the spray grew small, then large, until he tired and expertly flipped her over and caught her in his arms, his skin now sunset red, streaked with rain.

24

AT SARATOGA, THE hands of time moved only in one direction. Diana wondered every day: Had she made Ash the way he was? As she pored over wallpapers and paint colors until she was sick of it, sick of Rose's boundless enthusiasm, sick, in fact, of Rose herself, she found herself racked with guilt. Finally she sat down with Rose, as Rose had said she would, in the sunroom, with their golden Manhattans, and she poured her heart out, confessed her sins, all the nights she didn't go, the years she didn't pick him up, the rashes, the avoidance of the shining beauty of her only son, the misery of her marriage.

Rose sat for a long time, sipping her drink. Eating peanuts, one by one, toying with each one like a cat with a treat.

"My sweet baby," she finally said. "You wholly misunderstand. Ash's . . . character, let's call it for the moment; no, let's call it what it is, his homosexuality—it has, I think, much more to do with the fake captain than with you. People always blame everything on the mother. I myself live on the dark side, spending whole evenings with dreadful catamites, mannish women dressed in white tie and tails, hair slicked back into pathetic ducktails, playing pool and smoking Cuban cigars. They're always whining about their mothers. My mother was a wonderful woman, and my father was a great man, an honest laborer who worked at the same dull job his whole life, in a factory that assembled washing machines in Connersville, Indiana. I felt I was suffocating in their house, just two steps above a shotgun shack. I thought I wanted the lights and the cars and the sophistication, but what I wanted was women.

"I wonder if it's not the same for Ash: he isn't making a choice, he was born wanting men. It's not what he does. It's who he is. You must embrace not just him, but everything about the way he lives. Believe me, it is a life filled with punishments and humiliations and grief. He needs you now more than ever. Don't let him push you away. Fight back with all the love in your heart. Have your fling with your young lover. Of course I know. Don't look surprised. That is your salvation and your right. But Ash has rights, too.

"And I have the right to another drink."

Calling for Priscilla, Diana reached for Rose's hand. "I understand," she said.

Eventually they moved on to talk again about paints and dadoes and carved mantelpieces, until they went in to dinner, Gibby sitting at the head of the table as though he had always assumed that position in the household, Lucius humbly off to the side, saying whatever he thought might amuse them.

And at night she lay in the arms of Ash's best friend, or so he had been, Gibby's taut muscles almost crushing her frail chest, her full breasts, her tiny waist, sucking the wind out of her, so that the only name she could call was Gibby's.

And Ash lay where? And with whom? Word had reached her, of course, about his escapades, and her face reddened at the thought. Fight back, Rose had said. Fight back with love. But this love, where was she to find it in her heart?

She always forgot, neglected to put into the equation, the degree to which Ash had loved his father, how he had learned from him to fly-fish, first on the back lawn and then in the river, the pride he took in every one of the boy's catches, even if they let them go, teaching him the practicality of hunting, a deer for the winter in the giant freezer, the thrill of the pull of the fish, the jerk in the line, the awkward battle for a seven-year-old, shooting a duck and hanging it on the back porch to season until Priscilla said it was ready to roast, how to sit astride a horse, how to take an oxer, even at seven, how sport was about not being afraid, about looking beyond the jump and never lowering your head as it approached. One of the great rules for life as well as the show ring: Keep your head high and look past the jump.

They sat together on the back porch one evening as the sun went down, shucking corn for the water already boiling.

Copperton said, "Who would you be if you were never afraid?"

"I would be a giant. I would be able to fly, Father."

"Remember this, son. Never be afraid, and only do the things you can do well. Choose carefully. And also remember: all people are alike. Rich and poor. Black and white. They all put their pants on one leg at a time. And they deserve your respect. Many of them need help. Always give it with an open heart. It is always possible to be kind. Whatever else you do in life, never forget kindness."

And at that moment, listening from the door, Diana realized that she, too, had learned something about love that she would never forget. And the love she had felt, once, for a time, for Copperton, blossomed again in her heart.

Copperton said to the boy, "One last thing: the Bible says 'Love is stronger than death.' Do you understand?"

"Not really." Ash looked at his father, afraid of disappointing him, but with a gaze that was so filled with love.

"It doesn't matter if you understand now. But can you remember it? Can you do that for your old papa?"

"Love is stronger than death. Did I get it right?"

"Perfect. Keep that in a little box in your mind, keep it safe, and one day you'll understand it. Now let's go in to supper. How long do we boil the corn for?"

"Five minutes."

"And not one second more."

Apparently Copperton could turn his affections on and off when he felt like it—especially for Ash—so days went by when the Captain didn't notice the boy in the slightest way. Ash would sit outside his father's door for hours, waiting for him to come out, but when he did, he would pass Ash without a word or a glance, as though he didn't exist. He would sit silent at dinner, drinking glass after glass of wine, grunting at the food, pushing it away in disgust, putting his boots on the table, a smirk at his wife that said "I dare you to say something."

Ash could never predict which father he would get—loving and kind, or the immutable rock. He lived a life of constant anxiety. Not that people called it that in those days. They would just say he was a nervous, moody child.

Ash never forgot any of it. He grew to be a deeply kind but nervous man, his eyes always beyond the jump. Diana, on the other hand, was still trying to make Copperton love her. The night after she overheard father and son discussing life as they knew it, she walked with Copperton up the stairs, carrying a very sleepy Ash in her arms. So big he was. She hadn't noticed. Together they gave him his bath, and put him in his pajamas, and then he sat on the floor while Diana brushed his hair dry and Copperton read to him from an illustrated book about King Arthur. Together they put him to bed and said his prayers, and kissed him good night, leaving the nightlight on because he was afraid of the dark.

Without a word, and with complete understanding. Diana

led Copperton to her bed, and took him to her in a way that hadn't happened since their marriage, with a tenderness and love that didn't need to be spoken.

He was soft and kind and considerate, and she began to think that perhaps they could truly be husband and wife, that they could tramp the fields and swim the river as a threesome, without all the anxiety and bitterness.

When it was done, he didn't immediately rise from the bed, as he usually did, but lay in her arms, idly kissing her from time to time.

"Cop—" She started to speak.

"Shhhhh . . ."

And so they lay, complete in their comfort for the first time in their marriage, the rages stilled, like the water of the river after a storm has passed, leaving a halcyon stretch of blue green, the ducks in V-shaped armada, the kind of moment when you suddenly see the natural world and find it the most amazing thing imaginable.

They made love a second time, more sweetly even than the first, and then he did rise from the bed.

"Copperton? Husband?"

He turned to look at her.

"I won't lock the door. Let's begin again. This minute. This second. Let's begin again and be a comfortable couple."

He came and knelt by the side of the bed and laid his head on her breast. He didn't say anything, and she didn't either. She just let him cry until he raised his head and looked at her for a very long time.

In his voice there was the rasp of genuine emotion. "I'll see you at breakfast."

At the door he turned. "Are you happy, darling?"

"I wasn't, but I could be. Let's be happy together. For us. For Ash."

So they tried. They tried so hard it broke their hearts.

They say that all families are either about the parents or the children. In the last months of Copperton's life, they tried to make their marriage about Ash. They tried to find their love through him. And night after night, after the bathing ritual, he came to her a different man from the man she had married, gentler, kinder, more attentive, and she in turn was more giving, more open. It wasn't ecstasy. It wasn't an explosion of passion. But she dropped her disdain and took him as he was, and he dropped his secret fear of her, his envy of her bloodline, all the things he could never be, and they found a kind of comfort they could live with, and that's more than most people get.

And they watched as Ash began to heal, to be more self-assured, less tentative, more adventurous. He had always acted around them as though something were about to happen, something he didn't understand. Now he sat with them comfortable as the ducks on the water, rising and falling with the tides. To him, they were no longer separate people, each filling a separate need; they were one being, interchangeable, and each was always willingly there when he needed one or the other.

Who would you be if you weren't afraid?

And then Copperton died. And then he stayed dead. He stayed, winter and summer, in a mausoleum he had designed, too grand, too lachrymose, in the graveyard on the hill, and Diana and Ash would walk up there every day and she would wander and watch while Ash spoke to his father, whispered, as though he still lived and breathed. At the end of each of these conversations, as darkness fell and Priscilla called from far away, in the kitchen, Ash would kiss the cold, ornate marble and whisper, "Love is stronger than death. I remember. Good night, dear Papa."

Then came the thin-fingered men and the reading of the will, and she, in her bitterness, forgot all the joys and comforts of their rapprochement.

Every baby is born with such tenderness and kindness in its heart, such a graciousness and a gracefulness in its way of going, as they say in equestrian circles. What had happened to Ash, to Diana before him?

Damage. It was all damage that could not be undone. Ash was risking his heritage for a forbidden love, and Diana was risking it all for the imperatives of her body and her long-unloved heart. Nobody could ever know what it was like to sit there in that behemoth day after day, alone, with one book after another from her grandfather's library, peaceful, so they said, lovely and peaceful, when the few sad aristocratic neighbors came to call, everybody calling each other Missus or Miss, women she had known for thirty-five years, but what it really was, was searingly lonely. The sadness when she pulled back the covers every night, the crisp whisper making her want to scream, to throw something, to look at the window and wonder if it was high enough.

This time the damage would be mammoth, and it could not be reversed. Her love for Gibby was like a wrecking ball ready to be swung at any minute. Months had passed, and he was still here, and she had a thousand ways of saying she didn't want him to leave, ever, but she didn't say them. She just let it all ride, and a peace formed in her heart built around his love, a peace unlike anything she had ever known.

With Ash gone, they explored the night like naked, provocative children. When Gibby made love to her, she wept. When he brushed away the tears and asked their cause, she held tight to his hand, but she looked far in the distance and kept her silence.

She should let Gibby go now, before the irreversible damage, the cruelty, the wreckage, began. But she would not, could not let go.

Let the house fall down around her, around them all, let the library at Alexandria burn again. She would burn the topless towers of Illium to keep him by her side.

She had harnessed his red hair, so startling, so fine, to her heart, and she would go, helpless, where it led her.

25

SHE OPENED THE door at three, naked. He stood in front of her, too shy to knock, even now, after countless nights, in his ratty wool bathrobe. He could see she was cold. He stepped toward her, opening the robe, and she stepped inside as he wrapped it around both of them. They were almost the same height, their skin ruddy on porcelain white, their hair ginger against black. She shivered, but not for any reason he could know.

At what point does desire turn to love? At what point does sex no longer matter, no matter how much of a joy it might be? He was walking her to the bed, their legs moving in unison, and she wanted to say, Can we not? Can we be together, just like this, until the sun begins to come up?

She had spent her days watching the river. It held all of her heart. It was her conversation and her memory. It was her Christmas present and her Easter basket. Some days it was smooth as plate glass, and she took her mood from that, placid, the brown of the shallows leading into the deep, deep blue of the deeper waters, the far shore, the Northern Neck, as it was called, as far as the moon to her.

She had hardly ever been there, except to go to Belle Isle, another grand house, where she played as a child and dined as a woman, from which she could see the sunset and her own house, massive even at a distance. It was like looking in Alice's mirror, exciting and somewhat disturbing. People live there, she thought, and then, suddenly, *I* live there. Those lights in the window always called her home.

It was the time just after sunset, that fifteen minutes after the great fire, when the embers of the sun spread across the blotter of the deepening sky, pink and orange and gold streaks, brushstrokes of light that lifted her heart out of her body and closer to the risen Lord of her childhood, the Christ who had abandoned her years before. Over her bed hung a round plaster Della Robbia cast of the baby Jesus, and she kept it there even though she no longer believed because somehow, as long as it hung where it had always been, her childhood, her lovely childhood, would not vanish. It held her in its embrace, and made her remember that she was loved.

So, alone, she was afraid, because she knew how it ended. The thoughts she always avoided came crowding into her head, like an addict dreaming of the house parties they used to have, the money they wasted, the love that was not love, all the years she did not look at the sunset, did not live in the afterglow, in the streaks and strokes of heaven's extraordinary palette.

Downstairs, in the darkened kitchen, sat Lucius Walter, in his underwear and his tatty bathrobe. His work had been finished weeks before, but he didn't want to leave, he couldn't. There was nowhere for him to go. So he told nobody, and nobody seemed to notice; the house was such a swirl of painters and plasterers and glaziers. He just kept out of everybody's way. He had become like a piece of furniture that had sat in the same corner for years. If asked, Diana would have looked at it with wonder, surprised to find it there, trying to remember where it might have come from.

Every night he sat in the kitchen as he always had, a book open in front of him, and the iron, picking the odd silverfish from the pristine surface, listening to the sounds of the house. He had figured it all out. He was not a stupid man, and he knew it would end in tragedy.

For Diana, upstairs in bed with Gibby, it didn't feel tragic. Lying in Gibby's arms, Gibby kissing her neck, Gibby's hands gently opening her up. She had always desired him, of course she had, since the moment she saw him, but now she was racing toward the moment he was inside her and she felt that unique feeling of being at home, at home in the dark, no longer a single person but a woman made of two people, she was racing toward that, but she bent back her head and said so that he could hear, "I love you." He didn't pause. She took his head in her hands and pulled him up so he could look in her eyes, "I said, and you have to listen, I love you, Gibby. I will love you forever. There are no secrets. Copperton used to hurt me. He belittled me and debased me. We had maybe eight happy months together." She started gently to cry. "But I love you now and forever. You."

He looked at her a long time, and then he laughed sweetly. "You talk a lot, you know that?" His whole face was illuminated with tears of happiness, and then he looked at her very seriously. "I've never had anybody. Shuttled around. Got where I was only because I could do the Iron Cross at fourteen. Plus I had an Ivy League brain, and that got me there, and that got me here. I never had parents. I never had girlfriends. I never saw much except the inside of a gym. It was a hard life. You are the only comfort I've ever known. And whatever happens—and I'm so sad to say this, but something will, I don't know what, but something. So believe me when I tell you when I say that I've never said it before, and I know in my heart I'll never say it again. I love you, Diana. I promise you that you have my whole self. I love you."

How could he lie on top of her with his whole massive body

and yet feel so weightless, like a light summer blanket? Did he even know what love was? Did she? Did anybody?

She raised herself up and kissed him until they were both breathless.

They drew apart. He smiled and said, "Now I've knocked at the door long enough. Will you let me in?"

They heaved and humped and slithered in their own sweat for half an hour, they turned and tumbled and grasped, until two people became one, until the music of time stopped, until thought became a vast desert in which nothing existed except this one being they had made, one thought, one body that was not a body but only a yearning, that was only what a kiss became, something like a deer in the rearview mirror, the narrowness of the escape, the realization that they had not hit him but glided on unfettered, no future, no past, no sky or sea, no war, no discussion of ideas, no art, no money, no youth or age, just two bodies conjoined to make this one, this one thing, until both were spent with no more to take or to give. She slipped from the bed and came back with hot linen cloths and bathed their slick bodies until the cloths grew cold and they shivered with the dawn air. She stood on the bed and spread her arms like an eagle, and then fell, knowing that he would catch and hold. Then they just lay there, hearing Priscilla coming in and beginning to make biscuits, so mundane, all these things that had been happening while they wandered in the desert, and each thought, silently, secretly, What was that? And there was no answer, there never was, so that in an hour they would be sitting at the breakfast table, dressed, calm, hardly looking at each other, taking part in the society of the house, Gibby and Lucius, Rose and Diana, sitting like normal people because they were normal people and the gymnastics of the night stayed in Diana's bedroom, and in the thoughts of both of them, and the question

What was that? What was that? separated the irrevocable from the rest as they talked about the war that was all they talked about anymore. France had fallen, London on fire, the fire and the noise coming every night, the people praying fervently as they lay in the dark, blackout trials everywhere, but Diana and Gibby knew something that nobody else knew: they had made love in the night, and, ephemeral as it was, it was also strong as steel and it could not be taken away, not even if they didn't understand it, not even if the dirigible were floating over Saratoga and dropping bombs on the very house in which they sat. How were they to go on, knowing what they knew? How were their bodies to disengage? What was war to them, except some far-off fire and noise? Headlines in the morning paper, so similar every morning they became inseparable?

Diana looked up from her eggs, and there was Lucius, humble, insinuating Lucius. Why had he been brought here? Oh, yes. The library. But surely that work had been finished weeks ago? Surely his mission had been accomplished? Was she still paying him? She hardly knew.

"Lucius, darling," she said. She didn't want to have the conversation in front of everybody.

He whitened, but answered with his usual joviality, "Yes, my good madame?"

"I'd like to take a look at the library. I haven't been in there in weeks. Can you give me a tour after breakfast?"

He whitened further. He hesitated and then said, "Well, of course. There are still some odds and ends to be done, but we can overlook those. I think you'll be pleased."

"Can we first look in the freezer?"

As everybody got up from breakfast and went their separate ways, Lucius heaved opened the freezer door. There were two shelves, each holding about twenty books. "The ones on the top are ready to be ironed. The ones on the bottom are still drying out." His eyes were shifty, secretive. Diana instantly knew what was going on, but she said nothing. One of the books was Sir Walter Scott, which she had been reading just last week.

They took a cup of coffee and walked into the library. It had been totally restored to its former magnificence.

"Lucius, it's gorgeous. There's not a flaw."

"Well, there's a bit of tweaking, and some books left to do."

She looked at him closely. "Lucius, I know what you're doing. You're taking books you've already dried and ironed and wetting them again so the whole process can start all over."

"I . . . I want to do my best work."

"You want to stay on in this house. By your plan, your work will never be done."

He began to argue, but then his face crumpled. "This has come to be my home. I have nowhere else to go. I don't cause a moment's bother to anybody."

"Lucius, my little duckling, what I'm trying to say is that your work is done here. We'll be sad to see you go."

"Please, do I have to go? You don't have to pay me. In fact, you haven't paid me in weeks." Tears began to stream down his face. "I have nowhere to go."

Diana found it both touching and repulsive to see a man crying, but she barreled on.

"What about the university?"

"School is finished for me. I've gotten my degree. There's nothing for me but to try to find a job. But teaching library science to a horde of pimply prep-school boys? God, I'd rather die."

"I'm terribly sorry, but the answer has to be no. You have

so many charms, and I'm sure you can find other people with libraries like this one that need restoration. I'll write some letters for you. But you can't stay here. It's already complicated enough."

"I know what you do in the night. You and Gibby. And I know about your son. I know everything."

Her eyes went dead. "How dare you try to blackmail me? I was going to tell you that you could leave in two weeks. But now, I think it's best you leave tomorrow."

He burst into tears. "I am so sorry. I should never have said that. I . . . I adore you. Your business is private, and it's dreadfully wrong of me to poke my nose—"

"Tomorrow, Lucius. That is the end of our discussion. Priscilla will iron the last of the books. I will write you a glowing recommendation and give you five hundred dollars in cash, but I don't want to see you anymore. Thank you for such excellent work." Her voice was frigid with disdain. She looked out at the blue-brown river, calm today. When she turned around, Lucius was gone, and he wasn't seen the rest of the day. Nobody noticed his absence. Not one of them.

Conversation was thin. They went as usual through the papers, avidly reading about the war. The painters worked away. The upholsterers unrolled bolts of cloth under Rose's watchful eye, she often shaking her head and sending the cloth back where it had come from. Now it was no longer a matter of whether they would enter the war, but when, and like the rest of the nation, everything hung in suspense. America was like an enormous firecracker with a fuse that stretched to all parts of the globe. It would explode with the first spark.

That night in bed, Diana looked at Gibby and thought of Ash. She thought of war, and how he could not bear it; some way must be found to keep him safe. She told Gibby about her cousins, all gone now, about sweet little Uncle Charlie, and Gibby laughed and shook his head.

Then, soberly and surprisingly, Gibby recited "To an Athlete Dying Young," and after that they lay in silence, until he kissed her and left her in the cooling bed.

The next day passed in a crushing silence. She sat in the south study with a cocktail and watched the sunset, really watched it closely, and there it was, the second the sun went down behind the horizon, a brilliant, instantaneous green flash, here and gone in a second, a little thing, everything, her mother, her childhood, the whole weight of Saratoga, her life and what would become of it, here and gone as quick as the green flash itself. They say life is long. It's not. It's over in an instant. Things are seen up close, and then almost immediately at a great, unreachable distance, and you are left withered on the shore, old, bent, as thin as the memories that haunt you.

She saw nothing of Lucius. She assumed he was packing, talking on the telephone, making a plan. She had paid him handsomely, and he had spent nothing; he must have accumulated a little pile to make his way in the world. She had Priscilla take him some dinner on a tray, but he wasn't in his room. She left the tray for him on his bed.

That night, after she and Gibby made love, pledged again eternity, knowing that eternity was about to collapse around their heads, after they turned from their good-night kisses and she watched him go as she always watched him go, with stealth, she fell into bed and drowned in sleep, so deep, her breath and her dreams coming like one single drawn-out note on a stringed instrument, so eternal that neither she nor Gibby heard the pop, the one pop in the night, so nobody knew that Lucius Walter had used a safety pin to trip the lock on the gun cabinet and taken out a Colt 1911, neatly, quietly cleaned it, loaded it with one bullet, and taken it down beside the moonstruck water, where he put it in his mouth, pulled the trigger, and blew his brains out. By the time they noticed his absence, in the late morning, birds were already picking at his eyes.

26

WHEN ASH GOT home the next day, he took charge of everything. He had Priscilla wash the body and sew it in gunny sacks from the barn, and then he and Gibby lifted it into the walk-in freezer.

They called the university, but got very little help. Yes, Lucius Walter had been a student, graduated two years ago. He had been hanging around since then, trying to look useful. In his records, there was very little information about family. An aunt in California. But when they called, the number had been disconnected, no forwarding. Beyond that, they couldn't help. He had emptied out his lodgings when he came to Saratoga, and even at the university they had had no idea where he had been these last months. He had received no mail in his absence, mail that might have given a clue as to where he was from or who his friends were. He was a complete enigma from nowhere, Lucius Walter, and now he was just a corpse in the meat locker on the hands of people who didn't even know him. Priscilla knew him. Their paths often crossed when she came in to start breakfast, and he was still diligently ironing at the kitchen table. She knew him to be kind, and respectful, and funny and fascinating. He talked to her as an equal. Her coming was supposed to be the signal for him to go to bed, but often he didn't. He sat and talked to Priscilla until the house came alive. Then the others, in their beautiful bathrobes, made their sleepy way into the dining room, always sitting in the first chair they had sat in when they arrived, but now each one fraught, charged with secrets and lies and love and fear. At the first sound, Lucius crept up the back stairs, not to be seen again until dinner, except by Priscilla, who took him a sandwich and a lemonade at lunch.

ON THE MORNING after Lucius Walter put a bullet through his brains, Diana did not appear for breakfast. The boys, however, ate like horses, and after breakfast went down into the basement in search of something suitable to build a box. They found an old two-legged table, immense, and they thought they would use that. There were many things like that down there, broken things, waiting for the day when somebody would take an interest, fix and restore them, and they would arise like the phoenix from the ashes.

The boys in their jeans and their Carhartt jackets dragged the table from the basement into the barn and built a box. They weren't very good carpenters, and it wasn't a very good box, but it would have to do. They needed the freezer back.

All day, Priscilla bristled about something, and it finally came out. She wouldn't let them bury Lucius wrapped in gunny sacks in a pine box, like some poor black man with no family. They explained it wasn't pine, it was mahogany; they pointed out that he, in fact, had no family; but nothing deterred her. She'd seen white folks' coffins, rich and soft, like babies' beds, and she was determined to have that for Lucius. Before he died, he had given her a shoebox tied with a school tie, and told her to open it if anything should happen to him. "Like what, honey?" she'd asked, and he'd shrugged and said, "I don't know. Just something." Then, as an afterthought, he asked her to share with Clarence, and asked if he could hug her, which she let him, and then said good night. In the morning, after they found the body, she and Clarence counted the money in the shoebox, laying out the bills in two piles on their bed, and Priscilla just said, "Praise Jesus, he was a nice boy. Never hurt a fly." By their lights, they were rich. It was his whole salary since he came to Saratoga. But this was too much. She'd simply loved him. She'd loved their secret breakfasts together, when he treated her with such respect and affection and good humor. She laughed the whole time she was making the biscuits, and he taught her to hang a spoon from her nose. And when they were all having dinner, she could hear his voice, and when he spoke, they all laughed when he'd finished, and by her lights, that was enough. To her eye, none of them did anything anyway. White people. They just lounged around, telling anecdotes about that war that was almost a hundred years ago, about who had had lunch here once, about the time so and so did what and where—useless talk, and expecting food on the table exactly when they wanted it, and them dressed up like Mr. Roosevelt was coming to dinner.

Priscilla went into the attic and found some purple brocade curtains fringed with weighty gold bullion. Nobody used them anymore. There was a time when the house was religious, when the curtains in the south study were changed for the ecclesiastical seasons—red and white and green and so on. Purple was for Lent, the season of repentance and redemption.

She found an old moth-eaten mattress and ripped out the horsehair batting and lined the coffin with that, and then she went in the freezer, afraid as she was of dead people—haints—and sewed him into his heavy purple silk brocade shroud, tucking and sewing so that the bullion went down the front of his body and around his face. Then he was ready, and they nailed the box shut and carried it to the family plot, and lowered him into the hole Clarence had dug. Ash and Gibby were fairly drunk by this time, and it was gray and drizzling, so that at the last minute the strap broke and the coffin fell with a thud into the muddy, collapsing hole, helter-skelter, and Priscilla yelled out, "Sweet Jesus!" but by this time the pale sun was setting through the thin cloud cover, and there was no time to do anything, so that's the way Lucius Walter was to spend eternity. Only Priscilla wept.

Dinner was cold salads, served late. Priscilla entered the dining room regally with her tray, a large silver spoon hung from her nose, but nobody noticed, a joke gone bad. Diana maintained her absence, so Gibby and Ash took the opportunity to get really drunk and have mock fistfights and jump on the furniture like children half their age. As though they had forgotten. Finally forgotten the death in the river. And then that turned into the emotional part—*I love you, buddy, you're the only real friend I've ever had*—until about midnight, when they struggled arm in arm up the stairs.

That night, when Gibby knocked his usual knock, Diana lay still and cold in her bed and did not move. He knocked again. And then one more time.

She got out of bed and locked the door. She drew the heavy velvet curtains, turned out the nightlight so there was nothing but darkness. She had to feel her way in the black. There would be time. Not much, but some. She was safe only in the dark.

There was a final soft knock, at five, and this time she opened the door. Gibby stood, concern and love in his eyes. She didn't move aside so that he might come in. There was a long silence in the dark.

Finally Diana spoke.

"I'm pregnant," she said, and closed the door.

27

WHY DO TERRIBLE things happen in such splendid weather? Two days later, on a dawning day in late October, Gibby and Diana left in first light for Richmond and her regular doctor, whom she had been seeing since she was a girl.

The silver sliver of a moon still hung in the lightening sky, the river smooth as mercury on a plate, waiting for the thin golden veil that would fall on everything when the sun came up, the leaves russet and scarlet, one of fall's gifts, the warm golden dawn.

They might have had a picnic, chicken salad sandwiches down by the river. They might have gone riding. They might have made love on the secret rock. He might have twirled her over his head again, his arms bulging, Diana feeling like the ducks flying over the river, the freedom of being above the ground, her wings spread.

There might have been so much joy. They might have been freed from the shackles of age, on this explosive fall day, just two bodies joined in every way two bodies can be joined, coming home with grass and sand inside their clothes. They might have forgotten Ash's pain, and his rage.

Instead, they pulled the ancient Rolls out of the garage while everybody else was sleeping and headed for Richmond and this awful, awful thing that awaited her, awaited him as well, his lesson in being a grown-up.

The weather so pristine, sullied only by the event that was to happen. A girl. A boy. A human bean just six weeks old. Gone into a bucket. Louisa Regina. Thomas Maitland. Never to be. Sleeping peacefully curled now in her womb. In another time, another society, the child might have grown to term and emerged and lived. There might have been a christening with the family christening dress, yellowed with age. But she wasn't that brave. She hadn't slept for forty-eight hours, trying to find the courage to defy them all, to tell them all to go to hell, the first families of Virginia, the whisperers, with their smirks, but it just wasn't in her.

Like dominoes stacked to fall, the knowledge would get out. First to Ash, and it would kill him—his tiny baby brother or sister, the next in line—or he would kill Gibby, for trespassing, for his evil audacity. Either way, there would be blood, and a coffin, and the sliding into the earth, into the eternal dark, either way, her life's love gone into the ground not to return, then a reception at the house, ham biscuits and chicken salad, and the gracious smiles and the thanks for coming and then the quiet that would never ever end. The ticking of the clock. The perfect morning. The fetus in a bucket.

They drove in silence. Diana shivered. Gibby turned up the heat in that car until it was tropically hot. Still she shivered in her fur coat, her grandmother's purloined mink from Montaldo's. The landscape went by them. She turned her face to the window so Gibby wouldn't see her tears.

They were two entirely separate people in the same car.

Several times Gibby started to speak, then cleared his throat and shut his mouth, jaws clenched to keep the words in his heart. Now was not the time for revelation or words of consolation.

Finally he said, as the skyline of the city came into view,

"Dr. Howland is going to help you. Everything will go on, until today is yesterday, and all of this is a fading memory."

"You don't understand a single thing. Not about women's hearts. Not about me. Not about the way real life grinds you down. Dr. Howland will give me his congratulations and a big hug and wish me well."

"Then why are we seeing him at all?"

"We have to start somewhere. I hope he'll know somebody, a retired nurse. An alcoholic doctor, somebody. I hope he'll be generous and kind."

They rode in silence for twenty minutes. The day grew more gorgeous with every moment as the sun rose and they entered the streets of the city.

Diana rolled down the window. The cool wind rushed into the car, lifting the silk scarves they both wore. She turned on the radio and through the static said, "Give me a cigarette."

"You don't smoke."

"I want a cigarette."

He reached into his pocket and pulled out his Luckies and lit two, one for each of them. She barely drew the smoke into her mouth before she blew it out. She turned off the useless radio.

"Gibby." Her tone was flat, without affection. "Except for my parents, except for Ash, I have never loved anybody until I met you. So please listen to what I'm going to say." She threw her cigarette out the window.

"I love Ash beyond anything. He comes first, whoever he is, whatever happens. I would lie down on the railroad tracks for him. He came out of my body and that creates a connection and that connection can never be broken. It's blood. Not ever. Not for you. Not for anybody. He's my son.

"You have given me something I have never had, and I want

to have it forever. There is not a moment in the day I don't want you with me. You have my body, forever. It's a gift I'm giving you, and I hope your fascination with it never fades. You could have anything I have, and I have a lot of things.

"We come from a noble family. I have been told that since I was a baby. The Cookes of Virginia. Now I'm . . . I'm . . ." Her voice caught, and she was silent for a moment while she gathered herself. "I'm throwing one away, like garbage after a dinner party. Unless Ash has children, and that possibility seems to have vanished like smoke, there will be no more. All that fine breeding. An historical child. But you, I ennoble you. You are the king of my heart. And you always will be, and yes, I would marry you. Yes, I already have married you. And we could step into the light—the beautiful dress, the veil, light as air, flying like a cloud behind me as I rush down the lawn to meet my love, my heart, my . . . husband, if, if only . . ." She stopped again, this time for a very long time.

"And there is the end of the story. We are the king and queen of If Only. There is no more. There is no after."

Gibby stared straight ahead and drove. He had, in his young heart, a thousand things to say that would never be said. But there were too many secrets. Secrets and silences.

He realized that this was her decision. It was her body, and her reasons lay so deep that he could never reach them, much less change her mind. She was forty-one years old. She could have this child.

But she lived in a world where propriety was everything, and to step outside the bounds of what was acceptable was death, true death. This is where their sexes divided them. She was caring not just for her place in society but for the history of hundreds of years, for the stern gazes of the portraits that hung everywhere in the house, the governors, the signers of documents, the upright and the righteous of the long line that led to here, to her, to this moment that would remain forever secret. What she was doing was not only her choice but also her duty. That's why she didn't cry. That's why her face took on the waxen look of a death mask.

Because she must, she had to, in her heart of hearts, want this child, which would at least be born out of love, unlike Ash, who was born of animosity put aside in favor of that same sense of duty. Ash, who was the end of the line, Ash, who had a beautiful seat on the back of a horse, who could take the jumps, who could shoot a turkey from fifty feet with one shot, who could drink massive quantities of bourbon with the men up and down the river who lived in the other great houses, Mount Airy, Blandfield, and never lose his composure, never put a foot wrong or stray from his perfect manners or lose his perfect posture. Ash, who was a homosexual, a fact that, if known, would remove him completely from the society into which he had been born, in which his many virtues would become useless in light of his one singular vice.

They drove up to the Medical Arts Building on Cary Street. The sun was just rising. They had to wait half an hour before Howland's office opened. Anxious and sad, they took a walk, watching the city come alive. They were so obvious in the Rolls, that behemoth of a car, and they wanted to put as much distance between themselves and it as they could. Gibby took Diana's hand in his, and they walked.

"We've never walked on a sidewalk, like normal people," said Gibby, kissing her gloved hand.

"It's nice, isn't it?"

"If you were willing to give up Saratoga, and move to Richmond, we could marry and do this every day forever."

She stopped on the street and screamed at him. "You don't

understand a thing, do you? Not one damned thing. You don't understand what it is to live in the house your family has lived in for five generations."

He shouted, "Life is not some ossified history lesson. Life is bodies touching, and sweat and blood and hope. And digging in the dirt and, yes, going to the beach in the summer and seeing Niagara Falls and going to Europe and not staying in the Ritz even if you can afford it. There is always hope. Life is change. From the rocks to our bodies to the houses we leave behind. Let it all fall down."

"You're an idiot! You don't understand anything! That house is considered to be one of the most beautiful houses in the country. People come from all over to see it. We don't let them in. They wander the grounds, like deer. Important things happened there. The country, the United States of America, was invented in that sitting room. My life's duty is to take care of it and embellish it as best I can."

"Let Ash have it and walk away."

"And where would I go?"

"*We* go. Where would we go? It's my child too, you know. Never ever forget that. *We* could go anywhere. The grandest house in Richmond, if you want. Or New York or London. And there we could raise *our* child."

"There *is* no child. Not now. Not yet. There is only the tiniest idea of a child, and it's inside my body, and I want it to come out and that is my decision and you can't stop me."

She started sobbing and collapsed into his arms, almost invisible wrapped in his camel-hair coat. She could not control her tears, and there was no way to make it work, no sense fighting. So they paced, their hearts secret, their voices mute, drawing their coats around them, their sorrow deep and piercing, until it was time to see Howland. When she pulled away, her face was like carved marble.

The office had just opened, and she was the first patient to enter. She walked up to the receptionist, a crisp woman in a blue suit, and asked to see the doctor. "He's very busy," the receptionist said, "chock-full, but I'll ask him if he'll fit you in right away before the first appointment, Mrs. Copperton."

"Cooke," said Diana.

"Oh, you changed it back," said the receptionist. "Probably for the best. Be right back." She was gone less than a minute before Dr. Howland's office opened, and the receptionist motioned her to come in.

"Do you want me to come?" Gibby asked.

"Absolutely not," Diana said, and she went into the office.

"How nice to see you again, Diana," said the doctor. "Your next appointment isn't for a few months. So there must be something wrong. What's up?"

He was a big man, with big hands, which always made her dread her visits to him, and he was one of those men who, in his late sixties, had stopped trimming his eyebrows, so he had full bushy wings of white hair where his eyebrows should be, above spotless wire-rimmed glasses. She had been afraid of him since her first visit when she was twelve, but he was the gynecologist of choice to all the finest families in Richmond. She found him repellent, and hated for him to get his face close to hers.

"I'm pregnant."

"How wonderful! I always love to help bring a new life into this world."

"I can't. I won't have this baby."

Then she panicked, and tears began to course down her cheeks, running her rouge into a mess.

"Of course you'll have the baby. You're just scared."

"I'm not scared at all. I'm not having another baby. I have no husband. There is no father."

"Of course there's a father. Marry him."

"He's of no consequence. This is my decision. I won't have this child."

He turned stern and put his face, now hateful, close to hers. "Then why come to me?"

"I want to get rid of it." She couldn't even say the dreaded word. Abortion.

"You know I won't do that, both because the law forbids it and because of my own morals."

"Then what am I to do?"

"I pity you, and I respect you. I've treated every member of your family since long before you were born. But I cannot, will not, help you. You're not the first woman to come to me with this . . . problem. And I have done the only thing I can do to help.

"I will make one call for you. One. Do exactly as I say. Go stand on the steps of the museum. A man will come. His name is Larry. After that, you're in his hands. You need to have five hundred dollars in cash in your pocket. That's all."

"Thank you." She fought the tears that hung in the corners of her eyes, and got up to go. As she reached the door, Dr. Howland called after her gently.

"You understand, to my sorrow, you are no longer my patient. I'm old. I don't understand these modern morals. I can't treat you anymore. This secret will go with me to the grave, of that you can be sure. I owe you that."

"I understand. Thank you for all you've done for me, for the family."

"It was my pleasure and my honor. Good day."

Gibby was tender as he put on her coat, as he led her to the elevator, his hand under her elbow. He said nothing, just listened closely to her instructions so she wouldn't have to repeat them. As he drove, she would point to the left or right, to indicate how to get where they were going. And then they arrived at the deserted museum steps. The car slipped quietly into place. Gibby kept the car running, so it stayed warm. Neither spoke. There was an inescapable sense about it all. The sense of an ending.

28

THE WIND WAS blowing hard, a cold wind in a big open space. Gibby sat in the car discreetly twenty yards down the street. Diana was grateful she'd chosen to bring the fur, even though she had thought it ostentatious. They sat in front of the museum where she had spent so many happy hours as a child, her mother's hand holding hers as she explained the blocks of color and light, pictures of grand and ghostly ladies and strong, ruddy military men, letting her linger over the opulent collection of Fabergé eggs, which needed no explanation. She longed to be that little girl again, start over. When she thought about it, her life had not turned out well. Those enraged years at Farmington, the husband who wore her like a diamond signet ring on his pinkie, fake family crest and all, the son who had literally been lifted out of her arms, just as she was getting to know him, the long years of solitude in which her only purpose seemed to be to watch her parents die, and now this, this unholy mess. She had chosen a lover over her son, and now, no matter how discreet she was, how sensible Gibby was, this would get out, get around, and then the house would fall down, fall down after two hundred years, one of the grandest houses in America.

Guilt is the thing that eats your heart, and then the rest of you, until the sun of your life is eclipsed and you're nothing but shade.

A black Packard pulled up right in front of her. It had some definite age on it. A man got out, and all he said was, "Larry." Larry also had some mileage. The thinnest of overcoats blew around his shoulders, the collar standing up around his bull head. He hadn't seen a razor in a week.

She walked down the steps, legs wobbling just a little, and got into the car. Larry pulled away. "You got the money?" She handed it over to him.

"You don't have to count it."

"Wasn't going to."

He took out a scarf and gave it to her. "Tie this tightly around your eyes. It's silk," he said, with a touch of braggadocio.

She carefully folded the scarf, which was silk only in Larry's dreams, and tied it around her eyes. In the sudden darkness, she no longer had to look at the grease stains and cigarette burns on the car seat, but she smelled it.

It smelled like fear.

Not just her fear, which was palpable, but the fear of the dozens, perhaps hundreds, of women who had ridden in the back of this car, blind to everything passing. The fear of women who were too young, or married with lovers on the side, or married with brutal husbands, the fear of all the women who suddenly didn't know what to do with their bodies, who felt betrayed and in danger, who, for the youngest of them, might never have children again. The fear of the women doomed to living with a secret when their husbands asked how five hundred dollars had disappeared from the bank account. The fear of women who would live with a secret all their lives, who would never be free again, if they lived.

"What do you do with the bodies?"

"What bodies?"

"Well, some must die. It must happen."

"Don't talk."

"Do you have a cigarette?"

"I wouldn't have figured."

"You figured wrong."

He pulled a Camel from his coat pocket, lit it and handed it back over the seat. "Now, shut up."

She did as she was told, just sat and smoked with her trembling hands, as the big car rolled on, first on smooth streets, then on cobbled streets, until it finally came to a stop.

"Don't take off your blindfold until I tell you. There are stairs. Sixteen stairs. I'll help you." So greasy Larry helped Diana, whose name he didn't even know, through the door that he unlocked and then another door, also locked, and up the sixteen stairs, a landing, another locked door, and into a very warm room where he removed the blindfold at last.

It was an immaculate room that must have once been a kitchen that had been turned into a makeshift operating room. A door opened and a jolly, heavy woman walked in. She was wearing a crisp white dress, rubber-soled shoes and, oddly, a string of large fake pearls. "I'm Miss Louisa," she said. "How many weeks?"

"Fourteen, I think. Maybe sixteen."

"It makes a difference, you know. Well, we'll see what we see."

Diana faced again that overwhelming feeling that she had committed a crime for which she would be caught but which she couldn't remember.

"We don't have last names here, for obvious reasons. I am a nurse, a registered nurse. I've done this hundreds of times. I have not had one calamity."

Diana had a fleeting vision of a beautiful girl, hair flying, on horseback, taking the jumps as they came to her, dressed all in white, as she was once, a debutante, but her dream came up short. Whose arm would she take as she walked onto the floor? There was nobody.

"I can't have this baby."

"Well, then, let's get started. It'll only take a few minutes. There will be pain—I'll try to spare you as much as I can, but I don't want to lie. I'll give you a little chloroform, more for panic than for pain. I'm not a butcher. I think women should not be subjected to this medieval torture, but the law is the law, and when we have nowhere else to turn, I'm glad women come to me instead of some butcher who doesn't know what he's doing. Oh, the stories I could tell you. You won't be one of them."

In the room was the familiar table, the angled back, the stirrups, the sheet of paper drawn down to cover the whole thing. Diana was told to take off her panties, which she did, and put them in her pocketbook.

She got on the table, lay back, and put her feet in the stirrups. A gauze pad with chloroform was put against her nose, and everything suddenly became very hazy. She was awake, but dizzy. She felt wonderful, not afraid at all. Then everything went mercifully dark.

There was silence in the big clean white room when she opened her eyes. Saratoga. She wanted to go home. In just a minute she would rise from the table. Just a minute.

Miss Louisa came back in, all smiles. After she'd removed the chloroform mask, she took Diana's hand, stayed with her and held her hand until Diana stopped trembling with the pain. Diana's breathing, still a rough rasp, calmed, and the whole room came back into focus, every sound, the ravishing heat.

"You'll need a napkin. You're bleeding quite heavily. That will stop in a few hours. It may start and stop for a few days. Don't panic. You are not going to die. Just rest for a few minutes, and then Larry will take you back to where he found you. It was a total success. Quick and simple."

"Was it a boy or . . . ?"

"There's no way to know. At fourteen weeks, it's hardly a speck. No way to know the sex."

"Poor little thing."

"If you start hemorrhaging badly, go to the ER. I'm not perfect, and sometimes accidents happen. Then you'll have to have a full D and C, or even a hysterectomy. I don't think it'll happen. I just wanted you to be aware. Still feel dizzy?"

"No."

"You can have another baby. That's a good thing."

"Is it?"

"Larry!"

He came into the room, still in his greasy overcoat, holding the fake silk blindfold. Diana felt this ridiculous urge to say thank you, but she didn't. Even still, she knew that she was one of the lucky ones, at least so far. There had been no coat hangers or forceps or cold steel instruments that bore no resemblance to anything medical. There had been no paregoric or throwing herself down stairs or any of the other voodoo treatments that poor women had to go through.

There had been a real nurse in a string of pearls, a clean white room, and greasy Larry, who suddenly seemed like her best friend, just as Miss Louisa seemed like her kindly, secretive aunt. She wanted to kiss her on the cheek as she left, but she realized how grossly inappropriate that would be—this woman who had just taken a fetus—so she just put on her coat, and let Larry tie the blindfold and help her down the stairs.

It took much less time to get back to the museum, where Gibby was sitting on the hood, rolling and unrolling a pair of pigskin driving gloves, smoking. He opened his arms, thought better of it, and said, "Front or back?" to which she indicated back, which they had strewn with down pillows.

"I'm still bleeding," she said, which Gibby heard with blind curiosity. He had no idea what had just happened. He thought it no more than a teeth cleaning, until he saw her face, and then the weight of her grief punched him in the stomach and he couldn't breathe for a minute.

"Are you . . ."

"Yes, all right, yes. Just take me home," and, as he started to close the door, she said, weeping, "I hate myself. I hate you," and Gibby just collapsed, head and shoulders bowed, then raised his head to bring in great gasps of air, as though he had run a mile at top speed, and they both started crying.

"Just take me home. One day, not even very long from now, this will just be an awful thing that happened on a bright fall day in Richmond. Someday, I'll look you in the eyes. But not today. Just drive home. Get me to Saratoga."

For the next three hours they drove in silence. When they got there, Ash didn't come to greet them, thank God. Gone for a walk, perhaps. Shooting ducks and drinking bourbon.

As the car drove into the driveway, only Priscilla came out of the house. She opened the back door of the car and took Diana's extended hand.

"Priscilla. Priscilla, my dear. Just get me upstairs and into my own bed. Tell Clarence to do nothing. Gibby will clean up this mess back here. It's . . ." She looked at his tragic face. "It's the least he can do."

She got out of the car, wobbled, and almost fell. Before Gibby could catch her, Priscilla was there.

"Baby, what did they do to you?" as she swept her in her arms and picked her up off the ground.

"Just get me in my bed. Use the back stairs." She wanted to avoid Rose and her chatter about paint chips and wallpaper samples, the workers with their light dusting of plaster. And into the darkness she went. She didn't reappear for three days, by which time she was completely and utterly her old self. So it would seem. She carried within her, in her heart, and would until the day she died, her little bean, and the blood may have stopped, but the pain would never go away. She would carry it deep inside her as long as she lived.

Priscilla knew exactly what had happened from the second she saw the lines of grief on Diana's face. She changed the cloths, hid the blood, kept watch.

The history of the world is the history of the unspoken bond between strong women.

29

MORNING BROUGHT NO sunrise, no familiar ball of fire rising over the opposite shore to glint on the gilt around the edge of Rose's breakfast cup. It was just a slight lightening, the water barely moving, stippled with black. Rose woke from a short nap, as she always did, in despair. She was a lonely woman in a narrow bed, not old but getting older, a genius at what she did, producing splendors up and down the East Coast and, before the war, all over the world. Without extravagance, she was horrid, and she knew it. She was horrid to look at, beyond strange, so she made herself stranger, more extravagant, so that people would look beyond the stooped posture, the fingers crooked by arthritis, the hooked nose, all like something out of a child's nightmare.

They looked at her various getups, and took them for the whole. Nobody ever saw the kindness in her heart, the true generosity, the longing for love. She desired these things as a man dying of thirst in the desert craves water, but there was no oasis. People thought her a splendid ogre, no more.

She took her breakfast hastily and bathed in the huge claw-foot bathtub, washing carefully with the Roger & Gallet soap that always traveled with her, carefully washing the few clumps of hair that dotted her scalp, unseen by anybody, ever, not even her random lovers. She had been struck by alopecia in her twenties, only then learning that her mother had it, too, hidden by wigs and glorious hats. The doctor said it might go away of its own accord, so she had begun wearing turbans, at first fanciful and colorful, amusing. But it never went away, and she switched to black, as though she were in mourning for her lost hair. They always wanted her to take her turban off, those men and then women who took her to bed out of pity or desperation, and who were usually zipping up their pants by midnight.

She finished washing her paper-thin body, so thin she was almost weightless, emaciated beyond fashion, beyond desire, and dressed as extravagantly as she knew how, wondering why, if she loathed herself so much, she was driven to call so much attention her way, to shine the spotlight always on herself, when she longed to hide in the shadows, pricking her thin arms with a needle, her own tattoo of hatred.

She sat at her dressing table in an expansive bedroom in one of the greatest houses in America, adjusting a cascading garnet pin on her tightly wrapped turban, and when everything was done, everything finished, she paused for a minute before she got up, and spat at her face in the mirror and watched as the spit ran down the crystalline surface, shattering her reflection, so that her face ran down the glass. Priscilla would clean it up, as she did every day.

She arrived in the dining room all smiles and sparkles, ceaselessly on the move, like a black hummingbird. Like a hummingbird, if she stopped for a moment too long, she would die. The speed of her speech gave off a draft like a hummingbird's wings, and she wanted nothing less than to know everything. She knew something had happened, something monumental, something that changed the music of everything, but she couldn't figure it out. Things seemed to be as they always were, everything held in place by Diana's obvious sorrow as Priscilla brought out one steaming dish after another, eggs, bacon, grits, oatmeal, sticky buns, ham on the bone, enough for an army, everybody eating as though it were the last meal on earth, except for Diana, although she almost never ate anything at breakfast, anyway. Diana's eyes were like tightropes, noticing every turn of the head, the whip that tamed the lions in the cage.

They were silent for a while, the clatter of knives and forks the only sound. Diana had been absent for three days, lying in her bed, attended by Priscilla, although nobody, out of politeness, remarked on this unusual fact. This is what Rose wanted to know. Where had she been? What sea change had occurred during those three days? Diana hadn't been sick, of that she was sure. Diana was never sick.

Ash spoke first. Looking directly at his mother, he said coldly, "Mother, did you love my father?"

Diana stared at her son, white-faced, and said nothing.

"I'm leaving here in half an hour. I need to know."

"Leaving?"

"Yes. Leaving. I don't belong here anymore, not after . . ." He looked at Gibby, who looked down at his breakfast, congealing on his plate.

"After what?"

"I don't want to talk about it. Did you love my father?"

"I'm sorry to say that no, I never did."

"Did he hurt you?"

"He never meant to, but, yes, he hurt me. I hurt him too. People always hurt each other, married people."

"How did you hurt him?"

"I made him feel small."

"What a cruel woman you are."

Diana whitened, but said nothing.

"One more question. Do you love Gibby? I know you are lovers, but do you love him?"

Gibby shot up from his chair. "Ash!"

"Shut up!"

"Do you love Gibby?" His stare was cold as blue ice.

Diana paused a long time, as though paralyzed. She looked at Ash. She looked at Gibby, still standing in shock, and back to Ash. Rose sat silent and still as a rock.

Finally, she whispered, "Yes. Yes, I do. With all my heart."

"Then it's over. That's the end. You're dead to me now. Both of you. I'm leaving this afternoon for Richmond. I'll be gone for a while, and when I come back, I want him gone. Forever. I never want to see him again. Can you do that for me?"

Knowing it was a promise she could not keep, she said, "I promise."

They were frozen around the great table, the platters and plates of food getting cold without another bite being eaten. They were frozen in space, in time, in their hearts, as though they were already a photograph in someone's album, glimpsed years later.

"Ash," she said, across the long length of the mahogany table. "You're my son. I love you with a love so strong I feel ashamed. I feel helpless in the face of my love for you. You have a home in my heart, a bed in my soul. Saratoga will be yours when I die. Don't underestimate the power of a mother's love. My love can't be thrown away like a sock with a hole in the toe. It can't ever be thrown away or broken, or forgotten or lost, like a hat on a train. Maybe you think I'm awful. But you came out of my body, and that cord can never be cut."

"I spit on your grave. You, my dear mother. Gibby, I will see you dead."

Ash rose and without a backward glance, hastily left the

room. She heard his car starting, and then spitting gravel as he roared out of the driveway. She sat completely still until there was no more sound.

Rose turned to Gibby. Her voice was harsh, demanding. Her turban was beginning to come unraveled. Her bony hands quickly flew to hold it in place. "Do you see what just happened? Are you so callous you can't see it? She risked her life for you. Do you understand me?"

"I . . ."

Suddenly ferocious, Rose stood up and shouted, "DO. YOU. UNDERSTAND. ME?"

Gibby sat, looking straight ahead, at nothing. He let Rose's words sink in, until the silence had settled, the way the water eventually smooths after you throw a stone into a pond. Then he said, in a quiet, soft voice, with tears trickling down his face, "I would die for her. You've probably never felt that. I don't think a lot of people have. But I have, and I know."

Diana turned to her and said coldly, "Rose, please wait for me in the study. We need to talk. And I need to be alone with Gibby. The whole world has come apart, and I can't bear the sight of you right now. Forgive me."

ROSE, SHUNNED AND excluded, listening for voices, waited in the study, as instructed. Diana never came. At one, Priscilla appeared with a tray of sandwiches, crab salad, cucumber, and peanut butter and jam, which Priscilla knew Rose adored. She ate listlessly, staring out at what was once a knot garden, the kind of thing that took years to perfect, the delicate up and over of the box and rosemary plants, the precision, like hearts entwined, and only a season or two to fall into ruination.

Like her life, she thought. Everything she told the world about her life was a lie. There was no Park Avenue, no cocktail with Billy Baldwin and Cecil Beaton and Gertrude Lawrence on a piano singing "Stormy Weather." There was only her third-floor walk-up on Barrow Street, her fat papillon and the Sunday crossword puzzle, not finished until Wednesday, the table lamps draped with scarves so that everything was always in shadow. There was soup out of the can and, yes, peanut butter and jam sandwiches. Even her name was not real. She was not born Rose de Lisle; she became her, through wit and imagination, like a picture in a coloring book. She loved men who dressed as women because they, like herself, were wholly creatures of their own fervent imaginations.

There were invitations. Mountains of invitations. She was not a nobody. Most of her day, when she was not actively working, was taken up with getting ready to go out for one cocktail or another, always in demand for her wit and her sense of the exotic. Her life, as described, was a borrowed one, and she loved the rich as a nun loves Jesus, because she could pretend that the miraculous rooms she created for them were her rooms, her chairs, her Aubusson rugs, her little lapdogs, her needlepoint footstools.

Rumors that she was in fact a man abounded, and that only added to her allure.

She was considered brilliant at what she did. A Rose de Lisle room was a room for history. A room for the camera.

But it always came back to this, peanut butter and jam on a piece of bread with the edges cut off. She hadn't cast off all civility, after all.

30

SHE WAITED ALL day. What Diana and Gibby were doing all that time was a mystery to her. She didn't like mysteries, but with the river flowing by the windows, it was not unpleasant. She had picked, whatever Diana said, a room that faced east, toward the water, and its endless fascinations beguiled her. The sun had long come up out of the thin orange horizon; a razor moon was fading as it rose into the cerulean sky. She wished for change, for violence in the weather, but it was just a nice, fair, cold day, the oystermen already having filled their nets and gone home. She stirred beneath her harem pants when she watched their massive forearms pulling in the nets, their thighs like tree trunks in their canvas pants and leather boots covered with salt. If only . . . if only she could go home with one of them, be his woman, buy his beer and kiss his round, hairy belly and feel his strong forearms pull her to the bed. Her life was a high-wire act of degradations and mirages. And she always plummeted to her tea and her sandwiches and Butch, who ate the rest of her sandwiches after she fell asleep, snoring.

She had a knot of fear in her stomach. She knew Diana was about to fire her, and the indignity was too much. She had learned certain things in her life, and one of them was that if you think you're getting fired, you are.

But, as she had learned from Priscilla, there's no point in

crying tomorrow's tears today, so she lost herself in the new gardens, what they would look like in the spring. Perfection was the answer. The gardens now were cold and dead. But they would come alive, all of them, the monstrous blue and pink hydrangeas in the summer, the hideously expensive tulips that might or might not survive the ravenous deer, each bulb planted with a clove of garlic tied to it, the narcissus, the old Edwardian roses. Diana, like all gardeners who don't know much about gardening, had asked that everything bloom all at once, and Rose, after trying to explain that the lilac never sees the lily, gave in and pretended that she was giving Diana what she wanted, knowing that she would not be here to see the magical succession of bloom that was the true miracle of a great garden. She gave her Beverley Nichols to read, and Diana was delighted by the thatched roofs and the cows in the narcissus, but she was not educated by the small books.

Except for the lawn, there were scrub pines all around—not a beautiful landscape at all. Now that the gold and rose were gone from the deciduous trees, it was like living in a hostile forest of gray-fringed spikes, some reaching to the moon, some tilted in despair, waiting for the woodsman's ax. This ugliness was what made those beautiful fires in the house's eighteen fireplaces every night so necessary, when the dark brought with it a cold that wouldn't be denied. These old piles were unbearably cold; the furnaces put in in the twenties never worked when it got cold. The beautiful fires never worked, either. People just froze, either sitting in steaming baths for hours or in their sweaters in the Great Room, fires going, what the English called bum warmers at every fireplace and always in use, alternately, lap robes for everybody, and strong cocktails.

Then dinner in the frigid dining room, both fireplaces going and of no use whatsoever. Sometimes they ate in their coats.

Then upstairs to their warm bedrooms, where fires had been going since four, and then sleep, the sparkle of the molten embers leading into dreams and leaving them there during the night, so they woke frozen as ice cubes and raced to dress in tweed or cashmere dressing gowns and race down to breakfast, the men sometimes in full hunting gear, silk long johns, flannel shirts, and so many pieces of clothing they could hardly reach to eat. But warm.

This all was Rose's surmise as she waited. At exactly four thirty, as the far shore was lit up by the sun sinking behind the house, as the needle point of every scrub pine turned from ash to gold, Diana walked into the room, followed by Priscilla, with two icy cocktails on a silver tray—a perfect Manhattan for Rose, who had never wanted one more, and a frosted old-fashioned in a silver cup for Diana, with fresh mint (from where? In November?) as a garnish. Along with the drinks, the inevitable sterling bowl of peanuts and, of course, ham biscuits, which meant that this was business and not pleasure.

Diana still had on her riding boots and a stock shirt under her moth-eaten cashmere sweater. She'd been galloping. The seat of her pants was wet with sweat. She threw herself casually into a wing chair next to Rose's and flung her boots up on the same enormous ottoman. Rose delicately removed her feet and hoped she wasn't noticed. It was then that Rose noticed that Diana held two checks in her hand. The dustman was being put in the dustbin.

"Rose, sugar"—and in that beginning, Rose knew just how powerfully mendacious the rest of the conversation was going to be—"you know, I hope, just how fond I am of you."

"Well, I haven't broken anything."

"You've brought such excitement to the house, it's been such an amusing ride. But it can't go on."

"You're firing me." Rose sipped her Manhattan and lit a cigarette.

"Yes! Yes! Let's smoke!" Diana took a large gulp of her old-fashioned. "God, I love drinking. How had I forgotten that? Let's get really drunk. Firing you? No, dear Rose. Nothing so dire as that. I'm just saying we stop here. We're mostly painted, even the dadoes, a word I had never heard before you came into my life, like so many others. We're waiting for the no doubt exquisite curtains. And that's it. *Finito.* Priscilla?" she yelled out, as Priscilla came into the room, right on cue. "Two more of the lovely cocktails, please, and don't be stingy. Make them like you made them for my father."

"You gone get crazy, like him."

"Exactly the point."

"You gone start crying."

"Worse things have happened. Now get your butt in the kitchen and make us our drinks."

While waiting, they watched the water in silence, like children waiting for the magician to pull the rabbit out of the hat. The drinks came, and they resumed their conversation.

"Firing?" repeated Diana. "Nothing so gauche as that. I'm just saying the work stops here. I want everything brought back from wherever you've hidden it and put exactly where it was."

"But it was a mess. A yard sale with a roof over it. The rug in the living room is a pathetic scandal."

"There are dozens of rugs in the attic. There's no need to look further. Rose, you've gone to a lot of trouble, and I thank you with all my heart. Maybe, in your words, they're a bit tatty. Maybe they're not ready for the garden club tour, but I don't want all those women tramping all over my house anyway."

"I don't know how to do that."

"I do. I remember where every teaspoon goes."

"You brought me all this way to slap on some paint and make some curtains? This could have been the most beautiful house in America."

"It *is* the most beautiful house. To me. To. Me. I want it as close as possible to the way it was. Tell the painters to finish what they're doing, then put down their paintbrushes and go home. There are checks for all of them in the kitchen. Tell the floor sanders to wax and then go home, the plasterers the same. Nothing half done. Nothing overdone."

"But . . . ," Rose tried.

"I know. I don't want the most extravagantly beautiful house in America. I want the house I grew up in, the house where everything was treasured and nothing was lost or ever thrown away. Yes, the pictures are valuable beyond anybody's wildest dreams. But I don't want a house that calls attention to itself. I like my shady lady. What do you suppose a Gilbert Stuart is worth, a Sully, a Stubbs, and on and on? The biggest Turner in America? Incalculable. The more the house calls attention to itself, the greater is the possibility of thieves in the night. Nobody knows they're here. Ash has gone to Richmond. He may never come back. You know the reasons. When I die, it will all be his. He can do whatever he wants. Part of what I pay you for is your silence. You must never speak of this house once you leave. Let Ash tart it up like an Easter bonnet, if that's what he wants. I'm sorry. I thought I wanted that. But I don't. I don't. Did you know that I was run over by a car when I was a little girl? I was. Memory. This house is a museum to memory, and it's memory I want. The South and my life, my place in it, is built on that. I want to be warmed by my memory, not live in a spread in a glossy magazine."

"I think I understand."

"You could never understand, not fully, and that's not your

fault. You are a creature of the imagination, wholly created from the ground up, and I admire that, I really do. I am all bones and history. The chains of history. My great-great-grandmother Catherine Esten sat in this very chair having her cocktail, just as we are, except that her liquor was made up in the woods, I can show you where. Who would erase that, just wash it over with a color named Eating Room Red? Or Jesus knows what. We are trammeled by where we came from. The bloodlines, like horses. We were Americans before there was an America. My aunt, somewhere back there, was Pocohontas. How could I put that in a wheelbarrow and send it off to auction? That ormolu clock you so casually dismissed was my grandfather's wedding present to my grandmother. Underneath, right below 'Cartier et Cie' it says 'Per Sempre,' and maybe he didn't know his languages, but he knew his heart, and I will not turn it over to some newly rich lawyer on Park Avenue or some movie mogul in Hollywood. Okay, end of sermon. There's no way to put it into words, but I hope you understand a little bit, just a fraction, of my heart now, what it all means."

Rose reached out her hand and took Diana's in hers. Her voice was softer and kinder than it had been since she was a child in the Midwest, genuinely loving.

"It doesn't matter whether I do or I don't. It's your house. You can do anything with it you want. Anything. With my blessing. Not every lily needs gilding. Or painting, as the poet actually wrote. It was my dream, not yours."

"I have a check here for three thousand dollars for all the work you've put in so far."

"I'm flabbergasted."

"And here's another check. This one is for five thousand dollars, and it's for the project, miracle really, you're going to pull off for me in the next two weeks."

Rose was stunned. Eight thousand dollars was a fortune. She could buy an enormous apartment on Park Avenue, after all, make it a world-class showplace for her work, invite smart people over. These smart people would spread the word to other smart people. Her phone would never stop ringing from both aristocrats and the new booboisie, asking her to make a palace on a shoestring (the boobs) or with budgets so vast the mind reeled (the aristocrats.) The future unfurled like a golden carpet in her mind. She squeezed Diana's hand even harder, and when she spoke, you could hear the tears behind the voice.

"One doesn't know what to say. I've never seen so much money."

"The budget for this project is limitless. You may have noticed. At the four corners of the big house are four of what the old folks used to call dependencies—for cooking, I suppose, for washing laundry, for the farm manager to keep the records, and one, hidden from the eyes of the rest of the house, far from the west corner of the house, the biggest but also the most secret, a model of Saratoga that my father built as a playhouse for me. Probably also as a place for secret trysts of his own devising, I'm ashamed to say. He may have lost a leg, but he still needed pleasures my mother no longer would provide.

"It has four rooms—a kitchen, a drawing room, and two bedrooms. I used to go there when I was blue. It's sort of my Petit Trianon. You have complete freedom to make it the most beautiful little house in the world. There is one condition. This is what I'm really paying you for—your absolute and total secrecy. Not even my son can know where it is, or what its purpose is. Not even you will know what its purpose is. Are we of the same mind?"

"You have my word. When can I see it?"

"Let's walk over there now. There's enough light left. Priscilla will make us a shaker of cocktails to take with us, and you can see the whole thing. It's kind of marvelous, really."

So, drinks in hand, they set out, through the kitchen door, toward the setting sun. It was a ten-minute walk along a hidden path through the pines, set in a grove of rhododendron and magnolia, the whole wrapped, almost totally obscured, in what had once been climbing roses, pink, probably for a little girl, now gone wild, the canes shooting as much as twenty feet above the slate roof. And it was astonishing, a perfect miniature of Saratoga, built as a birthday present for a ten-year-old girl. A Georgian jewel, invisible from the house behind thick screens of privet—invisible from everything, in fact. Rose thought she had never seen anything so beautiful. They walked in through the unlocked door. She was amazed she'd never seen it, but then her infrequent walks had always been toward the river, not away from it, and it was so perfectly situated, so perfectly hidden, that anybody who wasn't specifically looking for it would miss it.

Inside, there were four graceful, perfectly proportioned rooms with arched doorways framed by columns, surprisingly high-ceilinged, two fireplaces, and a bathroom, with a big marble Roman bathtub. Obviously he had spared no expense, her father, and his eye for detail had made sure that everything was just right.

In the kitchen there were still the paraphernalia of a child's fantasy: a play stove, bowls and wooden spoons, hand towels with her initials on them, everything pink pink pink. The bedroom faced the water and, miraculously, had a view of the sunrise and the river. The largest room, the sitting room, also had a fireplace and a sliver of river to catch the eye. Everything was filmed with dust.

Diana's voice caught when she spoke. "God, I haven't been in here for years. Decades, probably. How I loved this place.

Nobody, not even Ash, knows it's here. Imagine. Ten years old. My own house. I give it to you to do with it what you want. You know me. You know what I'd like. I'd like to use as much stuff from the big house as possible—rugs, china, pictures, things like that. It's all in the attic. Nobody will even miss them. I'll pay all expenses. You can hire whomever you want, bring them from anywhere.

"There's one thing I'd like. I'd like a bedroom that's painted, walls and ceiling, with a high-gloss green so dark it's almost black."

"You said I had complete license."

"Just give me this one thing. Decorate it however you want. But that color. That exact color. The color of the iron railings in London."

Rose was in some sort of a trance, her mind racing. "You must leave me alone now. I want to spend what light is left here, alone. I'll be home for supper. Tomorrow I'll come back with my book and a tape measure. Just now I want to *feel* the house, catch its spirit like rain in a bucket. This is probably one of the finest examples of Georgian architecture in America. And nobody, nobody knows it's here. And nobody ever will, at least from me. That's both a joy and an enormous burden for me. I don't want to fuck it up. Excuse my language. You say I have a free hand. Do you really mean it?"

"Cross my heart. There's a flashlight in one of the kitchen drawers. Maybe it still works. I'll see you at supper."

Dusk was coming on fast, the way it does on the river. Rose had, at most, twenty minutes of light left. She used it well. When she appeared at the dinner table, along with sad-eyed, mute Gibby, her face was flushed and she ate quickly, impatiently, as though she had someplace important to go. And she did.

She was up all night with her books and her swatches and

her telephone, picking carefully her accomplices in the transformation she had two weeks to accomplish. "Darling!" she would start every conversation. "You won't believe!"

She already had a thick book of ideas for the big house. The challenge was to take those ideas and write them small. Little Saratoga would be the most beautiful small house in America. In two weeks.

BY MORNING, WHEN Priscilla arrived with her coffee, she was ready for battle. At nine she picked up the phone, and at eleven she put the receiver back in its cradle. She ordered marble busts, obelisks and minarets, and boxes, and certain curiosities that only she and the dealer would recognize as valuable. He was to pack them in a crate and put them on the train that morning.

She ordered cotton chintzes, cabbage roses and wide stripes and narrow stripes and dupioni silk in a color like unwashed cement.

She went up into the attic and explored the hidden stash of china. She picked Chinese ginger jars and beautiful vases, French and English, porcelain and silver, from small to large, and had them brought down and sent to a tiny man who could make them into lamps.

The next morning Rose got up very early. Each worker, as he got up, was made to sign a confidentiality agreement, under threat of a million-dollar lawsuit. You could have built a skyscraper for that money in 1941, so it tended to get their attention.

The workers already bustling about, Rose had herself driven to Richmond, to the art school at Virginia Commonwealth, and asked to see the portfolios of the very, very best students. They shyly stood as she went through their work, looking in particular for figure drawings after the classical. She found plenty, and bought every one she liked, paying each student a dollar per drawing. She dyed them all in weak tea and hung them on the clothesline to dry. She pressed them with a hot iron while Priscilla shook her head and thought about her sweet Lucius.

And Diana was true to her word. She kept her distance from the project. She spent her days wandering in and around her house. She saw Gibby only at night. She napped in the afternoons in Ash's room.

Ash. Oh, Ash. He had outgrown the night terrors, and now he had outgrown her. He had entered a strange netherworld of which she knew nothing, to which she had no entrance, no access. He was gone, and who knew if he'd ever forgive her, ever come home? She was truly bereft, but when she heard Gibby's foot on the stair, she was overcome with longing all over again, consumed with desire for her lover, for the man, the coup de foudre, that she had chosen over propriety, over her own son.

31

FOR THE NEXT several days, Diana and Gibby walked by the river for hours, holding hands like schoolchildren, sometimes lying down in the sand to make love. And every night, joined by Rose, they behaved quietly and with grace as they ate their lavish dinners and raided the best of the wine cellar. They drank a lot, and the lovers went to bed early so they could feel each other's skin, hers cool, his radiating heat, the only thing they had a true appetite for.

He had actually gone to the drugstore and, in a highly embarrassing encounter, bought condoms, so they made love without restraint.

He told her, "The guy, the old man in the drugstore, when I asked for condoms, looked at me, and said, 'I don't see no wedding ring,' and I said, 'I'm getting married on Tuesday. It was in the paper. Didn't you see it?' He didn't believe me for a second, but he sold me the damned things anyway. It's like having sex through an umbrella, but anything for you, darling."

For the first time since Ash left, she laughed.

Gibby said, "I would, you know. I would marry you on Tuesday."

"And regret it by Wednesday. Besides, this *is* Tuesday."

A quietness came over them. They were suddenly aware that

time was passing. Two weeks had already gone by. The alarm was ringing, and she turned it off with sorrow and fear. Ash could be home any day.

They slept chaste as babies. They lay in bed, exploring with their hands the body that would soon be gone, not in sadness entirely but also in gratitude. They didn't speak of it, but soon there would be no indentation on the pillow next to Diana, no crumpled sheets, no nightclothes casually tossed on the floor.

Gibby went to town, December winds blowing off the river and turning bone to ice. He had been at Saratoga almost a year. When he came back, in time for lunch, Diana was alone at the table, while Rose was busy at Little Saratoga doing whatever she did. His cheeks flushed with excitement, he said, as he sat down at his place, "I've joined up."

"Joined what?"

"The army, of course. America is going to enter the war any day, and it's my duty. If I join up, instead of waiting to be called up, I get a chance to choose what I want to do, and I want to fly planes."

"When do you leave?"

"First thing tomorrow. Don't worry. I'll stay out of the way when Ash gets back."

"You forget. He's coming today. We can't hide you or stash you in some bed-and-breakfast. You are my lover and my family. We'll just have to explain and face it. I would keep you here for as long as I live. I love you."

"Try to think clearly. What am I supposed to do? Ash will kill me. Diana, this cannot happen. I love you. I would crawl naked howling through the dirt to get to you. If I come back, I'll come back to you and stay as long as you'll have me."

"Forever."

"Forever. But now I have to go. The country needs men just like me. Brave and foolish. There's no reason to it, there's only the answer. Besides, I've signed the papers already. I get on the train tomorrow morning at six."

"I won't, I can't, come to say good-bye."

"Let's do this. Go upstairs, and we'll write each other letters. To be opened only when one of us dies. We'll say what's in our secret hearts. I'll carry yours in my uniform pocket, next to my heart; you will lock mine away in your dressing table."

They left the dining room, and spent the whole morning writing their letters to each other, hers on her lavender-bordered stationery from Mrs. John L. Strong in New York, his on plain yellow lined schoolboy paper.

"My dearest darling," they both wrote, and then they both put down their pens, paralyzed. After a few minutes, Gibby picked up his pen and wrote a quick note and sealed it in a plain envelope. His handwriting was surprisingly eloquent and fine. Then he sat and thought for long time, finally taking his note and tearing it up and starting over, and this time it took him a long time and several pages to say what he meant to say.

They dressed for dinner, she in a rose-and-turquoise dress from Dior that was fifteen years old, Gibby in his tuxedo that was beginning to take on a sheen. They behaved with perfect decorum; even Rose joined them, resplendent in a golden Chinese gown, with a red turban, held in place by an eighteenth-century miniature painting of a child's eye under glass, surrounded by tiny diamonds. Rose knew she wasn't to talk about her work, so, for the three of them, there was really no topic except the war and Gibby's recruitment.

"How splendid," said Rose. "Heroic and grand and perfectly right. In addition to which, dear boy, you'll look so sexy in your uniform they'll gobble you up in every port." She made a growling sound. "My philosophy, looking back at a life of lost opportunities, is to sleep with anybody who'll have you." Gibby and Diana looked down into their crab bisque. "Short women," Rose went on, "tall women, black and white, Chinese, Ethiopian, women with one leg. Ugly women. Women who smell nice. God, the life I could have had, and I regret it. I live with that regret all the time, every night in my skinny bed, always cold when I sleep, always struggling into alertness in the morning, if I do sleep at all. Tell them, 'Don't be here when I wake up,' and go at it, dive into pleasure like you're diving into a crystalline pool of warm water."

"Rose," said Diana, looking up. "We're at the dinner table."

"Oh, so now we're ladies and gentlemen. Do you want to talk about furniture? About demilunes and fauteuils and bergères? No, I thought not. Because one must talk about something."

"Not necessarily," said Gibby. "Silence is, as they say, golden."

"And all that glisters is not gold," retorted Rose, a bit too quickly.

Going on, she turned to Diana. "Your house is ready for you. Two weeks, you said. Tomorrow you can see it, and then I'll be gone. Not to the eight-room apartment on Park Avenue I told you about, but to my little Barrow Street walk-up, with my cat and my crossword.

"Now I will really live on Park, and my Chinese coats will sweep behind me up the winding staircase, and I cannot, cannot begin . . . I cannot begin to tell you how you have changed me with your generosity and with your love. Gibby, I sincerely wish you every safety, every happiness. You are not to die in the war. Promise me. Promise."

"I promise. If such a promise means anything, I promise."

Rose took from her finger an ancient rose-gold intaglio signet ring and slipped it on Gibby's little finger. "This will keep you safe."

They sat in stunned silence for a long time. It was Diana who spoke first.

"In the library there's a completely beautiful illustrated complete works of Shakespeare. Volume after volume after volume. I want you to have it."

"I've seen it. Moroccan leather. Seventeenth century, in perfect condition. Completely beautiful, and wildly valuable. The old Rose probably would have nicked it had you not made this wonderful gesture, which I accept with all gratitude. In turn, I want you to have this." She unpinned the brooch with the child's eye, a thing so rare and beautiful it made Diana gasp, and she pinned it on Diana's dress. "It is the eye of an angel who will watch over you. The diamonds, I admit, are small, but they're fine. It will always keep you safe from harm in your perfect house."

Rose merely bowed her head. She stayed that way for a long time, while Gibby and Diana exchanged awkward glances.

Suddenly Ash appeared at the door. At the sight of Gibby, he stopped dead in his tracks.

"I wanted you gone. I made it clear."

Diana stepped between Ash and Gibby. "Ash, he's joined the army. He leaves tomorrow on the bus at four in the morning. There was no place for him to go. Please. Be reasonable."

"Reasonable?" screamed Ash. "After what you've done? In the bed, in the house I gave to you?" He turned to Gibby. "And you . . ."

Gibby looked at Ash. "I'm so sorry, Ash. I'm sorry I hurt you. I've never had a better friend. I'm so sorry."

Ash ran from the room, Diana after him. Rose and Gibby raced to their rooms, slamming the doors behind them.

Diana found Ash facedown on his bed, sobbing. Very softly, she said, "I have something to say to you. You don't need to answer, just listen. You're my son, and I love you forever and always. There is no circumstance that could change that. I don't give a damn who you sleep with. I hope it gives you some measure of happiness. I hope you find a man, a true love, who will stand by your side for the rest of your life.

"I want you to know what I know now, where your heart goes when you're lost in love, when you step off the grand precipice, knowing that somebody will catch you."

Ash spoke softly, as well. "I've already known the only love I'll ever know. You took him from me. I'll never forgive you."

"You're only twenty-one. You look at your life now, and you see a desert because Gibby is leaving you. But even in the desert, there are hidden oases that offer comfort and ease, and one day soon, to your complete surprise, you'll find yourself in one of those, and you will lie down in love and luxury."

"I'll never forgive you, Mother. And I'll never forgive Gibby."

Sometimes some things are enough, just as they are. She gently took off his shoes and socks. She rubbed his feet until he was asleep, and left him, making sure the nightlight was still on. She slipped out to her own bed, closing the door softly behind her.

At three thirty she woke up, listening for sounds of Gibby. Turning on the light, she found a small blue box on her bedside table. Inside it was a ring, a wide band of gold. She looked carefully, and inside the ring was engraved in tiny letters, "Gibby loves Diana forever. December 7, 1941."

Without throwing on her robe, she jumped from her bed and ran to the door. Gibby was walking away from her.

"Gibby!" she called out. He didn't turn. "Please!"

He turned, and walked back to her, and embraced her. At

that moment, Ash's door opened, and he looked directly into the hall. His anger was so fierce, so turbulent, he hung on to the door frame.

"I told you," he said. "It's not like I didn't tell you. Step back, Mother. Step back now! I told you, Gibby. I shouted it with every look, every gesture. I love you. But you were blind to me. You never understood. You are the only one I ever loved. Ever will. Night after night, ten feet apart, listening to your breathing. So soft and quiet, all I wanted was to slip from my bed into yours, to hold you close to my chest, to my heart forever. You never understood. And now, you steal my mother from me."

Ash suddenly pulled a small blue-black revolver from the pocket of his tweed jacket.

Diana shouted with alarm, "He was just saying good-bye, Ash. I swear that's all it was."

Ash shot Gibby twice—in the heart and in the face, destroying his beauty forever. The noise in the silent house was the death of time, the end of history.

Gibby collapsed like a rag doll, and Diana collapsed with him, his head in her lap, blood and bits of brain everywhere.

The whole world was screaming—Diana, Ash, and Rose, who had rushed from her room at the sound. The waters of the black river rose up in horror and slammed against the shore. Ash, screaming himself, fell to his knees and, almost as an afterthought, shot Rose straight in the heart, so that she screamed and stood where she was, surprised, spouting blood, until Ash shouted, "Shut up!" and shot her a second time, causing her to collapse into a puddle of black and red, her turban undone, her blue-black wisps of hair wrapping around her bald scalp, her witchlike fingers clutching her heart, her many rings glinting in the moonlight.

Diana screamed, "Ash, why? Why Rose?"

And he answered, calmly, coldly, in a daze, "She bothered me."

And then the screaming stopped, and there was nothing but silence. Every room, every stairwell, was silent. The rocking chair stopped rocking. The clocks stopped ticking, time stopping forever at 4:07 a.m., December 7, 1941. And every portrait of all the men and women who had met and bred since 1607 in Virginia, in the house called Saratoga, looked down silently on complete emptiness.

32

SHE LOOKED UP to Ash, who was rocking back and forth on his heels, keening.

She crawled to him. "Ash," she said, to no response.

She shook him until she got his attention. "Ash, listen to me. You didn't have to do that. You didn't. He had just come to say good-bye. Please, darling, listen to me. Just to say good-bye. Give me the gun, and listen to me. Can you listen to me?"

He nodded. His eyes were bloodshot.

"Can you drive? You're in shock. But can you focus? Can you do that? Do you think you can get dressed and drive away from here?"

"Yes," he whispered.

"Then pick up your luggage and go back to Richmond and wait. Just wait. Eventually the police will call. Wait for the call. You have been in Richmond for the last five days. Listen." She shook him until he looked at her. "Do you understand me? Are you sure you can drive? You are not to die in a car crash, do you hear me?"

"Yes, Mama." He couldn't speak above a whisper.

"Ash, he was going into the army today. He just wanted to say good-bye. He kept his promise to you. We. We kept our promise. I want you to know that, we kept our promise.

"There's something we have to do before you leave. We have

to put their bodies back in their beds. It's the least we can do. Can you help me do that? Are you all right?"

Stronger now, Ash nodded, and he and Diana picked up first Gibby, so heavy, and laid him in his bed, covering him with his covers. The bleeding had stopped now, and Diana washed what was left of his face with a warm cloth, realizing that, warm or cold, it made no difference now. She put a pillow under his head, from her childhood, stolen from a resort hotel where they used to spend three weeks every summer. It was small, what her mother called a baby pillow, and it was embroidered in baby-blue stitching with the hotel's famous line: "Shhhh. . . . It's sleepy time down South." And there was an embroidered mammy, her finger to her lips, to watch over your dreams.

While she was doing that, almost a holy ritual, Ash picked up the practically weightless body of Rose and put her in her bed, covering her appalling nakedness first with her Chinese robe and then her elaborate silk bedcovers, sitting her up against her many pillows so that she could see the approaching dawn. What had he done? What, now, had he made of his life?

He stood at the doorway. "I've finished, Mama."

She came to him and hugged him fiercely, his tears wetting her hair, running down her cheeks. Mingling with her own, salt on salt.

"Now get in your car and drive and don't die. You may not see me for a long time. You might not see me ever. Do you understand how much I love you?"

He shook his head.

"Will you tell your children?"

Again he shook his head. "I'll never have children, Mama. You know that."

"Will you tell your lovers about the mother who once loved you so much she couldn't look you in the face?"

"Yes, Mama."

"Now go."

He went into his bedroom to dress and emerged, carrying his overnight bag, white as a ghost, trembling.

As he turned onto the grand staircase, he paused for a minute and looked at her. "I love you, Mama. You were my only love until I met Gibby. You held me in your arms all those years. Thanks for dancing only for me."

She didn't move, but she smiled the dazzling smile that had first attracted his father. "I love you to the end of the world." And she blew him a kiss, then closed the door of her room.

She picked up the box by her bed, and tried the ring inside on every finger. It didn't fit.

It was the end. The future held no promise, the past no refuge. She was alone, but free at last. Free of family, of the obligation to carry on. She could nurture and indulge her grief forever.

She would obliterate everything—hope, her Christian faith, her ancient southern blood, this mausoleum of a house, prison of the goddamned South that had held her captive since birth, with its traditions, the guilt at the sight of generation after generation of black faces, the slavery, the genocide, the sting of the lash on a young girl's back. Her lineage, her place in that long chain of guilt. She would break the chain, the shackles that bound them all to a time long past, the serene, evil faces in the portraits of her ancestors. And with it all, the vast bondage of possession, of things, the furniture, the Persian rugs, the china, the black faces that looked at her with mournful eyes through the tight noose of history, everything except her father's wheelchair, which was already in her secret garden, her living grave.

She hoped she lived a long, long time, long enough to forget, to expiate her crimes, the crimes of all her family, brave on horseback, flying into war against the Union, their rage spurring the stallions on into the fray, all to protect a way of life built on an evil principle, riding, whip in hand, plumed hats on their heads, strolling down the long dusty road that divided the shacks in which they housed their property, muslin curtains lifting gracefully in the windows without glass, the dirt floors, the freezing winters, until they picked some pretty young girl and went in, the birth of more property, counting their worth in the number of people owned.

Virginia, her beloved country, had owned more slaves than any other state, and those people, their children's children, still lived in bondage and fear, their every move watched, their moves dictated by the signs everywhere that read "White Only."

This was the Day of the Dead, her lover dead, his beautiful body, his tongue in her mouth, his sex moving into her with such kindness she wept every time. All dead now, all gone forever. She was complicit in every death that washed over her like the waters of the Rappahannock River. There was no undoing it, no salvaging the tiniest piece of all she had ever known.

And she looked up at her familiar, countless rooms, the rooms of history, never to be seen again, and her heart burst open, just broke in a thousand pieces like a shattered teacup.

And she realized, deep in her broken heart and then washing over her entire body until her hands trembled, until her whole body turned to ice, the deep truth of this dreadful, murderous moment.

This was her Independence Day.

Rise up, the voices said in her heart. The voices of the ruddy-faced men hanging on the wall, and the prim, weary women. Exhausted from the endless lying-in, the endless births, sometimes seven before they were thirty and dead. Rise up, the sorrow and the glory, all over now. Rise up, the voices of the dead, the dead at Antietam and Gettysburg and Bull Run and the Wilderness of Virginia, the boys at New Market, rise up. Rise up, black woman, black man, rise into true freedom. Never again. Not no more. And teach, as Sojourner did, teach the hatred, the belittlement, teach your own inherent beauty, your own truth and music, not borrowed, not nobody else's.

Rise up from the mahogany table and pull the damask tablecloth, pull down the crystal chandelier with all your might, until it all crashes to the floor, shatters in a billion pieces, the candles guttering out, the portraits staring down aghast.

Rise up, Diana, from love as you have known it. It poisons. It poisons everything. Rise up from your husband, who hated you. Rise up from the tenderness of your boy lover, the fluttering ribbon of your heart.

Rise, and run. Rise into the light.

Rise up, pretty girl with the pretty foot. You are all alone now. It no longer matters. Not one single thing is of value, on earth or in heaven. Rise up into the relief of hopelessness, of the certain knowledge that nobody will come, ever again. Nobody.

Independence Day. Take your chance, your only hope at love, at happiness, which consists of expecting no one and nothing, a century of curtsies and clothes now blowing into history and the grave like dust on a dirt road.

And rise she did. She kissed her lover, his blood staining her lips, and blindly, longingly, with hope of resurrection, she rose.

Rise up, O ye people. All ye people, rise up.

Rise.

33

SHE WAS IN the kitchen before Priscilla. "We were up awfully late," she said to her, her voice just barely trembling. "I think there's not going to be anybody at breakfast."

"I thought I heard some noise. I said to Clarence, 'Maybe I should go over there, just to see if anybody needs anything.'"

"You're a sly one. You hate not knowing everything that's going on. Actually, we were playing charades. Mr. Ashton has already gone back to Richmond. Mr. Gibby has left for the army—he had to be at the bus at four, so we all just decided to stay up until he had to leave. And Miss Rose is leaving today. I'll take her to the train. Here's two hundred dollars. I want you and Clarence to go into Richmond and stay in a grand hotel and have a grand dinner and come home rested and happy. After this, it's just us again for a while. At least until Ash comes home."

"Well, I don't know . . ."

"Priscilla, did you ever even have a honeymoon?"

"Not really."

"Well, now's the time. Do what I tell you."

Priscilla reluctantly put down the apron she was putting on. "When do we come back?"

"When your money's all gone."

"Lawd. That could be a whole month. Mebbe more."

"Then that's it. I'll do for myself. I'll eat down at Lowery's in Tappahannock."

"That new place? You know we don't go to no restaurants."

"Well. We will now. Go." Diana couldn't stand much more of this. She had to get them out of there, get on with it.

"Clarence just going to lose his mind."

"Just come back in one piece."

Priscilla bustled out the door, and half an hour later, the two of them could be seen loading up their old car, Priscilla in a hat that would have made Rose green with envy, and driving out the long drive.

Diana changed into a sober, proper dress, got into the Bentley, and drove carefully to Big Mike's filling station. His father was called Little Mike, oddly, since he was half the size of his gargantuan son. She got three ten-gallon containers of gas. Even though each one weighed sixty pounds, Big Mike hefted them into the trunk as though they were nothing.

The total cost for the gas was $3.60. Annihilation costs so little. It's really rather cheap to destroy everything forever.

As she drove home, her hands shook on the wheel, and she almost ran the car off the road several times. The fever was now so intense it glimmered behind her eyes, leaving little sparkles of fear and excitement. Did she have enough? She had to have enough. And how would she lift it? How would she carry sixty pounds up all those stairs?

She pulled to a reckless stop in the front of the house. The fever was now her heartbeat. It breathed in and out as she did. She had never felt so alive, so intent.

She opened the trunk, and there they were: three red metal containers containing the end of everything. The end of class and her place in it. The loosening of the shackles. The end of things.

She went upstairs, put on Rose's most extravagant Chinese

robe, and carefully wrapped a black turban around her hair. If anybody saw her, they would assume it was the mysterious stranger who had lived in the house for the last seven months, rarely seen but once seen, never forgotten. The whole town knew about her—the robes, the turbans, the jewels, the beak. That crazy woman—they'd heard the stories from the workers who ate in the diner. Unfair, but Diana couldn't bear the responsibility. It must be somebody else who was doing this. Somebody far crueler than she could ever be.

She carefully pinned Rose's sacred eye over her heart.

But the fever, the rage, was on her, and she could not be stopped. Southerners are born with a wistful longing to live in the past, to wrap themselves in it like a homespun garment and live there forever. There is also the constant and eternal desire to tear it apart, to cut the shackles of history and walk freely, to pull down the family portraits and cut out the faces. They see themselves as ghosts in glass dollhouses, pulling behind them the weight of every man and woman on the long chain behind them, the chain that reaches to the beginning of time. Too much. It is too much.

She went back down to the car and picked up the first of the three red containers. It was light as a feather. She carried it like the desperate woman who lifts the car off her child. Robe flowing behind her, she ran up the stairs and began to sprinkle gasoline everywhere. Going back down, she saw the Sargent they had overlooked, the one of her as a white muslin girl, and she tried to lift it off the wall, but it was secured strongly at all four corners. Her hands were shaking so badly, she couldn't begin to figure out how to get it off the wall, so with enormous, heart-rending regret, she left it where it was. Back at the car, she took another container and began to sprinkle it over the downstairs, and so on with the third. The smell was overwhelming and she almost fainted, but she went back up the stairs to grab her jewel case from the safe in her room and, almost as an afterthought, with sheer brute force, pulled the Sargent from the wall.

She stopped in Gibby's room. He was cold and blue, which made his hair look even redder, and she had to force herself to remember that it was Ash, and not she, who had killed him, she felt so complicit in his death.

She whispered the poetry to him he had once whispered to her in the night, and then she kissed his cold blue lips, covered his face with the linen sheet, and left him to his fate at the hands of God.

She had never felt calmer, or more at peace, but also more in a rush. In the kitchen, she picked up a box of kitchen matches. She stood at the lintel of the dining room and lit one and threw it in. She had expected the fire to start slowly and build. Nothing prepared her for the instantaneous conflagration that was suddenly all around her, leaving her little room for exit. All over the house, upstairs and downstairs, balls of fire shot up throughout the house. The fire was so sudden and so violent it singed off her eyebrows, which would never grow back, giving her, for the rest of her life, a look of continual surprise. She barely made it out the back door, Sargent and jewels in hand, before the whole thing exploded.

She ran through the glimmering dawn to Little Saratoga, robe flying, and peered through the windows as the entire history of her august family burned. Port Royal had a volunteer fire department, a ragtag collection of six volunteers with one truck, and she could hear them approaching from the distance, but it was, in every way, too late. In the end eight volunteer fire squads arrived, each equally sincere and equally incompetent, and there was nothing to do but stand and watch as one of the greatest houses in America burned and burned and burned.

The car exploded in a ball of flame, shooting fire twenty feet into the air. They tried to look for her, for Diana Cooke Copperton Cooke, but it was far too hot to enter the house. Every now and then, a ball of fire would go off and shoot into the sky, like a roman candle. One of these landed on the schooner, and it caught fire, and burned and sank, unsalvageable, beauty inseparable from fire and water, the brass trimmings on the boat melting with fire, curling into grotesque shapes, the sails themselves flying free with flame. The horses raced from the barn, panic-stricken, and out into the fields through the gate she had left open for them.

Nothing was untouched. Nothing was left. Papers that added to the train of history curled and crackled into ash. Paintings shimmered and crackled on the walls before they caught fire and fell into the inferno. Whole sets of French porcelain cracked and slid off their burning shelves. Everything that could burn did burn, and everything that was inflammable melted into lifeless lumps, unrecognizable.

And all it took was three dollars' worth of gas and one kitchen match. So cheap, Armageddon.

The firemen stood by, smoking, as the roof beams caught and cracked and the giant roof collapsed. It was no longer a house, or even a building, just a patch of smoke and flame that could be seen all the way to Port Royal.

It burned all day, through the magnificent sunset, the winds sending fire everywhere. Fire companies came from as far away as Richmond, but there was nothing, nothing to do except smoke cigarettes and talk about other fires, and companions lost to flames, and children burned to death in tenant farmer shacks, after which a silence fell, for the children, for their brave companions, heroes who lived forever in their hearts, myths made entirely of fire.

In Richmond, Clarence and Priscilla sedately shimmied in a coloreds-only nightclub, and then went back to their hotel and made love the way people do who've been married for twenty-seven years, gently, sweetly, with complete knowledge of each other's bodies.

Diana, the debutante of the century, eternal widow to a boy she hardly knew, stood in her big window in Tiny House and watched it all. Occasionally a fleck of ash or fire would land on her roof, and she would panic that her little house would go up in flames, but they bounced off, lost their heat, and fell harmlessly to the ground, and she knew she was safe.

The fire burned for three days, and smoked for three weeks. After that the scavengers came. She watched as they picked through the ashes, hoping to find a fork or a teaspoon or a plate. Scattered in the ashes were Rose's big rings, and pins, and these were the prizes, and big shouts went up as each one was found. The others looked for weeks, and for years people would come occasionally to look for things that were not there. For things that had been consumed by a fire beyond heat, an inferno that left nothing in its passing.

They were looking at her, her family. Their faces asked only this: Why? And she had no answer except this: It was time. She was the daughter of time, and all the clocks had stopped. It was too much to bear. The grief. The weight of history.

She could live in luxury for the rest of her life. Clarence and Priscilla, their lips sealed, would take care of her. They would ask no questions, and tell no tales.

No tales. No tales except this: It begins with a house, and it ends in ashes.

And this: Love burns.

Epilogue

COLOR AND LIGHT and dirt and water. But mostly water. That's what everything is made of. And you poke through these to find some undiscovered remnant of the past, a hopeless task. The house burned down more than fifty years ago. Hundreds, even thousands, have picked through this sodden landscape of ash. How could there be even the slightest remnant left?

In New York, where you live and work, people are sitting down to lunches composed mainly of hope, matter created out of nothing. They glitter. They do deals with a flutter of an eye. Their clothes fit smartly; every woman's wrist glitters with expensive bangles, watches that cost as much as cars, while you bat away black flies, hoping that you will find something, anything.

The only way to find something in the well-trodden battlefield of tragedy is to turn over every stone until the scorpion sinks its curved stinger into your wrist. You have to leave the part of the earth that everybody else has looked at, hoping to find the famous emerald, the essential Meissen. Because what you're looking for is not here, hasn't been here for decades.

Ash had the area fenced off, locked, that was the first thing, while the smoke still rose, burning the eyes, and sent in a team of private investigators to look for something, anything, that might have survived. Looking, of course, for her, the sizzled corpse of his mother. But she wasn't there.

The ash was so hot it melted the firemen's boots. It curled the random silver fork that was left behind, curled it into grotesque shapes that bore no resemblance to anything that might have revealed its original purpose.

Ash kept his guilt hidden, and stood silent as the bones were found. There had been people in the house, but who? How many?

And he raged. She didn't have to do what she did. The last of her cruelties, her crimes.

He forgot his own crimes. He wanted only money. Her money. His father's money. What should have been his. He sought her lawyers, her accountants, but there was nothing, no note to give him any comfort. Then the big shock. Almost all the money Ash had given her had disappeared along with her. There was no trace of the fortune that he had given back to her.

His rage became unbearable; the last of his love turned to hatred, a light switch suddenly switched off. He abandoned Saratoga and never went back. He moved to Richmond for good, a lawyer now, seeking love in dark alleys in the dead of night. He bought the most magnificent house on Monument Avenue. In the course of his ordinary life, he became prosperous in his own right and amused his friends by saying frequently, after his second old-fashioned, "Someday I'll be very, very rich," after which his friends would howl with glee.

Ash did manage to marry, in his forties, one of those *mariages blancs* so common in the South, and even produced two boys, Powell and Page, who grew up completely ignorant of the past and their place in it, but at least he had done his duty in making sure the line did not end with him.

But you haven't come about Ash, whose history you have learned through dozens of phone calls, whose name suddenly took on an ironic twist that his friends never failed to remark on. He died of a sudden aneurysm about ten years ago, not long after he finally had Diana declared dead.

She is here, somewhere. You can feel it. You know it beyond knowing. She is off the beaten track, here, deeply here, everywhere around him, but with so much land, five thousand acres, which track do you follow?

Then you see it. It's not a path. Most people would never have spotted it. It's just a place three feet wide that's less overgrown than the land on either side. It could be deer, but you follow it anyway. Then you smell it. Something living. Somebody cooking. Somebody moving from room to room. The smell of color and light and water and dirt. The path disappears. You hack through with your machete knife, swinging wildly with excitement.

It can't be her. It's somebody, but it can't be her. She would be ninety-nine years old.

Then it's in front of you, surrounded and concealed by a high hedge of privet. A slate roof, still wet from the night's drizzle. Beneath the roof, there is life.

There is an opening in the privet, a mazelike way through the density of the shrubbery, and you follow it, until it opens on a solid, square brick house with a woman looking out of the window, a pistol pointed straight at you.

You feel foolish, but you raise your hands, just like in the movies. She motions with the gun to move to the right, around the side of the house, and you do, until you come to a thick door, where you wait while the three dead bolt locks are laboriously opened, and then the door springs wide, and there she is, the famous Diana Cooke Copperton Cooke.

She is calm, and incredibly old, although her face is almost unlined. You feel as if you have found the Hope Diamond.

"Good afternoon. I'm—"

"I know exactly who you are. You're a reporter come to find me, like so many others. Except you have. They never did. That's worth something. For what it's worth, which isn't much, if you ask me. I have a gun pointed at your head. I have no idea how to use it. Where does that put us?"

"Is it loaded?"

"I think so. I don't really remember."

"Is there a lot you've forgotten?"

"I remember everything. Everything. The tiniest detail. Like in a photograph. I remember everything."

"Will you tell me?"

"I guess so. Perhaps. But you have to make a promise."

"What's that?"

"First come in. Where are my manners? I haven't seen anybody in so long I don't know how to act anymore." She turns and leads the way into the spectacular yellow room, fallen into disrepair now, but still remarkable.

She is wearing jodhpurs and riding boots, a white linen shirt, and a tattered Chinese court robe, bloodred, embroidered with gold dragons; the peculiar smell of age fills the room. Her long gray hair is worn in two braids down her back. She sits grandly in what is clearly her favorite chair, surrounded by books and Turkish cigarettes and an ashtray from Hermès.

You sit across from her. "It's a beautiful room," you say.

"It's the most beautiful room in America. Nothing has changed in fifty years."

"Who takes care of you? Cleans? Makes dinner?"

"I thought I would learn to cook, after Clarence and Priscilla died. A tragic mistake. I don't know. There's a girl from town. I don't even know her name. She comes. She does what I want. And she keeps her tongue in her mouth. She knows it's the most important thing. I pay her an exorbitant amount, mainly for that reason. She broke so many things I told her to keep away from cleaning. Her food is horrible. Nobody knows how to cook anymore. I would kill for a ham biscuit. But she knows how to keep a secret, as I hope you do. Give me your word."

"I promise."

She has been twirling the pistol in her hand when it suddenly goes off, causing you to scramble behind the sofa.

"Oh, that's how it works. Put the promise in writing."

"First put the gun away."

She does, stiffly, in a drawer, and you write your pledge, and you both sign it.

"I'll tell you the whole story, but you have to know it's rather long and rather complicated, so you have to listen closely, because I'm not going to repeat so much as a single word. It's about love and beauty and death. But then, isn't everything?

"Poor you. You come all this way to find the thing that everybody's been looking for all these years—debutante of the century, hah!—and you find it, her, me, and you leave with nothing, not so much as a teaspoon.

"People have always wondered how it happened, but I did it. I burned down the house. I was possessed with a cruelty so immense it wasn't even a choice. And I buried Gibby's medals in the family graveyard, along with that library fellow."

"Lucius Walter."

"Was that his name?"

She talks through the brilliant sun of afternoon, the jeweled brilliance of the late sun on the river, the blue mist of evening's approaching.

At sunset she rises, and makes two stiff old-fashioneds, never slowing her narrative as the ice cubes clink in the crystal glasses, the color of the bourbon matching the shining amber of the moon's rising and its settling into the night, the sky pocked with stars, her voice strong, pausing from time to time to absorb what she is saying, as though she has never heard it, showing you the ring and the key on the golden chain, and the jeweled child's eye, making more cocktails before leading you through the house, room by room, explaining every artifact, showing you her bedroom, the black-green she so long ago demanded, showing which side of the bed she sleeps on and which side is Gibby's. She tells her story, and the story of her love for Gibby, two hearts entwined, the rose-colored lightbulbs turned on one by one as they pass, and you are aware of the cruelties of being left alone in time's boat, and the actual one you hope is still waiting for you at the ruined dock.

Her voice is tender, another layer of softness wrapping itself around a grief that has never faded or left her for a single moment in half a century.

Sometimes, you think, even in the midst of the color and the light and the water and the earth, in the greenery and the flutter of the bird's wing, sometimes there is no appeasement. Sometimes you are left in a small life made of genius and sadness, and that's all you get.

It's late. She is ninety-nine years old. She will live out the century into which she opened her eyes. Her sins will be forgiven. You forgive them, right this minute. Your silence will be unbroken. You will not splash it in the paper or whisper it in your lover's ear.

You will not talk about her exquisite house. You will not talk about her standing firm at the doorway, gun in hand. You will not talk about the fact that, at ninety-nine, she looks sixty, or how she keeps the Olympic pool heated year-round and swims fifty laps every day.

You will, in fact, not talk about her at all, not even at your own clever dinner parties over the caviar soufflé.

Some secrets are born secrets, and they're meant to stay that way. She has built a completely invisible life, possible for her only because she's enormously wealthy. You couldn't build this life. Only millions of dollars can build it.

What will you write about? The tragedy of love and its aftermath, nothing that hasn't been explored before. The ladies on Park Avenue with their lapdogs and breakfast trays, opening first to the style section in their morning newspapers, will think they have learned something new, something tragic. They will never have heard of Diana Cooke Copperton Cooke and her mysterious disappearance. They will marvel at her archived pictures, the cloche hat with the diamond swallows, the famous jewels, the magnificent graduated pearls, unavailable today, the Beatons, the Horsts. The Man Ray. The iconic pictures, the one sad fallacious novel that was written about her in the sixties. But nothing of her today, two days ago, with her girlish braids, her genteel, still gamine, boyish ways, and the Persian rug covering the safe in the floor in which all the unbelievable jewels lie. The tea dress she changed into, Chanel, a dress older than most of your readers, priceless. You will describe the pin—the child's eye surrounded by diamonds—and they will come back into vogue; you have that power.

But they will have learned nothing, even though your editor, who never has a kind word, will think it a masterpiece of journalism, and miss the story that floats right before his nose before it's gone. It will be the most e-mailed story for two whole days, and then he will find some new way to make you miserable.

You stand at the door. On a whim, you take her hand and kiss her ring. You adore her. You've never seen, there has never been, anyone like her. And there never will be again. It is no longer possible to be Diana Cooke Copperton Cooke. You ask if you can come again. She pauses, and thanks you, but says she doesn't think that's such a good idea.

You start to leave, into the starlit darkness.

She says, very softly, "No, please. Forgive my rudeness. Come whenever you like. As long as you remember I am an invisible old woman. I am a ghost. Even to myself." And then she softly closes the door and locks it.

And for the days and months and years and decades following the great fire, you, who live in your safe house that will never catch fire, with your glowing children who sleep safe in their beds and get into the college of their choice, you who marry and lead a married life of adoration and then betrayal, of longing and eventual comfort, with your two immaculate cars in the drive, who go on vacations to the same place every year, you want to go, but you don't.

You want to go because you want to ask what happened after, even though you know the answer.

There is no after.

Acknowledgments

SO MUCH KINDNESS. So many coronets. This is for them. For Richard Abate, agent superior, and Lynn Nesbit, dear friend and helpmate. For Sara Nelson, who made me work harder than I thought possible, and cherish every minute. She is both diligent and brilliant, and she has my eternal thanks.

For Ruth Geer and Anna Fugaro. Ruth for generosity beyond what should be legal, and Anna for fifty years of unwavering friendship and cheer. We'll be together in heaven.

For Chuck Adams, who has turned more scribblers into writers than any man in America. Our gratitude stretches from here to the far Antipodes.

For Joe Nelms, a brilliant writer and a dear friend.

For Lynn Grossman, without whom I would never have written a word.

For all those who reached out a generous hand in kindness when my circumstances were dire, you have my heart.

For Dana Martin Davis, who never lets me stray from the biblical way. Except in Paris, when she made me buy those sneakers.

For Stephen Carriere, my real father, and Marie de Premonville, my brilliant translator.

For all these, and so many more, I wish I could have been stronger, braver, kinder.

But I promise you this, as I put a coronet on every head, I did my best for you.

ABOUT THE AUTHOR

ROBERT GOOLRICK is the author of the bestselling novels *A Reliable Wife, Heading Out to Wonderful,* and *The Fall of Princes,* and the acclaimed memoir *The End of the World as We Know It.* He lives and works in Baltimore.